CELEBRATING BOSMAN

A Centenary Selection of
Herman Charles Bosman's Stories

Compiled by Patrick Mynhardt

WITS UNIVERSITY PRESS

Wits University Press

1 Jan Smuts Avenue
Johannesburg
2001
South Africa

First published 2005

© in the Preface, Biography, Glossary and this compilation, Wits University
Press

ISBN 1-86814-416-X

Cover design and layout by Resolution
Printed and bound by Creda Communications, Johannesburg

Contents

Preface

It was during 1968 that the popular Springbok Radio personality Victor Mackeson invited me to participate in a 'theatre-dinner-by-candlelight' at the then fashionable Boulevard Hotel in Pretoria. Radio personalities would be reading short stories by highly acclaimed authors. I was to bring a South African flavour to the evening by reading 'Willem Prinsloo's Peach Brandy' by Herman Charles Bosman. At this time, I was not familiar with Bosman's work and, not having done this sort of thing before, I was reluctant but, with encouragement from actor Hal Orlandini, I accepted the offer. This decision drastically changed the course of my already successful but nevertheless precarious career, for it would provide me with plenty of work and a good living for the next thirty-six years.

The Bosman story turned out to be the highlight of the night, perhaps because South Africans could easily identify with it. This success inspired me to devise a one-man show based on Bosman's works. After choosing the stories I needed a title. Since Bosman published *A Cask of Jerepigo*, I considered *A Soupçon of Jerepigo*, but it sounded pretentious, and not many would have known what 'Jerepigo' was anyway, let alone 'soupçon'. Jerepigo is a sweet Cape desert wine, popular in the Western Cape and, in the region's inimitable accent, is pronounced 'Die Djigge Pik Djou' – 'die Here pik jou' ('the Lord strikes you'). As does a snake, the inference being that if you over-imbibe, you are punished with a terrible hangover. To my rescue came the late Rita Elferink with *A Sip of Jerepigo*, and that was it!

Next step was to find a venue and, if possible, an impresario. So, I presented my idea to the late Michal Grobbelaar, C.E.O. of the Johannesburg Civic Theatre. He jumped at the idea, and offered to present me at the 128-seater Pieter Roos Theatre. Opening night, Tuesday November 4th was approaching rapidly, and to our consternation Percy Tucker of Show Service (forerunner of Computicket) informed us that only 17 seats had been booked. At a price of only one Rand per ticket, inclusive of a glass of Jerepigo wine and a programme, we were in for a potential disaster. Wisely, Michal 'papered' the house with free seats for specially invited guests, at the same time gently warning me that, because of the appalling booking, we'd be forced to close on the following Saturday. An eleven-day run!

On opening night he and I sat in the dressing room, both of us sweating profusely and chain-smoking. Then came the dreaded 'beginners please' call which allowed me ten minutes for sticking on my moustache. It was gone from my dressing table, and nowhere to be found. As I was about to have a total nervous collapse I glanced at my dresser-prompt who was bent forward and peering into the rubbish-bin. There, beautifully draped across her backside, was my moustache! While watching me doing my make-up she'd leant against my table and the static in her dress had attracted the moustache.

I went onto stage in a terrible state of nerves, dreading the endless marathon ahead. But by the interval I knew that the first half had worked and, while I was changing costume for the second half, the audience enjoyed a sip of Jerepigo in the foyer. At the final curtain call there were shouts of 'MORE!', 'MORE!' and we were ecstatic. But the critics were not and generally the reviews were not good. Next day there was some activity at Show Service, and slowly bookings picked up as a result of word-of-mouth recommendations. Before long we were sold out days, then weeks and eventually months in advance – *Jerepigo* was a hit. I played from 4th November 1969 to 5th June 1971, a record run of one year and seven months, and closed only because I was to be married for the first and only time in my life. That, alas, did not last, but the *Jerepigo* has, for thirty-six years!

I followed *A Sip* with *More Jerepigo*, and this with *Just Jerepigo*, all of them highly acclaimed. In 1982 I opened my stage autobiography *Boy From Bethulie*, subsequently presenting a combination Bosman / Mynhardt show titled *The Best of Bosman and Bethulie*. I celebrated twenty years of Jerepigo successes in 1989 with *Another Sip of Jerepigo*. To commemorate my fiftieth year in the theatre in 2003 I had my complete autobiography *Boy From Bethulie* published, at the same time staging *Tjeerio Jerepigo* (cheerio), not as a final farewell gimmick, but because I liked the alliteration in the title, and wished to revive Bosman's superb *Cold Stone Jug* prison material.

I am frequently asked which is my favourite Bosman story. I refuse to have one as I have over the years got myself too involved with each and every one of them. This in fact has been the case with every role I have played. The acclaimed Russian actor Alexei Gribov of the Moscow Art Theatre gave a classic reply to the perennial question: 'Which is your most favourite of the parts you have played?' Gribov replied, *sotto voce*, 'I can't tell you that because you see, it would make the other parts jealous.'

Way back in 1981, having received much acclaim for my one-man shows based on the works of Herman Charles Bosman, I was invited to compile a personal selection of this author's works for publication, called *The Bosman I Like*. It is with delight that I now, in my thirty-sixth year of Jerepigo presentations, and my fifty-second year in the theatre, in salutation and celebration of Bosman's centenary, look forward to the publication of this new edition. Although Bosman's stories were all written in English, they are a rich blend of the vernacular language of South Africa of the time (early twentieth century) and thus contain a colourful strand of Afrikaans words and phrases – particularly when referring to the landscape, flora and fauna of the country. For the sake of the modern reader and those less familiar with such terms, a glossary has been included in this volume. Bosman's use in many of the stories of the term 'kafir' to describe a black South African would today – quite rightly – be regarded as offensive but, at the time that Bosman was writing, it was the norm and did not carry quite the same insulting and pejorative tone that it does now. Indeed it is fair to say that most of Bosman's references to black South Africans are filled with irony. They reflect the langauge and ideas of his characters and, far from denigrating black people, usually show up the ignorance, self importance and unthinking cruelty of the white men.

The problem with this prolific writer is that one is overwhelmed by how much good material there is and in constant turmoil as to what to choose. So, having re-read the old as well the more recently published works, I find myself sticking almost entirely to my original selection. I think that with thirty-six years of Bosman involvement and fifty-two years on the stage, my instinct has guided me wisely.

I hope the reader will agree!

PATRICK MYNHARDT

A cartoon by Jock Leyden of Patrick Mynhardt in the role of Oom Schalk Lourens, in the Bekkersdal Marathon and as the young Herman Charles Bosman in the condemned cell.

Herman Charles Bosman

A BRIEF BIOGRAPHY

Herman Charles Bosman was born in 1905 at Kuilsrivier in the Western Cape. His family moved to the Transvaal where he attended Potchefstroom College and later – in Johannesburg – Jeppe Central School, Jeppe Boys' High, Wits University and the Teachers' Training College. He was deeply involved in literature and excelled in languages but had no interest in Science and Mathematics which repelled him. In his matriculation exam he answered the paper on Algebra with a beautifully phrased essay, explaining that he felt he might dispense with the knowledge of this subject since his ability in English was exceptional.

Apart from contributing to the school magazine, he was, at the age of sixteen, writing a series of amusing short stories for the *Sunday Times*. Although he preferred the school library to the playing fields he never became a studious recluse. At Wits University, on winning the third prize for his entry in a student's poetry competition he revealed that the piece had actually been written by Shelley! At about this time his father was killed in a mining accident and his mother remarried soon afterwards.

After receiving his degree, Bosman was appointed to a teaching post in the Groot Marico district of the western Transvaal. This was a most fruitful period, for the place and people enthralled him – they provided him with the background for his best known works, the Oom Schalk Lourens stories and the Voorkamer sketches. When he returned to Johannesburg for the June holidays, his visit ended in an appalling tragedy. In the house of his mother and stepfather he fired a hunting rifle at his stepbrother, killing him. He was found guilty of unpremeditated murder and sentenced to death. Subsequently he was reprieved and the sentence commuted to ten years imprisonment with hard labour. He eventually served three and a half years before being released on parole. Bosman relates his prison experiences in *Cold Stone Jug*. On his release he started his own printing press and associated with a colourful group of journalists and authors in Johannesburg, writing the first Oom Schalk Lourens stories in *Touleier* and *New Sjambok*.

Bosman then spent nine years in Paris, Brussels and London where he wrote more Oom Schalk stories, later compiled as *Mafeking Road*. At the outbreak of the Second World War he returned home where he worked as a journalist and literary editor for several newspapers and, in 1944, translated the *Rubayat* of Omar Khayam into Afrikaans. In 1947, after *Mafeking Road* was published, the stories were broadcast on the BBC's Third Programme under the auspices of the South African poet Roy Campbell, who considered them the best stories ever to come out of South Africa.

Bosman loved to entertain and his parties were famous for the brilliant and witty conversations which went on far into the night. Two days after a house-warming party he complained of severe chest pains. His wife took him to Edenvale Hospital. On arrival he was asked, 'Place of birth?' Herman replied, 'Born Kuilsrivier – Died Edenvale Hopsital'. A few minutes after he entered the examination room, the doctor could be heard roaring with laughter. Herman emerged and told his wife he merely had indigestion. A few hours later he collapsed at home. He died as he was being wheeled back into Edenvale Hospital. The date was 14th October 1951.

Cold Stone Jug

'Murder,' I answered.

There were about a dozen prisoners in the cells at Marshall Square. It was getting on towards the late afternoon of a Sunday that we had spent locked up in a cell that was three-quarters underground and that had barred apertures opening on to the pavement at the corner of McLaren and Marshall Streets, Johannesburg. I had been arrested about fifteen or sixteen hours before.

Those first hours in the cells at Marshall Square, serving as the overture to a long period of imprisonment in the Swartklei Great Prison, were the most miserable I have ever known. By standing on a bench you could get near enough to the barred opening to catch an occasional glimpse of the underneath part of the shoe-leather of passing pedestrians, who, on that dreary Sunday afternoon, consisted almost entirely of natives. The motley collection of prisoners inside the cell took turns in getting on to the bench and trying to attract the attention of the passers-by. Now and again a native would stop. A lengthy discussion would follow. Occasionally (this constituting a triumphant termination to the interview), a piece of lighted cigarette-end would be dropped in through that little hole in the wall against the pavement. This was over twenty years ago. But it is still like that. You can go and look there.

For the rest of the time the dozen inmates of the cell carried on a desultory conversation, a lot of it having to do with what appeared to be highly unbecoming activities on the part of plain-clothes members of the police force, who seemed to spend all their waking hours in working up spurious cases against law-abiding citizens. Then, when it was getting towards late afternoon, one of the prisoners, a dapper little fellow who had done most of the talking and who seemed to exercise some sort of leadership in the cell, felt that it was time we all got sort of cosy together, and started taking more of a personal interest in one another's affairs.

'I'm in for liquor-selling, myself,' he announced to a man standing next to him, 'What they pinch you for?'

'Stealing a wheel-barrow from the P.W.D.,' was the reply, 'Not that I done it, mind you. But that's the charge.'

'And what are you in for?' the cell-boss demanded of the next man.

'Drunk and disorderly and indecent exposure,' came the answer.

'And what's your charge?'

'Forgery. And if I drop this time I'll get seven years.'

And so this dapper little fellow who was doing the questioning worked his way through the whole lot until it came to my turn.

'Say, what are you pinched for?' he asked, eyeing me narrowly.

'Murder,' I said. And in my tone there was no discourtesy. And I did not glower much. I only added, 'And I'm not feeling too good.'

'Struth!' my interrogator remarked. And his jaw dropped. And that bunch of prisoners in the cell, the whole dozen of them, moved right across to the other side, to the corner that was furthest away from me.

✱

I remember that I had company in the condemned cell. There was another man there, also under sentence of death, when I arrived. We were separated from each other by two rows of bars and wire netting, which formed a little passage in which the warder on duty paced up and down. The warders watched us night and day, working in four-hour shifts, with the lights on all the time. That other man's name was Stoffels.

✱

I can remember the jokes Stoffels and I made, talking to each other through two sets of steel netting and bars, with the warder in between. And the questions we asked the warders about life inside the prison. We had to ask these questions of the warders, we two, who were in the prison but not of it. And the stories the warders had to relate to us, in the long nights when we couldn't get to sleep, made life as a convict inside a prison seem very alluring – just simply because it was life. And when we heard the convicts march out to work in the mornings, their footsteps heavy on the concrete floor of the hall far removed from us, their passage sounded like the tread of kings. And when a warder mentioned to us the fact that he had that morning had occasion, in the course of an altercation, to hit a convict over the head with his baton, I know how I felt about that convict, how I envied him, how infinitely privileged I felt he was to be able to be regarded by a warder as a live person, as somebody that could be hit over the head. For no warder would dream of hitting a condemned man with a baton. To a warder a condemned man was something already dead.

Because we had been sentenced to be hanged, Stoffels and I were accorded certain privileges. For one thing, we didn't have to get our hair cropped short, like the other convicts, with a pair of number nought clippers. And when I was taken out on exercise, into the prison yard, twice a day, and I saw other convicts from a distance, and I saw how short their hair was, and I understood what my long hair signified – then I didn't feel too good. I even hoped that, somehow, by mistake, somebody would come in and say that the chief warder had ordered my hair to be cut short. Just so I wouldn't have to flaunt, in the exercise yard, that awful thing that made me different from the hard-labour convicts. Long hair and the rope ... A short rope.

Of course, Stoffels and I affected unconcern, there in the condemned cell. We spent much of our waking hours in pulling the warders' legs. We didn't know, then, that we were in actual fact engaged in a time-honoured prison pastime. We didn't know that 'kidding' to warders was a sport regularly indulged in by prison lags, and that this form of recreation had venerable traditions. We didn't know all that. We merely followed our natural bent of trying to be funny, and we found, afterwards, that we were all the time conforming to accepted prison custom. It must be that prison was, after all, the right place for Stoffels and me. Because to this aspect of it, at all events, to the part of it connected with pulling a warder's leg, we took like ducks to water.

There was one warder whom Stoffels and I nicknamed the Clown. He had not been in the prison service very long and had only recently been transferred to the Swartklei Great Prison from a native gaol in Barberton. We joshed him unmercifully. He was a young fellow in his early twenties, but Stoffels and I addressed him as though he were a man of the world with infinitely wide experience and an oracle of learning. He afforded us many nights of first-class entertainment, during the dreary hours between ten at night and two in the morning, when we could not sleep and were afraid to trust our heads to the hard pallet, in case when we woke up in the morning it would be to find the sheriff standing at the door, with the death-warrant.

The Clown had a very simple heart. One night, through a process of not very subtle flattery, we got him to acknowledge that he could dance rather well. We also got him to admit that, in general, men were envious of his ball-room accomplishments, and that, behind his back, they said many nasty things about him, such as that he danced like a sick hippopotamus, or the way a duck waddles. All because they were jealous of him. We even got him so far as to show us a few of the latest dance-steps. For this purpose he took off his heavy warder's boots. At the Clown's demonstration, in his stockinged feet, of the then-fashionable black-bottom, Stoffels and I laughed uproariously. We explained to him, of course, that we were laughing at the thought that jealous males could have come to such ludicrously erroneous conclusions about his dancing, merely because they viewed everything he did through the green gaze of envy. Thereupon the Clown joined in the laughter, thus making Stoffels and me roar louder than ever.

'Didn't they perhaps, in their jealousy, even say – ' I started off again, when we all suddenly stopped laughing. For a key grated in the outer door and the night head-warder entered.

'What's all this?' he demanded, 'The convicts the other end of the hall are complaining they can't sleep, the way you men in the condemned cell keep on laughing all night. And this isn't the first night, neither.'

The night head-warder looked at us sternly. There seemed something gravely irregular in a situation in which two condemned men were keeping a whole prison establishment awake with indecorous laughter.

'You condemned men mustn't laugh so loud,' he said, 'The hard labour convicts got to sleep. They got to work all day. You two don't do nothing but smoke cigarettes all day long and crack jokes. You'll get yourselves in serious trouble if the Governor finds out you keep the whole prison awake night after night, romping about and laughing in the condemned cells.'

I wondered, vaguely, what more serious trouble we could get into than we were already in. But at that moment the night head-warder happened to look down at the Clown's feet. So it was his turn to laugh. The Clown certainly cut a ridiculous figure, with shapeless pieces of feet leaking out of his socks.

'Where's your boots?' the night head-warder demanded, his tone midway between a threat and a guffaw, 'Don't you know you can't come on duty improperly dressed? What sort of an example do you think you are to these two condemned men. And look at all them pertaters in your socks. I never seen so many pertaters in a sock. More pertater than sock. With all them pertaters you ought to be working in the kitchen. Come on, now. Quick about it. Put on the other boot, too. What you want take them off for, anyway? To show these condemned men your pertaters, I suppose. Or maybe you got bunions. Yes, must be bunions. I suppose you got bunions on your feet through walking about the streets looking for trollops.'

With that sally, and still guffawing, the night head-warder departed. There certainly seemed to be something in the atmosphere of the cell adjacent to the gallows that was provocative of a spirit of clean fun. The condemned cell air seemed to be infectiously mirth-making.

'Now, isn't that just what we have been saying?' Stoffels asked of the Clown when the three of us were alone together on more, 'How do you like that for jealousy? The moment the night head-warder sees you he starts picking you out. What do you think of that? And so ridiculous, too. How can he say you got those bunions on your feet – '

'But I haven't got bunions,' the Clown asserted, 'You know as well as I do that I took off my boots to show you my – '

'Those terrible bunions,' Stoffels persisted, ignoring the Clown's remonstrances, 'How can he say you got those corns and bunions *and blisters* walking after whores in the street? Has he ever seen you walking after a whore in the street? Come on, answer me, has he ever seen you?'

'I don't know what he's seen or what he hasn't seen,' the Clown answered, 'I only know that the only times I've ever walked about looking for a whore it was in the other end of the town from where he stays. It was – '

*

I have explained that the warder walks up and down that little passage between the two condemned cells. The warder is also locked in. They do that so as to keep a condemned man doubly secure: first, locked inside his own cell, and, secondly, locked in with the warder in a larger cell, comprising the two condemned cells and the warder's passage. But the warder is all right, there. He's got a revolver. Only, he can't get out during the four hours of his shift. The section-warder has to come and unlock him. But he's got a bell-button that he can push whenever there's trouble. Each warder, when he enters the cell, is provided with a tin vessel, cylindrical and about a foot high – like a native's dinner-pail, but taller – containing drinking-water. When the Clown came on duty, at ten p.m., it was customary because of the lateness of the hour, to put two tins of water into the warder's passage, one for the Clown and one for the warder who came on duty after him. That meant that the cleaner in the section did not have to be awakened at two o'clock in the morning to get the next warder a tin of drinking-water.

But because the Clown had been transferred to Swartklei from Barberton only recently, he was not conversant with all the niceties of condemned cell routine. Consequently, he thought that both tins were for his own use. He would drink water out of one tin, whenever he got thirsty, and regularly, about ten minutes before the next warder (whom we nicknamed Jannie) came in to relieve him, the Clown would wash his hands in the other tin of drinking-water. He used my soap and towel, or Stoffels's soap and towel, whichever was nearer to hand. (Unfortunately, I find that I must again interrupt with a parenthesis. But that is the prison's fault, not mine. I can't help it that prison routine should be so absurdly complicated. Anyway, each time, last thing at night, after Stoffels and I had had our supper, the section-warder would order us to put our empty enamel dixies outside – and also our pieces of soap and our towels. This measure was probably incorporated into the regulations in order to prevent condemned criminals from suffocating themselves with the towels, or from making themselves unnecessarily ill through eating pieces of prison-soap.)

Anyway, two pieces of soap and two towels – mine and Stoffels's respectively – would be lying in the corner of his passage when the Clown came in, and there would also be two tins of water. As I have said, the Clown would regularly drink up the water in one tin, and wash his hands in the other.

Most nights, Jannie, the warder who relieved the Clown, would stay on duty right through until six o'clock, without getting thirsty. But those nights when he wanted a drink of water and he picked up the tin that the Clown had washed his hands in, Jannie would curse the whole prison up and down. Prison-warders as a class are not distinguished in respect of being particularly clean-mouthed. And Jannie seemed to be much more fastidious about what went into his mouth than he was about what came out. In fact, what came out of his mouth each time he tasted that water in which the Clown had performed his ablutions, were words and expressions that I felt no soap in the world would ever wash clean again.

'The cleaners,' Jannie would splutter, 'The – water tastes – soapy again. The lazy bastards of – of – cleaners are too – lazy to wash the – blasted soap off from the inside of the – tin when they put in water for me.'

This went on for about a week. Some nights Jannie went off duty without having a drink of water. That was all right. But whenever he drank the Clown's soapy water he would get into a rage that had him cursing for the better part of the night. Stoffels and I never thought of enlightening Jannie about the true state of affairs, preferring to let him blame it on the cleaners. Similarly, we did not think it worthwhile to inform the Clown that every time he washed his hands it was in another man's drinking-water. The situation seemed pregnant with possibilities that we didn't want spoilt.

Then, one night, it happened. It was past one o'clock. The Clown was somewhat circumspect about ringing the bell for the section-warder in a matter of nature ...

Stoffels and I said no word to each other about what we had witnessed. We went to lie down under our blankets, and lay hoping for the best. The Clown went off duty, Jannie coming in to relieve him. Nothing had been noticed. Could it really be possible that so unique a piece of enjoyment could come the way of two sorry felons such as Stoffels and I? Surely, it was too much to hope for ... Could two men, condemned to death, resting for a brief while at the foot of the gallows, be placed in the way of so rare a thrill? The genius that watches over criminals was with Stoffels and me that night. In the early hours of the morning, when I could hardly stand the tension any longer, Jannie got thirsty. I heard the bottom of the tin grate against the concrete of the floor. I heard Jannie draw in his breath before drinking. Then, oh, rich and ineffable and unforgettable ecstasy, oh, memorable delight, I heard – glug, glug, just like that – I heard Jannie drink. And he went on drinking. Eventually, he sighed, deeply, and I heard him put down the tin.

'Yes, I am thirsty, tonight,' Jannie muttered, half to himself. I couldn't stand it any longer.

'Meneer,' I said, 'The tin. The tin you drink out of. There was no soap in it tonight, was there?'

'No,' Jannie answered, 'But it tasted funny, all the same.'

'Like – like what did it taste, meneer?' I enquired, struggling hard to keep my voice level.

'Well, if I didn't know better,' Jannie said, 'If I didn't know that it was quite impossible, I would say that it tasted a lot like –.'

So Stoffels and I both jumped up from our blankets and informed Jannie that it was.

✳

As my companion in the death-cell for more than four weeks, Stoffels had done a good deal to cheer me up. And yet, on the morning of his execution, there was nothing I could think of saying to him. I could think of no last quip to make. I could think of no final word of comfort. In the shadow of the gallows, I had found, a jest or a solemn speech meant just about the same thing. But even if I could have thought up something to say, I would have had no opportunity of saying it. For early that morning two warders came and fetched me out of my own cell and locked me in a cell two doors away. They didn't lock the door, though, but only the grille gate. And from the sounds I heard later on, when the hangman came to perform his office, it sounded as though everything went off very efficiently. There was the tramping of feet on the iron stairs and the sound of doors being locked and unlocked, and no sound of voices. No orders had to be given. Each man knew what was expected of him, even Stoffels, – who played his part tolerably well, considering the fact that he was not rehearsed in it and was getting no pay for it.

The rest of the actors in this early morning drama of the gallows – the Governor, the warders, the doctors, the hangman, the chaplain – were all salaried officials of the administration. Only Stoffels was giving his services free.

I heard what sounded like a quick scuffle, then many footfalls. And then a muffled noise in which I recognised Stoffels's voice, but with difficulty, for only part of that noise seemed to come out of his throat. The rest of it seemed to have come out of his belly. More heavy footfalls and doors creaking on hinges. And still no rapped out words of command. Then a mighty slam that shook the whole building, rattling the pannikin on the floor of the cell in which I was. And it was all over. I looked at the warder guarding me on the other side of the grille. His face was a greenish-white. Then the bell rang. And there were voices, and the sound of much movement, and the noise and commotion of a prison with six hundred convicts beginning the day's routine. I was not as badly shaken by this experience as I thought I would have been. Perhaps it was because, as I have indicated, I had not felt in Stoffels's veins and lungs the blood and breath of life any more during the period of our having known each other.

✳

I don't want to waste any more time writing about the condemned cell. I want to get on with the next part of this story. In fact, I want to get out of the condemned cell as quick as possible. As quick as I got out of it that afternoon when the Governor came up and informed me that I had been reprieved. I was asleep on my blankets on the floor, that afternoon. I was dreaming, but I forget what about. And I awoke to find the Governor and the chief warder and the section officer and the warder on duty in the death cell, all together standing in a ring around me. I woke up and rubbed my eyes. The Governor was talking. And on a sudden the import of his words and his visit dawned on me. It was the Governor who had called on me, and not the sheriff. Not the sheriff. Then I got the gist of it. The Governor was saying that my sentence had been commuted to a term of imprisonment with hard labour for so many years. I got out of that condemned cell in such a hurry that I didn't hear all of the years. And afterwards when I did find out (because they took me down into the hall later on and got the number of years written on my ticket) that knowledge did not sober me up.

✳

During the fourth year of my imprisonment a very beautiful thing happened to me. I was working in the carpenters' shop, still. A bracket had to be fitted into a guard-post on the pavement in front of the prison. The head-warder sent me out to do the job. I went there escorted by a discipline-warder and accompanied by another convict. It was a wonderful adventure. Even now, when I think of it, twenty years later, that old thrill comes back to me once more.

'Get your tools,' the head-warder said to me, 'And the timber for a bracket.' To the discipline-warder he said, 'Get your gun.'

So we went out through the back-gate of the prison, the warder, the other convict and I. At the gate the warder got his revolver, which he slung over his shoulder on a strap. The other convict and I were searched. The outside warder opened the gate. Slowly, much too slowly, the gate creaked outward on its heavy iron hinges – and we saw the outside world.

Stout Cortez seeing the Pacific for the first time, from a peak on Darien ... All that sentimental rubbish. As though one piece of ocean could be different from any other piece of ocean ...

But in that moment of the gate swinging open very slowly, I saw the outside world again, after a period of four years.

'Forward,' the discipline-warder said.

It sounded like the voice of Divinity talking. It meant we were going down that road which I had seen only once before, four years ago, and the sight of which had made my throat contract, because I had been under sentence of death, then, and as we had approached the gloomy exterior of the prison, and those forbidding-looking portals had reared up before me, it was with an unutterable despair that I had looked on that same road, for the last time.

We continued down that road, towards the front of the prison, where the guard-post was. Several times the discipline-warder had to shout at me to pick up my step. For every moment was ecstasy to me. I walked with an awful deliberation. I wanted to miss nothing. I wanted to go as slow as possible; those moments that we were outside the prison had to be stretched as long as days and hours and years; oh, we hadn't to go at more than a snail's pace. And I saw to it that we didn't. The warder could shout his head off. This dreadful ecstasy had to linger.

I have never in my life, before or since, beheld a scene as entrancing in its splendour as what I viewed from that dusty road, that was impregnated with a heady fragrance – that dusty red road skirting the prison. I have seen Funchal from the sea; I have walked those cobbled roads, green with young grass-blades like sprinkled confetti, and I couldn't see what there was in Madeira to thrill the tourists, who all said, 'Oh,' and 'Oh,' as though it was paradise. And I have seen middle-aged men standing in St. James' park and looking over the bridge at the part of London other side Whitehall, with the early light of a summer morning on it: and I wondered what they saw in it. And the Paris boulevards, and in Brussels the Avenue Louise, and all sorts of other places and scenes – and among them, not least, the Hex River mountains from the train window. I have seen lots of sights – since that day when I walked out of the back-gate of the prison, to go and put up that bracket at the guard-post. And all those sights have left me cold.

I don't think that even love has had for me the warmth and the beauty and the deep-drawn delight that came to me on that road, red with perfumed dust, skirting the prison. Love. Well, I was young. And I was in love with the whole world. And life had not yet been made sick for me through the poison of introspection. And so I walked slowly, in spite of the discipline-warder's bellowings, in order to miss nothing, in order that this incredible joy that had come to me, suddenly and undeservedly, should fill my entire being, dropping rose petals on the places where my shoulders were bruised.

It was a dream-world that I walked into. For four years I had been dreaming of a moment such as this was. I was outside. It was all *world*. I was walking along a road where free people walked, where members of the public walked – men and women and children: and above all, women. Sunlight and shadow and distance played queer tricks with my eyes. Because I had been confined within cramped walls for four years, my eyes were unable to accommodate themselves to the majesty of distance. To be able to see far away – fruit trees a long way off, for instance, and a white-washed fence at the bottom of the road: all these things were very beautiful. They were invested with the magic of strangeness. I was in a painted world, queerly different from what I had expected the outside to be. I had so forgotten common things, that when I saw a couple of fowls in a backyard I stopped and stared at them in an unspeakable joy.

For four years I had had only memories of what the world was really like. And what I saw now, distance and hues, and pale lights and patches of grass: they no longer corresponded to my ideas about them. They were quite different from my memories of them. And they were even more lovely than I had expected them to be.

For years I had dreamt of the world. I had tried, in the nights when I had lain awake, to recall that gaudy lost world that I had known up to the time when I was twenty. And I saw now that it was less brightly-coloured than I had pictured it to be. But I was not disappointed. On the contrary, this pallid reality was something infinitely more exquisite than my black and scarlet visioning of it had been.

We got to the guard-post much too soon. But before we entered it a woman and a girl came past: the wife and daughter of a warder. And they didn't look at us, of course. Because this was on the prison reserve, where they lived; and so they were used to seeing convicts.

But I stared at them, at this woman and girl. I couldn't look at them enough. I had to see them, and I had to remember. I had to remember everything about them, every detail of how they looked, and what they *felt* like. I had to remember everything about what that divine moment of their nearness did to my senses, and every single detail of their faces and their bodies and their eyes and their dresses, and the folds in their frocks, and the crinkles in the woman's legs, at the back of her knees, and the way their bodies swayed when they walked, and the way their light, summery dresses fluttered in the breeze when they walked. Above all, I had to remember that sublime impact on my soul, on my blood, of their having passed close to me. I must not forget that feeling of thick silence that was fragrant with the inside of them.

For I had to remember all that when I was locked up again. I had to treasure it all up; not a drop of it was to be spilt; and I did, as a matter of fact, succeed in keeping that memory vivid for at least a year after that – perhaps even longer.

The woman's dress was short. I hadn't expected that. How was I to know that women's fashions had undergone so much change during the four years in which I was shut away from the sound and sight of all women? And the little girl's frock was a washed-out sort of blue. I don't mean that the colour really was washed out, of course. It was only that I had expected the colours of materials to be more startling-hued than what they actually were. And I knew, instantly, that those really were the colours of the outside world, the colours of trees and the colours of dresses. I knew immediately that that girl wasn't wearing a faded dress. It was only that I had, during the years, come to imagine, in waking dreams of the outside world, that there was a brilliance about the things of living and the acts of living which was not really there.

But, of course, this pallor only enhanced the incredible miracle of the life that people lived. It made the mystery all the more refined. The glitter was all the more alluring, because it was subdued. Life was washed out, faded. So its attractiveness was a haunted thing. The outside world was deadly artistry.

After the bracket had been nailed into place, the convict who went with me having made holes in the wall with the cold chisel in the places where I showed him – mine being the higher-up job of hammering in the plugs and securing the brackets – we went back along the road we had come. But this time the convict who had come with me joined with the warder in making us hurry up. For it was getting on towards lunchtime, and my convict-colleague was hungry. He was only a short-timer; so in the walk between the guard-post and the back-gate of the prison there was little novelty for him.

But this time I didn't mind hurrying. I had already seen so much. I had a whole world of things to remember in the days to come. I had been allowed into fairyland. I had thrilled to the earth and its beauty and its secrets. The faces and the figures of that woman and girl had not come up to my expectations in respect of the dark loveliness that I had come to associate with woman. But their beauty seemed all the more ethereal because it was not held fast in swift contours and vivid colouring. And their beauty had become all the more intangible because it made contact with my senses not as spirit but as clay. Paradise was so much nearer to me than the soil, during those years of my dreaming of the outside world. And what there was of clay in that girl and woman was a thing of far greater mystery to me than their quality of soul.

Reality was more trancelike than a vision, more breath-taking than any dream.

During the many months that followed, of my sojourning inside the walls, that saunter along the dusty road was a warm and luscious memory for me. It was an excursion into realms of gaudy adventure where my sight had been dazzled with shining fresh flowers and my ears had been filled with the sound of old gold. And life had been broken open like a ripe pomegranate, and tropical fronds had bent low in laughter, and spring had exulted in the stillness of young growth.

I had tiptoed down the corridors of ancient palaces, richly arrassed and niched with armorial bearings; my footsteps had wandered through sacred groves. And I would look at my feet, alone in my cell for many nights thereafter, and I would think that these feet, shod in these same boots, had walked down that road, once, and had got red dust on them, had walked in the same dust in which people of the outside world had walked, in which that girl and that woman had walked. And thinking like that I would not feel cut off from the world at all. For my boots were tangible proof that I was one with the earth and with life; proof – that any court of law would accept – that I belonged with people.

And, of course, the immediate effect of my adventure into Avalon was that my dreamings of the outside world became again exotic things of black and scarlet, heavy with perfumes, low-hung with the night. In my visionings the world outside the prison was invested with more vivid colours than ever before ...

(Only the other day I passed that same spot again, by car. After an interval of twenty years. And the red road had been tarred. And I saw then that the whole distance we had walked, the distance from the back-gate to the guard-post, which still stood there on the corner – with the bracket still in place, no doubt, for I nailed it in solid – was less than a hundred yards.)

✱

After my walk down that road, there seemed to be a spirit of liberation in the air of the prison. And I began to entertain queer hopes of being released shortly: of getting a special discharge – to use the official terminology. Now, any convict will tell you that when once a man starts getting hold of ideas like this, it is the beginning of insanity. And that was what began happening to me, of course. Although I held on to the hope, all the time, that the thing that was coming over me was only a form of neurosis, and not insanity at all.

✳

And it had to happen, of course, just at that particular time, that a convict did go mad. This sort of thing seemed to happen in bunches. Anyway, the convict's name was Krouse. He was a first offender. He was one of the cleaners in the section, and it had been noticed that he had got very quiet, lately: there was a suspicious sort of calmness about him. At least, that was what the other convicts said after he had started raving and the warders had locked him up in a solitary cell, through the peep-hole of which they were inserting the nozzle of a high-pressure hosepipe at intervals.

And then a most awful thing occurred, too, a couple of nights after Krouse had been removed to the solitary cell. Some convict in one of the sections suddenly climbed up on to his stool and put his mouth as near to the bars as he could, and he started howling like a dog. Or a wolf. Or a hyena. But mostly, I think, it was like a dog. That was the first time something of that description had happened during the years I was in prison. So I got terrified: not at the man's doglike howling, but at what followed. Because, almost immediately afterwards, a convict in another cell took up that howl. Then another convict joined in. Before long there were several scores of convicts, standing on their stools and getting their mouth as near the bars as possible, emitting the weirdest sort of sounds into the night.

More and more convicts joined in. And yet more and more. It was a most contagious kind of thing. The noise each convict made, while it differed from the sounds emitted by his neighbour, nevertheless had one thing in common with this general howling, and that was that it had a warm animal ring: but it wasn't so much like an animal on heat as like an animal dying – or an animal smelling the stink of death. I know I didn't join in with this general howling. I pulled the blankets over my head and lay on the concrete floor of my cage and shivered. I was very frightened, that night.

Hours later, when the howling was still going on, spasmodically, throughout the prison, I noticed a pale refulgence at the barred cell window which served three of the cages. I recognised that gleam. I had worked it out month after month. So I knew what that pale light was, now. In a few days' time it wouldn't show itself at all. Not through that barred aperture, anyway.

It was the full moon ...

✳

No convict would talk about that night. I dared not go up to any convict and ask him, 'Did you hear those weird noises, last night?' I dared not ask that question, for fear that the weird noises had existed only in my lunatic imagination. And no other convict would dare come and ask me that question, either, ... in case I would think, in my turn, that he was going crazy ... And the terror of insanity dominates the whole prison, asleep or awake.

✳

One evening as we were marching back to the section, I overheard one convict ask of another why mules were sterile. And the other convict said, well, there had to be order in nature. You couldn't have too much bastardisation, or where would the world be? A human male and a female baboon could have intercourse, he explained ('Talking from experience?'– I wondered, idly, because my brain was sick) but they couldn't have any progeny. Otherwise it would be an impossible world, he said. What sort of a monstrous thing, for instance, wouldn't the progeny of a pig and a rooster be, he said, by way of example.

By the time I got back to the cell, after having overheard that last remark, my mind was in a state of fever. I was locked into my cage, and my mind revolved, over and over again, the import of that dreadful picture. A pig and a rooster would have sexual intercourse: and the offspring they would produce would be half pig, half rooster. A snout and a comb, and a curly tail and feathers. And pig's trotters with spurs. It was a nightmare thought that strangled me. And it wasn't so much a thought as a sensation. I could feel all this madness oozing up out of my belly. It was stomach insanity. All chaos had been let loose in my belly, and it was seeping through into my brain.

And this half rooster and half pig monstrosity – what if it went and mated with something else? With the progeny of the mating of an elephant and a frog, for instance, or the mating of a railway engine with my jacket – my prison-jacket, with the number on, and all? Part frog and part jacket and part elephant's trunk and the tusks of a railway engine, and part – I was going mad. I tried to control my feeling. It was useless. My mind was in a whirl of horror and chaos. A frenzied world in which no single thing would have a brother or a sister or a father or a mother, because there would be nobody to look like him. And if a snake's tail hung down from where my head should be, and there were pieces of fish-scale and red brick in place of my hand, and I walked on one foot and two sticks and one wheel: what in the whole world would there be, in animate creation or in the inanimate realm, that I could fall in love with? What female would there be even remotely in my image?

*

With my sanity in the balance, as I knew it to be, I went through hell. I am not going to try to explain what I suffered. Every moment, almost, I thought I would go right off my rocker and start raving. At other times I was obsessed with the fear of a warder or a fellow-convict spotting the madness in my eyes, and giving me a wide berth, in consequence: and I knew that whoever spotted my insanity would pass on that information to somebody else, and so on. And then, no matter how hard I played sane, I would be classed as a lunatic. And every time, at night, when the steel door was banged shut on me by the warder, and I heard the key grate in the lock, then my head would start spinning, and I would crawl round and round on the concrete floor of my cage, round and round, with great difficulty, on my hands and knees, because of the narrowness of the walls of the cage. I would crawl round and round, like that, until I would drop down from exhaustion. And yet I had a strange cunning, with all this. I would time myself. The warders, coming along the corridor at hourly intervals and looking in through one peep-hole after another, would never catch me out crawling round and round the steel cage. Whenever I sensed that the warder was almost due I would grab up a book, any sort of a book, and I would sit down on the floor and pretend to read. And as soon as I had seen the warder's eye appear at the peep-hole I would resume my crawling. On hands and knees, round and round. I got very good at this crawling, after a while. I crawled very noiselessly. And I had got the trick of pulling in my buttocks, in just the right way, at each corner, so that I just rubbed my backside against the steel partitionings each time I made a full turn.

One night the warder came back again, unexpectedly, after he had looked in once and had seen me sitting on the floor, pretending to read.

And so he caught me crawling, like that. And for a couple of moments after he had shouted out and asked me what I was doing, I was terrified. I thought he had collared me dead to rights, now, and the whole thing would come out and it would be me booked for the bughouse.

But I didn't lose my head. And I answered quickly.

'I am looking for my ticket-pocket, sir,' I replied, getting up from the floor and going to talk to the warder through the peep-hole.

'But what you want your bleeding ticket-pocket for this time of the night?' the warder demanded.

'The ticket-pocket came off my jacket, sir,' I explained, 'and so I started looking for it.'

'That's a funny thing to do,' the warder said, and he sounded non-plussed, 'Crawling around on your hands and knees like you're mad, looking for your ticket-pocket.'

'It wasn't the ticket-*pocket* I wanted, actually,' I said to the warder, 'What I actually was after was the ticket inside the ticket-pocket. I wanted to work out how much time I still got to do.'

My brain was working very fast. I felt I could outwit a dozen warders, and also the whole world. Lord, they'd never tumble to it that I was mad! I had all sorts of illusions of grandeur, suddenly. Let them all come! I could do the most ridiculous things, and I could get away with it. I had a brain that could think out the most plausible excuses for the blackest kind of insanity that came out of my mad guts.

The warder looked at the card on my cage-door. He read out my name, crime, sentence, date of conviction, date of discharge, prison number, religion and workshop.

'Well, you still got quite a few years to do,' he announced, after having, apparently, done a bit of mental arithmetic.

'Yes, sir,' I answered, 'But I wanted to calculate it exactly. You see, I get a quarter off, for first offender's good conduct remission, and six months special mitigation for the Flag Bill (we all got that off you know, sir), and two months off because of the Prince of Wales's visit, and another – '

'You bastards get far too much time off,' the warder interrupted me curtly, 'The authorities must be mad to give you time off like that.'

'Yes, sir,' I agreed with the warder, promptly. I was very glad of what he had said.

He had said that the authorities were mad. That gave me more confidence than ever. I didn't feel so lonely and cut off from the rest of mankind, in my insanity. Here were the authorities also mad. I had the warder's word for it. I had a sudden, vivid picture of the authorities also crawling round and round on the floors of their bedrooms. It cheered me up no end, that ridiculous thought of the authorities also having to be careful of the way they manipulated their buttocks round the corners ...

Those last eight months passed quickly. As a matter of fact, it turned out that it was a bit more than eight months. The clerk at head office in charge of my files had omitted to make certain calculations in respect of remission, with the result that, for some time, I was in the queer position of being a forgotten man. I have difficulty, even today, in explaining what that means. The day I was due for discharge I said to my section-warder, in the morning, 'I am going out today,' and I added, 'I suppose I stay in the section until they send for the discharges, sir?'

The section-officer said, no, he hadn't been notified. But he knew I was going out, of course, quite soon. I had it on my ticket. And he knew that I had been measured for a suit. Anyway, I showed the section-warder my ticket, and we got a pencil and a piece of paper and we worked it out together. There was no doubt about it. I was due for discharge, and right away.

'Anyway, I got no instructions,' the section-warder said. 'Fall in for work.'

And in the workshop I showed my ticket to the head-warder, and he also worked out the figures, and he scratched his head, and looked puzzled. 'But I can't do nothing about it,' he assured me. 'That's for the discipline staff. I am only a head trades-warder. So get on with your blooming job.'

And I showed my ticket to a whole lot of convicts, and they worked it out, also, not with paper and pencil, because they didn't need to. A convict who had done lots of stretches only had to take a single glance at my ticket and through some sort of sixth sense, because he had done so much time, he could see at once that I was due for discharge.

'They must a lorst your papers at head office,' one blue-coat suggested. 'That means you'll never get out. You don't exist for them, no more. I remember the case of – '

But I moved away quickly. I didn't want to hear any bad-luck stories. I was scared of ill-omened precedents.

Next day I saw the chief-warder in the office about my getting discharged. He also agreed with me that, as far as the law was concerned, I was a free man. It said so on my ticket.

'Yes,' I acknowledged, 'I am free. I am a free man. There's nothing to keep me here in prison any more. Nothing except the bars and the locks and the warders.'

Anyway, the chief-warder informed me that it was no concern of his. All these things were done from head office. All he could do was, when a discharge-warrant came from head office for a convict, to order that convict's release. And he hadn't got such a discharge warrant from head office for me. 'But don't you worry,' he assured me. 'The moment that paper comes along, I'll see you get out. *I* won't keep you here a minute longer than I got to.'

I thanked him very much. But was there nothing he could do about it?

'It seems to me like the clerk in charge of your file has sort of overlooked it,' the chief-warder said. 'Or he may be on leave. Or he may have forgotten to enter some of your remission – over the Flag Bill, perhaps. Or he may have lost your papers. I remember a case – '

But I asked the chief-warder please not to continue. I was afraid I might panic. If nothing was heard during the course of the next few days, might he perhaps take it up with the head office? He assured me that he would. 'If you don't hear any more about it,' he said, 'Come and see me again in about a month's time.'

I went to see him again, of course. And in much less than a month's time.

'But see, sir,' I said, 'I am here, am I not? And according to the details of my sentence and remission I have no right to be here. In theory I am not a hard-labour convict at all.'

'What do you want, then?' the chief-warder enquired, in a nasty tone, 'Do you want a job here as chief-warder, perhaps? Don't be afraid to ask, now.'

But I informed him, trying hard to keep sane, that I didn't want any sort of job in the prison, and that I wanted no part of the prison, and that my one desire was to get as far away as possible from any contact with and any thought of the prison.

'It's your file at head office,' the chief-warder explained. 'Yes, something must have happened about your file. I'll go and see about it next chance I get of slipping away from the prison for an hour or so.'

'Might that be today, sir, perhaps?' I enquired hopefully.

'Some time next month,' the chief-warder answered, 'Look, you've done a good long stretch, already, and we haven't had much trouble from you. I hope you aren't going to start being a nuisance now. What's a few extra months, anyway, on top of the time you have already done with a clean sheet? Just go back to the section, and enjoy yourself here a little longer, and it will all get fixed up.'

I passed through a period of the most utter desolation. I felt so completely helpless and frustrated. And there was nothing I could do about it. I still get nightmares about that period. Here was I, in the prison, a human being, of flesh and air and bone; I existed here, in the prison, as a physical reality. At least, that was what I had always believed. But I found that I wasn't that person at all. I wasn't me. I wasn't this individual sitting here on a stool eating mealie-porridge out of a tin basin. Oh, no. This person did not exist at all, as an entity. It wasn't me, the person that had got his suit made – the suit that was all pressed and hung on a clothes-hanger in the tailors' shop, waiting for me to come and fetch it away. No, I wasn't this person at all.

What was really me were a lot of papers, dog-eared and yellowed with the years, lying between two cardboard covers and tied up with green string, in a filing cabinet at head office ... I saw, now, why I had got claus-trophobia, in prison. It wasn't because of the prison. Quite enough air came into my cage through the barred window. But that person in the steel cage wasn't me at all. My real individuality, my real me, were those papers in that filing cabinet. So, of course, I had suffocation fears. Who wouldn't get claustrophobia, shut like that between two covers, and tied up with green string, and then locked into a steel cabinet – with more and more folders getting piled on top of me with each year that passed? How on earth can you breathe inside a steel cabinet?

But I don't want to go on piling up the horrors. It is enough to say that, shortly afterwards, through the friendly offices of the chief-warder, a vast stack of other folders were lifted from me, and I was taken out of the steel cabinet, and my covers were dusted, and the green string was untied ...

✳

As a result of this bit of confusion, I didn't get discharged from the prison, like other convicts, at nine o'clock in the morning. The warrant for my release arrived late one afternoon. It was marked urgent, in very large, black letters and it said that I was to be released immediately.

So they had to fetch a clerk from his home (because he had already gone off duty) to work out how much was due to me in gratuity and to make out an official cheque for me. Another warder escorted me to the stores, where they fitted me out with a pair of prison-made discharge boots. They went and dug up my suitcase, containing a couple of shirts that I had worn many years ago, before I was convicted. I put on a shirt with stripes. The cool, luxurious feel of light linen against my skin after all those years in which I had worn the coarse, stinking, degrading – oh, never mind: the sensation of linen lying lightly on my body was exquisite. There was also a tie in my suitcase, a bright piece of neckwear that had not faded, very appreciably, during the length of time in which it had been thrust away from the world, in a dark corner. They had not put me in prison, alone, but my few poor possessions also. I didn't realise, until now, that I had had my suitcase and my socks and my shirts to keep me company during the period of my incarceration. I picked up that tie with a warm feeling of intimacy. My friendly old tie; my companion in imprisonment; here we were meeting again; and he was still gaudy; he still had memories of former gaieties, brightly-dyed; he was still half-cheeky. I wondered whether I was like my tie in this respect; whether I also, at the end of my imprisonment, retained something inside me that was bright-hued. But I feared not. My tie didn't have to say 'Yes, sir,' all day long.

And then, of course, when I had it round my neck, I didn't know how to fasten that tie. Through all that long disuse my fingers had lost the trick of knotting a tie around my neck. A warder performed the office for me.

And then I found that I couldn't get my suit. It was locked up in the tailors' shop. They couldn't get the key. It was a blow. But they fitted me out with an ordinary prison discharge suit, called a pom-pom, which the Government supplies to short-timer discharged convicts. It didn't look very elegant, but they said it would do for the night. Next morning I could call round at the prison, at the front-gate, and my blue serge suit would be neatly parcelled-up there for me.

'Please see to it that they don't crush my suit when they fold it,' I said to a discipline warder. But I hadn't much faith that they would exercise the right amount of care.

The final formalities were gone through. I was given my discharge papers. It was explained to me that mine was a conditional release. I was being let out on ticket-of-leave. The conditions of my discharge were read out to me: they were contained in two pages of print. Then I shook hands with the warders about me and I took up my suitcase and my prison-discharge boots sounded clumsy on the cement floor of the court-yard before the main-gate. And the gate swung open. Not very much. Just enough to let me out.

And I was free.

The guard at the gate shook hands with me. And he called me by my name instead of by my number.

'Look after yourself, now,' the gate-warder said, 'You know boob is a bastard. See you don't come back.'

I answered, 'Yes, thank you, sir.'

Forgetting that I no longer had any need to call him 'sir'.

✳

This is really a love story – a story of adolescent love, my first love ... Her eyes were heavily fringed with dark lashes, like barred windows. Her bosom was hard and pure and cold – like a cement floor. And it was faithful and chaste love. During all those years of my young manhood, in whose arms did I sleep each night, but in hers?

The Old Magistrate's Court

A few days ago I stood in a spacious courtyard surrounded with dun-coloured walls. The doors opening into the courtyard were few but massive; the windows were covered with rusty bars. Many years before, when I stood on that same spot and looked at those barred apertures, I thought that they were like a woman's eyes, heavily fringed with dark lashes. Now they seemed to be simply like windows with iron bars stuck in front of them.

The place where I stood was the yard of the Old Magistrates' Courts, in Johannesburg. Today the building is no longer a courthouse, but is used as offices of the Governor-General's Fund and for other purposes. But they don't seem to have found any use for the yard itself, which for half a century was the temporary place of detention for the city's awaiting trial prisoners, Europeans and natives, men and women. Whatever was the charge against them, those accused of transgressing the law were brought into the yard of the Magistrate's Court. They came on foot, handcuffed and under escort, or they were conveyed there by Black Maria.

Through the forbidding-looking portals opening on to New Street South the prisoners were conducted – quietly led, in most cases, cajoled or enticed, sometimes, or occasionally, simply pushed from behind – into the yard, there to remain until their cases had been disposed of. Which meant that they were either sentenced or acquitted in a summary trial by the magistrate, if the charges against them were not serious; or else they appeared on a preliminary examination, to be committed for trial at the Supreme Court.

It was warm and sunny, that afternoon of a few days ago, when I stood alone in that courtyard, at the beginning of a new Spring, and I was surprised to find how little the place had changed. The walls had always seemed just so dilapidated, with the same patches of weathered plaster, yellow like old parchment, and the same extensive areas of exposed and discoloured brickwork. There seemed to be still the cracks in the dirty grey of the cement floor; those fissures might have widened and deepened a little, with the years; but I couldn't tell. They seemed just the same, anyway.

And the blue enamel basin, fixed to a wall under a tap, was invested with that peculiar sort of squalor which becomes imparted to all inanimate things that have for long lived very closely to the raw things of human life.

The place had not changed. The walls were redolent of yesterdays that had lost their bitterness; they breathed of spectral long-agos, of ancient, sullied things.

The only way in which the present differed from the past – in which this afternoon was not the same as some other, vanished, afternoon, when the same sun shone down on brick and stone and concrete – was that now the prison-yard was silent. But it was not an oppressive stillness. It was a tranquility charged with a spirit of gentle melancholy, like when a single late violet is left growing on a bank where a little before there were a myriad clusters.

And as in the perfume of violets, in that quiet there was a heady fragrance, maddening to the senses, so that that prison-yard seemed to come alive again, for a little while, and the fat gaoler seated in front of the heavy door, in the far corner, was not a ghost but a stony reality; and the native warders were again marshalling their charges, making them stand up or sit down in rows; and the white prisoners, if they were new to the ways of a goal, were clamouring at a little barred window about getting messages sent to their friends for bail – to the cynical amusement of the police and the old offenders, who did not expect to see the outside world again for many years, if at all, and who had other, more serious concerns. And a couple of street-walkers were once more looking into the cracked piece of mirror over the blue enamel wash-basin, putting paint on their lips and then wiping it off again, uncertain as to what would make a better impression on the magistrate who was to try them for soliciting.

For a little while, because of the silence pervading that yard which for 50 years had been a prison and was now open to any member of the public to stroll about in, there resounded once more within those walls the clank of fetters. In that dilapidated yard there was awakened again, for a few moments, that sombre activity of men and women languishing in bondage that is more stark than the dilapidation of crumbling plaster. Deserted of its tenants for ever, the yard in the Old Magistrates' Courts, for the first time since it was built, did not seem to be derelict.

I would recommend who is interested in that strange and brooding and carnal-twilight thing that we call 'atmosphere' to pay a visit to this place. For I don't suppose it will be long, now, before they pull those old buildings down. And remember, as you walk the yard and your footsteps echo because of the silence, that there are ghosts from the past that walk beside you.

And for a few moments may the place come alive for you also.

The glint of the Spring sunshine on the handcuffs. On tarnished people and on dreams that have gone. The gaudy scarf which a man will wear around his neck only a little longer: the scarf is shortly going to be replaced with a rope. The stained handwriting on the letter from his sweetheart which the forger pulls out of his pocket, surreptitiously – gloomily wondering why there is such a thing in the world as handwriting. The blue haze in which a native prisoner is puffing at a dagga cigarette, in the lavatory while his accomplice watches the door. The crimson lipstick on the mouth of the harlot, as vivid now as it was twenty years ago. And the *corpus delicti*. And the placid clouds in the sky overhead. And the detectives. And the pallid terrors in the hearts of men.

As for me, I found when I eventually turned to depart, that the massive door, because it moved so heavily on its rusted hinges, refused, for a few moments, to open.

Johannesburg

Taken out of its ancient African context, Johannesburg is one of the world's newest cities. I don't know whether any of the old 1886 pioneers survive. Perhaps there are still here and there a few genuine pioneers, who came to Johannesburg with the first gold rush: it won't be at all extraordinary, because they all seem to have been remarkably tough. But there are any number of men and women living in Johannesburg today who were children in Johannesburg's childhood, and have seen the city change and grow and develop as they themselves, leaving childish things behind, have grown to a maturity which is already passing into a dignified or dissolute old age.

Quite recently I spoke to a gentleman who made reference to certain steps chopped into the sides of the railway cutting just off Twist Street. That was before there was a bridge over that part of the line.

'We had gone to school across the open veld, there, for several years,' my informant said, 'and then the Netherlands Company excavated that cutting and laid the tracks, and so we schoolboys had to dig steps of our own into the sides of the cutting, in order to continue with our education. I was the youngest of the group and the older boys had to help me up by pulling on my satchel.'

This gentleman also informed me that those old steps, crudely carved by the hands of school-children, had suffered much from erosion during the many years of disuse, and he didn't think they were there any more. But he still had the straps of that satchel in a suitcase, somewhere, he said.

'They didn't issue any certificates in that school,' this gentleman explained, 'so I kept those straps from the satchel to show my prospective employers that I had had a schooling. And I have still got those straps – just in case.'

You can still come across lots of people who can tell you about the spirit that prevailed here in the early days when Johannesburg was a roaring, wide-open mining camp, in which every citizen was imbued with the one laudable desire of making all the money he could in the shortest possible time. It was an all-in-scramble with no holds barred. The place teemed with short-cuts to a gaudy opulence. And venturers from all parts of the world heard that there was money going in Johannesburg, and they flocked here to get some. And through some of the quaint whimsicalities of the Roman-Dutch law, which was the basis of legislation in the Transvaal Republic, some ways of making money were regarded as being less legitimate than others.

Thus when members of a spirited fraternity, hailing in the main from Australia, alighted at Park Station and started getting busy with their luggage, their activities gave rise to a good deal of unfriendly comment. For the sole luggage that these gentlemen had brought with them were home-constructed sandbags which they wielded on the populace, left and right, with a singular effectiveness.

The members of this fraternity, perhaps not unjustly, resented the discouraging attitude which officialdom adopted towards their industry as an unfair discrimination, based on the fact that they were newly-arrived immigrants who still had to ask passers-by the way to the Stock Exchange or the Rand Club, when they wanted to go and look for customers. The point of view of the authorities seemed to be, 'You can see for yourself that we impose no restrictions. You can do anything you like to a man in order to take his money off him. Only you must not hit him with your luggage.' Even today this seems an unreasonable sort of distinction to make. Not allowing a man from foreign shores to contribute his luggage to the building up of a new nation and a new culture.

And talking about culture, I believe that Johannesburg has got all those attributes, mainly in the form of very raw material as yet, which will enable it eventually to occupy a leading place in the world of art and letters.

I would like to put forward my naive views on this subject in such a way as to try and avoid, as far as possible, anything in the way of controversy. But I believe, frankly, that as a source of new cultural inspiration to the world Europe is finished. Europe has got a background of unrivalled magnificence. Almost every town and city of Western Europe is impregnated with ancient splendour. But as far as the spirit of the peoples of Western Europe is concerned, these are glories that have run to seed.

For this reason it is most depressing to find painters in this country –

some of them not without a good measure of creative talent – slavishly following the tricks of technique which contemporary European artists are employing with an ever-increasing complication of subjective subtleties as a substitute for individuality. Nothing can take the place of the raw inspiration of life itself, expressed with all the strength of a creative personality. Nobody knows this fact better than the European artists themselves, who are not glad that their inner force has decayed, but who simply can't help themselves.

It is therefore all the more regrettable that our South African artists, as a whole, should have no clear sense of values in this matter. You can learn all the technique you like from Europe. That's what Europe is there for. But if you don't put your own spirit into what you paint, either because you haven't spirit of your own or because you don't know how to express it, then what you produce cannot be anything more than synthetic rubbish.

But I believe that this is only a passing phase with South African artists. They are not trying to meet Europe on her own ground – which in itself would be an impossible enough task – but they are actually trying to copy Europe on her own ground. And this is pure clownishness.

But this stage will pass. And I believe that after that South Africa, with Johannesburg as its cultural centre, will find itself in an era of inspired creation, sprung forth out of the passion of love for this country, when we shall produce art that will reach heights of real grandeur because the note it strikes is authentic, and whose beauty will endure because it is our own.

We have got everything for it here. What has already been achieved in Afrikaans literature is a fine augury for the future. America has produced Edgar Allan Poe and Mark Twain, two sublime literary figures whose true influence is being felt only today. But Africa has not spoken yet.

I believe that it is possible to see Johannesburg as it really is only when we view it as a place of mystery and romance, as a city wrapped in mist. Is there any other city that is less than sixty years old – and the origin of its name already lost in the shadows of Time?

People who were present at the christening of Johannesburg say that the town was named after the second baptismal name of President Kruger. Others with equal authority say it was called Johannesburg after Johan

Rissik. Other candidates – and in each case their names are put forward on most excellent authority – include Christiaan Johannes Joubert, Veldkornet Johannes Meyer, Johannes Lindeque, and Willem Gerhardus Christoffel Pelser (the latter, possibly, because his seemed to be the only set of names that didn't have Johannes in it).

There are at least another dozen claimants. And you need have no hesitation in supporting any one of them. The evidence in each case is indisputable.

With its skyscrapers, Johannesburg is today no mean city. These tall edifices of concrete and steel would look highly imposing anywhere, leave alone just being dumped down in the middle of the veld. But we still bear one or two traces of our mining-camp origin. For instance, there is the Public Library.

The Standard Theatre

The trouble with me is that I never know what is going on in the world. I do not keep abreast of the latest developments in the field of politics, commerce and industry, culture and finance and philosophy. Consequently it was only at the tail end of the controversy about the closing down of the Standard Theatre that I got to hear of what was happening just about two blocks away from where I work. Nevertheless, if anybody had come to me at any time while the arguments pro and con the closing of the Standard Theatre were in full blast, I would have been able to say authoritatively and at any time: 'No, the Historical Monuments Commission will not place a blue plaque on the Standard.' I would have said: 'They will pull down the Standard Theatre like they have pulled down all the old buildings, theatres, gin-places, doss-houses, temples, shops, arcades, cafes and joints that were intimately associated with the mining-camp days of Johannesburg.'

Because I know Johannesburg. And I am satisfied that there is no other city in the world that is so anxious to shake off the memories of its early origins. If other cities took the same pride in obliterating the architectural remnants of their past there would be no figured obelisk tapering by the banks of the Nile; there would be no Westminster Abbey with its dangerous fan ceiling, consisting of thousands of tons of masonry that curves down like Madeira embroidery: the visitor to Westminster Abbey walks carefully and softly, on tiptoe, almost, in reverence of the Abbey's storied past – and knows that if he doesn't exercise caution the ceiling will come down; there would be no Erechtheum on the Acropolis, no tall columns beside the Tiber. No Zimbabwe.

No, they are not going to demolish the Standard Theatre because it is a menace to life and limb, because one day it might catch alight. Next to the Standard Theatre fire hazard, as I have said, I give you Westminster Abbey's tons-of-masonry-nine-centuries-old-fan-ceiling hazard. I give you – oh, well, it doesn't matter. We of Johannesburg know why the Standard has got to come down, and we know also that no power on earth can save it.

It was in this spirit that I paid a visit to the Standard Theatre premises a couple of days ago. I could see that nobody hanging around the doors of the Standard Theatre at that moment cared very much about the fate of the old building ...

So I went into the pub instead. 'Is this Frascati's or is it McCarthy's Beer Hall?' I asked of the bar-tender. It was something that had often puzzled me. The bar-tender's explanation was lucid enough as far as it went. 'It's Frascati's Pub, Pat McCarthy's Beer Hall,' he said. 'If you come in through the Standard Arcade – that door there – then it's Frascati's Pub. If you come in through the Market Street door, then it's McCarthy's. Simple enough, ain't it?'

The bar-tender told me that his name was Mr. J. Hodder and that he had been in the liquor trade in Johannesburg for 43 years, and that he had never once been in court – not even as a witness. This history of the pub was interesting. It wasn't opened at the same time as the theatre, however. Mr. Hodder didn't know why. I would have thought that the pub would have been opened even before the theatre. But I found out the reason for this afterwards, when I was upstairs talking to Miss B., the caretaker, and she showed me a very early photograph of the Standard Theatre. The buildings on the other side of the passage-way in front of the theatre were erected at a date subsequent to the completion and opening of the Standard.

I left the pub by the Frascati door and went up the stairs to interview the caretaker. On her door – No. 64 – was a notice 'Out between 1 and 2.' So I knew she must be inside having lunch. Accordingly I turned the knob and walked in – but only for a distance of 18 inches, that being the length of the safety-chain attached to the inside of the door. That gives you an idea of Miss B.'s character.

After I had assured her that I lived on a farm on the Muldersdrift road and didn't require accommodation in the Standard Buildings, the caretaker undid the chain and we got talking. I promised her that I wouldn't mention her name.

The man who built the theatre was a gentleman named Scott, Miss B. informed me. He would have been able to tell me a good deal more about the early days of the Standard than she could she said. It was a pity I hadn't come round sooner – say 20 years ago, or so, when Mr. Scott was still alive. She didn't mind very much about the proposed closing down of the Standard Theatre, she explained, but what she did resent bitterly was the distorted impression which the S. A. Broadcasting Corporation conveyed to the public with regard to the kind of entertainment provided by the Standard Theatre in the old days.

'To judge from what we heard over the wireless,' Miss B. said., 'it would seem as though they put on only cheap variety shows at the Standard. Nasty music-hall turns. What about when Margaret MacIntyre and her company, straight from Drury Lane, presented *Traviata* – in 1894? You've never heard about that before, have you? Neither in the newspapers nor over the radio. And what about other well-known companies that put on some of the world's greatest plays? I'll show you the photographs.'

I accompanied Miss B. to an office in the Standard Buildings, where Scott and Mendelssohn (of Mendelssohn's Buildings) carried on their business in the 1890's. Miss B. showed me a number of photographs of stage celebrities of the last century – music-hall stars who played in the Standard when the gold paint was still new. But I was more interested in the furniture in the Scott-Mendelssohn office than in the photographs. High oak desks at which clerks had sat on tall-stemmed stools; the rusty old iron safe; bloomy, ponderous chairs and tables that had constituted the last word in Victorian business-house equipment.

Miss B. drew my attention to the photograph of a corpulent male actor. A high stick-up collar and plenty of bulging waistcoat and a jacket with straight, narrow lapels. A shaggy jaw, bull neck and low forehead.

Miss B. told me his name. And she added, in a low voice, 'He was the handsomest man I ever knew.'

And the light sigh she drew then seemed to linger on in the old office after we had gone out again and locked the door behind us.

Playing Sane

I converse fairly regularly with a gentleman who was confined for a somewhat lengthy period in what was known in the old days as a lunatic asylum and is today called by the euphemistic appellation of a mental hospital.

'They are all barmy there,' the gentleman informs me, 'male nurses, schizophrenics, psychiatrists, paranoics, pathologists, homicidal maniacs, keepers and attendants.' This statement did not strike me as being particularly novel, nor this ex-patient's assertions as to the strain that was imposed on him in his trying to preserve his mental balance in the almost constant company of mental specialists and asylum keepers.

The psychiatrists were very difficult, my informant states.

'There was one fat mental specialist with a queer glint in his eyes who kept on asking me if I heard voices. He meant when you heard voices and there aren't any. Well, I never heard voices. And if I did, I wouldn't have been mad enough to tell him. And every time I told him I didn't hear voices you should have seen the look of disappointment that came into his face. I had the uneasy feeling that he heard voices all day long, talking all kinds of blah to him, and why he wanted me to say I also heard those voices was so that he wouldn't feel so alone.

'I even got so, after a while, that I would sit for hours on end in my padded cell, just listening. I thought that if perhaps I could only hear one voice, just saying a few simple things to me, and I could repeat it to the psychiatrist, he would feel a lot better. But it just wouldn't work. During all the time that I was locked up in that madhouse I never once heard voices. And it wasn't from want of trying.'

Thus spoke a former inmate of a mental hospital who was discharged, I suppose, on the grounds that he was incurable.

Now, this whole question of insanity, officially classified as such, raises a number of interesting problems, some of them insoluble, except, possibly, by a lunatic.

There is Edgar Allan Poe's story of a man's visit to an insane asylum.

The visitor is taken round by a person whom he believes to be the doctor in charge of the institution, but who eventually turns out to be the chief lunatic, for there had taken place, unknown to the outside world, a lunatic's revolution at this establishment, with the result that the lunatics had taken the places of the medical men and the keepers, these latter being now kept in confinement under the surveillance of their former charges.

It is a gripping story. It is a story that has got everything. But what puzzled me at the time I read it, was the question as to how this substitution of authority was ever detected. I mean, how is it possible ever to tell?

I feel that a change-over of this description has taken place in many of the world's best asylums before today (you know how cunning lunatics are) and with nobody the wiser.

When once a change of this nature has taken place in the administration, it seems only too simple to keep the new regime in power for ever. Picture yourself as the visitor to this institution. The new superintendent (former head lunatic) shows you around.

The first patient he will confront you with, as a matter of course, will be the former superintendent.

'A very interesting case, this one,' the new superintendent will inform you. 'It's all frightfully intricate. We have diagnosed it as *dementia praecox* with diurgic aberrations of the left cranial tissues. It's a species of insanity that is mystifying Krafft-Ebing and Walters and other psychiatrists and schizophrenics who are making a special study of it.'

At this stage, of course, the former superintendent will announce his identity, which will be just what the new superintendent wants in order to establish his point.

'You're mad,' the former superintendent will announce to the man who has usurped his job. 'In fact,' – and he will try to approach the visitor confidentially, lowering his voice and looking knowingly at him – 'in fact, they are all mad, here. I am really the superintendent. The lunatics have taken charge of the place here and have locked me up. I am busy writing to the Department of the Interior about it. You ought to see the copies I have got of all the letters I have written to the Department of the Interior. Stacks of letters and I get no answer. I am beginning to think that the Department of the Interior is also mad.'

'Like I said to you,' the new superintendent will announce to the visitor, 'just about incorrigible. We give him all the pencils and paper he wants for writing. It takes his mind off things. But when once a man becomes graphomaniac, like he is, there isn't much hope for him.'

You can go on this way *ad lib*. Because, in actual fact, you don't know where you are, in this world. It's a frightening thought. Take any book on psychopathology, written by almost any authority on abnormalities of the brain, either in its structure or its functions, and after a couple of paragraphs, if you know anything about the art of letters, you can feel to what an extent graphomania has been the dynamism that has impelled the author to sit down and write the book at all.

You will also discover, after the first couple of pages, that the writer is going to impart to you his own individual theories, which are completely different from any theories any other psychiatrist has ever held, and from then onwards the writer enters a realm of marvellously disconnected fantasy, where he can let himself go just as mad as he likes.

Something that I have also learnt from my ex-mental-hospital-inmate informant – and it is something that has shaken me – is the fact that the patients in mental institutions are no longer required to wear a distinctive garb. Now, in the old days, it was different. The custom of making the patient wear a uniform decorated with stripes or squares or daisy-chains was very sensible. It gave you a good rough and ready idea as to who was who in a lunatic asylum. But today that has gone by the board. The present-day situation is one fraught with peril. In the rough and tumble of trying to establish, under prevailing conditions, as to who is the mental specialist and who the mental case requiring treatment, some pretty ghastly scenes must get enacted. And the strain, of course, is on the keepers.

The whole field of insanity is of absorbing importance at the present time. To all of us. It is enough if you have got a fixed stare in your eyes and you seem sure of what you are doing, for people to be impressed with you and to invest you with all the qualities of leadership. Human nature can't take in the idea that a man should look as mad as all that, and carry on in a mad fashion and on top of all that actually be mad. It doesn't seem logical.

You can see this happening everywhere, and not only in the sphere of statesmanship. Where a man with a one-track insanity type of mind comes along, normal people instinctively stand aside. They accord him all due respect straight away. They can't believe that a man can have all that insane energy, and still be wrong.

In this respect we are still very primitive. We stand in the same awe of energetic insanity as did any of the members of a primitive tribe. We are actually in a more dangerous position than are savages with their taboos and rigid caste systems – all aimed at keeping the lunatic out. We even go so far as to allow him to write treatises on psychopathology. This is a terrible thought.

As a result of all this, we civilised human beings are all caught up in a whirlpool of mental aberrations, our thoughts moulded in terms of chaos conceived by lunatics of both the past and the present. To take just a simple example. Almost every civilised person you come across will tell you that the earth isn't flat. It's like an orange. It is, to be still more technical, an oblate spheroid. And the authority he quotes for this is that some astronomer a few hundred years ago saw it all in a telescope. Copernicus, and he saw it all moving.

The point of all this, obviously enough, is that the earth is flat. And it doesn't move. These facts are so axiomatic that you don't even need to test them out for yourself. You have just got to look at the earth and see. And you can feel it doesn't move.

Our whole mental attitude towards life is hedged around with unrealities of this description. We live in a chaos of ideas thought out by cranks. We have been unable to protect our civilisation from the perilous invasion of the lunatic, whom we have been unable to keep out. The result today, when you reject insanity, and you depict things just as they are, and you see the sun as Phoebus, as Apollo, as Ra bestriding the heavens, and a red sky in the morning is the shepherd's warning, then it sounds as though you are trying to talk poetry. Whereas it is all just plain, factual stuff, based on simple observations and divest of insanity.

We all know the expression, 'playing mad'. In this mad world there are, alas, a good many of us who have to engage in the pastime of 'playing sane'. There is quite a lot of fun in it. Playing sane-sane.

Street Processions

For as long as I can remember, almost, street processions have been in my blood. When I see a long line of people marching through the streets – the longer the line, the better I like it – something primordial gets stirred inside me and I am overtaken by the urge to fall in also, and take my place somewhere near the end of the procession. I have no doubt that the reason why, many years ago – before Communism had the social standing and prestige which it enjoys today – the reason why in my youth I joined the Young Communist League in Johannesburg was because that part of Socialist ideology which consisted of organising processions through the streets, holding up the traffic and all that sort of thing, made a very profound appeal to my ethical sense.

And it has been like that with me all my life.

There is something about the sight and the thought of a long line of men marching through the streets of a city that fills me with an awe that I can't define very easily. And it has got to be through a city. A procession through a village or just over the veld isn't the same thing. And the people taking part in it should be mostly men. One or two women are all right, too, perhaps. But there shouldn't be too many of them. Banners are optional. And while I am not too keen on a band, I can overlook its presence.

The ideal conditions for a procession are grey skies and wet streets. And there should be a drizzle. My tastes don't run to the extremes of a blizzard or a tropical downpour. Thunder and lightning effects are out of place. All you want is a steady drip-drip of fine rain that makes everything look bleak and dismal, without the comfortable abandonment of utter desolation. Then through these drab streets there must come trailing a long line of humanity, walking three or four abreast, their boots muddy and their clothes (by preference) shabby and shapeless in the rain, and their faces a grey pallor. They can sing a little, too, if they like, to try and cheer themselves up – without ever succeeding, of course. And in this sombre trudging – the dull tramp awakening no echoes – of thousands of booted feet on cobbles or tarred road, there goes my heart, also. I get gripped with an intense feeling of being one with stupid, struggling, rotten, heroic humanity, and in this grey march there is a heavy symbolism whose elements I don't try to interpret for fear that the parts should together be less than the whole; and I find myself, contrary to all the promptings of good sense and reason, yielding to the urge to try and find a place for myself somewhere near the tail end of the procession.

Oh, and of course, there is another thing, something I had almost forgotten, and that is the *cause* operating as the dynamism for getting a procession of this description organised and under way. Frankly, I don't think the cause matters very much. I have a natural predilection for an unpopular cause and, above all, for a forlorn cause – a lost hope, and whether this peculiar idiosyncrasy of mine springs from ordinary perversity, or from a nobility of soul, is something that I have not been able to ascertain. And so, while I always feel that it is very nice, and all that, if the march is undertaken by the participants in a spirit of lofty idealism, because a very important principle is at stake, I am equally satisfied, provided that the afore-stipulated conditions of muddy boots and grey skies are present, if the spiritual factors back of the demonstration are not so very high or altruistic.

This weakness of mine in the way of desiring to make one with street processions, identifying myself with and merging my personality in a mass of humanity moving onwards to no clearly defined goal, has in the past resulted in my becoming on more than one occasion involved in a considerable measure of embarrassment. In my youth, for instance, when the Salvation Army moved up from the town hall steps at the termination of a Sunday evening open-air meeting, and I found myself marching on at the back, in a sort of trance, it happened at least twice that I followed the procession right into the Hope Hall in Commissioner Street, with the result that, each time, I wasn't able to get out again until I had been converted.

And then, only a couple of years ago, with the annual Corpus Christi procession to the End Street Convent, when I had again from force of habit taken my place near the end of the line and was proceeding down Bree Street, feeling very solemn as I always do on such occasions, I realised, suddenly, the incongruity of my presence in the company of priests in black vestments and stoles and choirboys in white surplices, and all carrying missals, while I was dressed just in civvies and half a loaf of bread under my arm, which I was taking home for supper ... as I explained to an abbot-looking gentleman in a mitre, who hadn't said anything about my being in that procession, but who seemed unhappy, nevertheless, in a peculiar sort of a way.

Similarly, I have, at different times, marched through the streets of London with Communists, Mosleyites, Scotchmen on their way to the Cup-Tie, unemployed Welsh miners and the Peace Pledge Union.

The last time I marched in a procession was as recently as last Saturday afternoon. I was on my way home, when from the top of the Malvern tram I spotted in front of Jeppe Station a street procession in course of formation. I could see straight away that the conditions were just right. It was drizzling. The streets were wet and grey and muddy. The sky was bleak and cheerless. I prepared to alight. Unfortunately, however, the tram was very crowded, with the result that I wasn't able to get off before the Berg Street stop. From there I took another tram back to Jeppe Station, arriving there just as the procession was moving off. I took my place somewhere near the rear. We marched in a northerly direction and swung into Commissioner Street. Trudge. Trudge. Drizzle. Mud. Wet boots and shapeless clothes. I didn't ask what the procession was about. I didn't want to reveal my ignorance and chance getting sneered at. I had been sneered at by a procession before today and I don't like it.

'It's that (so-and-so) Steyn,' the man on the left of me remarked by way of conversation.

'You're telling me,' I answered.

He *was* telling me, of course. Otherwise I wouldn't know what it was all about.

'If it wasn't for him,' the man on my left continued, 'us miners wouldn't be on strike.'

'Us miners wouldn't be,' I agreed, relieved to have discovered, so soon, what the procession was all about.

A middle-aged man in front of me, in a khaki overcoat, was singing rather a lot. A young fellow with a free and easy sort of look marched next to him. On my right was a stocky man with a grey moustache and a red rosette.

'You know,' this stocky, grey-moustached man remarked to me after a while, 'in 1922 it was different. In 1922 I was shooting yous. In 1922 I was in the police. Now I am one of yous.'

The imp of perversity inside me egged me on to pick a quarrel with Grey-Moustache.

'How do I know that you still aren't one of thems?' I enquired.

Grey-Moustache's neck went all red.

'I am a rock-buster on the Crown Mines,' he retorted. 'There's half-a-dozen men in this procession as knows I am a rock-buster on the Crown Mines.'

In this way what had at first promised to be an unpleasant incident was settled peaceably.

Only, I couldn't help feeling that in the depth of his most secret sincerities Grey-Moustache was still one of thems. As the old saying goes, if you're once one of thems, you're always one of thems.

So the march continued in the grey drizzle. Wet clothes and boots and mud-splashed trouser-tops. A number of low songs were sung. Various obscene remarks were made. Everything was in order.

A big fat man in a black overcoat was acting as a sort of lines-man for our part of the procession. They called him Oom Tobie. He was a kind of cheerleader. He would hurry on until he got about fifty yards ahead of our rank, and then he would stand on the pavement and shout out the slogans. These were in the form of questions to which the procession roared out the answers. As far as I could make out, it all had a lot to do with the miners' democratic rights.

'Do we want Steyn?' Oom Tobie would ask.

'No!' the procession would roar. That seemed to be the right answer.

'Do we want the capitalists?' Oom Tobie would ask again.

'No!' would come the thunderous reply.

Then Oom Tobie would look sort of arch, like a schoolteacher trying to tip his class off as to the right thing to answer, with the inspector present, and he would shout out: 'But – do we want democracy?'

I make the acknowledgement – and gladly – that a considerable proportion of the miners shouted 'Yes!' But it was also a fact that an equal number would answer, with the same degree of determination, 'No!' It seemed to me that Oom Tobie had not properly rehearsed them in their responses. He didn't seem to have given them the proper instructions on this point. I came to the conclusion that Oom Tobie wasn't himself too sure as to what was the right answer either.

Trudge. Tramp. Grey faces. Dirty songs. Everything was going very nicely. Then, near Delvers Street, somewhere, the procession came to a halt. Oom Tobie, water dripping from his black overcoat but his face beaming, came and made a further announcement. 'The West Rand boys is here, now,' he said, 'and we are going up Jeppe Street. And when you get to the *Rand Daily Mail* building, stand there and boo your guts out.'

Everybody, myself included, looked forward to booing his guts out in front of the *Rand Daily Mail* offices. But I don't know what good it did. There seemed to be only a few clerks and subs and typists looking out of the first and second floor windows, and at the first blast of all those raspberries they drew back and went and hid somewhere. But nobody appeared in any window of the works department. Thus, after twenty years in journalism, I was denied the opportunity – which had so nearly come my way – of telling a comp. what I thought of him.

It was after we had passed the *Rand Daily Mail* offices that I realised why the man in the khaki overcoat and the free-and-easy youth were singing more loudly than anybody else. By that time they were not only singing, but also staggering. They had a bottle of Jerepigo wine which they were passing backwards and from which they were taking surreptitious swigs. Grey-Moustache reported the matter to Oom Tobie. As I have remarked before, once one of thems, always one of thems. Nevertheless, I have rarely seen a man as indignant as Oom Tobie was at that moment. And I am sure that not even an underground manager had ever dressed down Khaki Overcoat and the free-and-easy youth in terms of vituperation such as Oom Tobie employed now.

'You are giving us all a bad name,' he shouted finally. 'Drinking wine like that out of the bottle, and in the street. And in front of the *Rand Daily Mail*, too. What if they had taken your photograph, drinking wine, when all the boys was booing? What if they got your photo like that in the *Rand Daily Mail* on Monday morning?'

'But we did boo, too,' the free-and-easy youth explained. 'In between.'

'Won't you have a pull at the bottle, too, Oom Tobie?' the man in the khaki overcoat asked. 'Just a small one, Oom Tobie?'

'Well, seeing it's you,' Oom Tobie replied, 'and because it's raining today – but not for any other reason, mind you – I don't mind if I just have a small mouthful. But don't let anybody see. Don't pass me the bottle until that tram has gone round the corner.'

A few minutes later the procession reached the town hall steps and I made a dash for home. But as there wasn't a Malvern tram in sight, I sauntered into a pub. I asked for a Jerepigo. I found it was good stuff.

Reminiscences

Iwas engaged for a couple of days last week in going through old files of newspapers and magazines, making a collection of stories which I had written over the past fifteen years.

In re-reading some of the Marico Bushveld stories that I had written as long ago as the early years of the 1930's I was surprised to find how intimate was my knowledge of life on the South African farm. I was also astonished at the extent of my familiarity with historical events (and the spirit of the times and the personalities who had figured in them) that had taken place in the ou Transvaal.

Anyway, in again perusing those stories, written long ago, I realised where all that local colour came from: I had got it from listening to the talk of elderly farmers in the Marico district who had a whole lot of information that they didn't require for themselves, any more, and that they were glad to bestow on a stranger. It was all information that was, from a scientific point of view, strictly useless.

That was how I learnt all about the First and Second Boer Wars. And about the Native wars. And about the trouble, in the old days, between the Transvaal and the Orange Free State. And about the Ohrigstad Republic. And about the Stellaland Republic. If any contemporary South African historian would like some fallen-by-the-wayside information about any events in the early days of the South African Republics, I could supply him with all the facts he needs; and, what is more important, with a whole lot of surplus information outside of just facts.

I regarded them as wonderful storytellers, the old Boers who lived in the Marico district twenty years ago. Most of them moved into that part of the Transvaal, next to the Bechuanaland Protectorate, in 1917. It was a part of the Transvaal that had remained practically uninhabited since the Anglo-Boer War. I still have vivid recollections of the Boers who lived in the Marico in those days. I was there as a schoolteacher for a little while. And I can only hope that the information I imparted to the children, in the way of reading, spelling and arithmetic, was in a minute degree as significant as the facts that were imparted to me by their parents, whom I went to visit at weekends.

I remember that there was old Oom Geel, who had been a Cape rebel and who still used to display a fragment of red-striped jersey that he had worn as prisoner-of-war in the Bermudas.

Because he was a Cape rebel, Oom Geel said, he had been regarded by the English not as a regular prisoner-of-war but as a convict, and so he had been sent to the Bermudas instead of to St. Helena. And he said that when he returned to South Africa after the Boer War the former Free State and Transvaal burghers, who had been respectable P.O.W.'s at St. Helena, used to look on him with suspicion, as though he was going to pick their pockets, and so on, because he had worn a striped convict jersey in the Bermudas. I can still remember the laughter that invariably followed on this straight faced statement of Oom Geel's.

Old Oom Geel had a very tall son, called At, and a shorter son, Jan, and a large number of grandchildren. And there were a family of Bekkers who lived on a farm, *Drogedal*. This farm seemed the size of a whole district.

I don't know how big the farm was, exactly, but in later years, when I was working for an educational publication in London, and I had to interview the principals of schools in the southern English counties, I remember that we would approach Tunbridge Wells or Sevenoaks and the man who drove the car asked me, 'Are we now in Sussex or in Surrey, do you think, or perhaps in Kent?' then I would think, 'Oh, well, all these counties together are less than the size of the Bekkers' farm in the Marico.'

And there was an Afrikaner family named Flaherty, with whom I boarded; and the old man Flaherty would regularly welcome me at breakfast with the greeting, 'Die beste van die more,' and it took me quite a while to realise that these words must have constituted a traditional family greeting, a literal translation of what the family's original Irish forebear, the first South African Flaherty, must have said habitually at breakfast time, 'The top of the morning to you.'

I must have known most of the families living in the Marico Bushveld at that particular time and some of those farmers had most interesting stories to tell, relating in a matter-of-fact way all sorts of unusual circumstances. And my mind absorbed whatever they had to relate provided that it was of a sufficiently inutilitarian order.

There was that legend of a spectre in the form of a white donkey that haunted the poort on the road to Ramoutsa. If you passed through that poort just around midnight, then at the darkest part of the poort, near where the road skirts a clump of maroelas, you would be certain to encounter an apparition in the form of a white donkey with his front legs planted in the centre of the road. Nobody was quite certain where the hind-legs of the donkey were planted, because the lonely traveller would decide to turn back just about then. (I visited that part of the Marico again about two years ago. The clump of maroelas by the side of the Government road have been cut down, since those days. But the donkey is still there.)

Amongst hundreds of other stories I heard in the Marico was a first-hand account, by an elderly man who had been a burgher in that particular commando, of the sartorial eccentricities of a certain Boer War kommandant. This kommandant was very fussy about his appearance and always insisted on wearing white starched shirt-fronts and cuffs. No matter under what adverse conditions the commando was operating, in constant retreat from the enemy, fording swollen rivers under fire and negotiating barbed wire fences between block-houses, every Monday morning was washing-day, with the burghers having to go into laager beside some spruit or dam (or a jackal hole with muddy water at the bottom) while the kommandant supervised the washing and starching and ironing of his linen by the native agterryers.

It wasn't that he was personally over-fastidious about such things, the kommandant explained. But it was necessary for the prestige of the Boer forces in the field, that a kommandant shouldn't go about looking like a Bapedi.

My informant, the ex-burgher in this commando, said that he could never feel that the kommandant's arguments carried any weight. Himself, he didn't care if he looked like a Bapedi, or like a M'shangaan, or like an orang-outang, even, he said, as long as he didn't get shot. But the kommandant was a capable officer, he said, and the burghers trusted him and admired him although in their ragged clothes they would be aware of a certain sense of inferiority beside the kommandant's starched magnificence: it was observed that when the kommandant addressed a veldkornet directly, giving him instructions, the veldkornet would say, 'Ja, Kommandant,' and would meanwhile be standing shuffling somewhat awkwardly.

There was something fine, I thought, about the way the kommandant led his force into a northern Cape village that the English had evacuated. He did it all in great style. He wore his best white shirt-front for the occasion. And he sat up very straight on his horse, riding at the head of his commando, with an occasional stray bullet still whistling down the street. And it was only when they got to the church square, in the centre of the village, that the burghers realised from the circumstance of his shirt-front having gone limp, and not being white any longer, that their kommandant would ride at their head no more.

Another of many stories that I heard in the Marico, and that was of particular interest to me, because it had to do with the building of a farmhouse (something that has always fascinated me) related to the sadism vented by a farmer on his stepdaughter.

After you have laid the foundations for a house you start with the bricklaying. To make bricks you dig a hole in a place where the soil is clayey, and then shovel in river-sand and pour in water, and you get the cattle to mill around in this sticky mud until it's all properly mixed.

Now, this farmer, who had subjected his stepdaughter to all sorts of bru-talities for a number of years (she was now sixteen) hit on the idea of mak-ing her mill around, day after day, in the clay-hole, along with the cattle, helping to tread the clay until it was of the right consistency for making bricks out of. Anyway, the point of this story is that this sixteen-year-old girl one day studied her reflection in a mirror and came to the conclusion that she was very pretty, with the result that she shortly afterwards clambered out of the clay-hole where she had been tramping about in thick mud that came up to her thighs, and she ran away from her step-father's farm to Johannesburg.

In the city, men found her desirable – as her reflection in the mirror had told her that they would do – and so she went wrong. But they say that in Johannesburg she dressed very fashionably, and that she looked ever so distinguished.

And through the years that have followed, pondering on that story, I have often pictured to myself that girl from the Marico clay-hole walking the streets of Johannesburg. I can picture to myself the grace with which she walked the paved ways of the city, on high-heeled shoes. And I have wondered if the experience she gained in the clay-hole did not do her a lot of good, after all ... It seems to me a good way for a girl to acquire an elegant gait. Stepping high ...

Thinking about the Old Marico in this way gave me a sense of nostalgia last week. I felt I wanted to hear more stories, at first-hand, of the Transvaal's bygone days. It was impracticable, at the moment, to take another trip to the Marico. But I might be able to meet some old Boer, here in the streets of Johannesburg, to whom I could talk, and who, because he had seen much of life, and was a veteran of the Anglo-Boer War (and even of the First Boer War, perhaps) and had lived through stirring times in the early days of the Transvaal, would be able to discourse, at length and entertainingly, about a world that had passed away for ever. And he need not be an old Boer from Marico, either. Any elderly-looking Afrikaner, who had lived for many years on the platteland would do for my purpose.

I walked through the streets, scanning the faces of the passers-by. But they all looked much too young. Then I saw a man lounging near a bar. He walked with a stoop. His face was lined. Many winters and summers had passed over his head: many winters, I thought. He seemed really decrepit. I invited him into the pub. Yes, he was an Afrikaner, all right. In his younger days he had lived in the Potchefstroom district. Good enough. I also knew Potchefstroom, slightly. Then he started talking. He was reminiscing, like I asked him to. But his recollection didn't seem to go as far back somehow. I wondered if his memory was perhaps beginning to fail him.

And then I asked him for his name again. And it suddenly struck me that I had met this relic from a venerable past many years before. In fact, we had been at school together, in Potchefstroom. And in the same class.

And only after I had told him who I was, and had reminded him of the old days, and he had said, 'Good God, I would never have recognised you. You look all gone in' – only then I realised what it is about the past that makes it seem so romantic, and I thought, *eheu fugaces*, I thought.

Home Town

L ast week I revisited Kuils River, a village that is a few miles outside of
the Cape Town municipal area and that enjoys the questionable distinction of being the place in which I was born. How shall I describe my
feelings on alighting at the shabby little railway station and gazing about
me at my unfamiliar birthplace, which I saw again, now, for the first time
since the age of four? I felt very lonely. There was nothing about the place I
recognised. And if it wasn't for the fact that Table Mountain looked quite
near – through its proximity at least giving me some sort of a clue as to
whereabouts I was – I feel sure that I would have caught the next train
back again. I felt so lost both emotionally and geographically.

I had only one conscious memory of Kuils River. That was when I was
about two. I was seated on the grass, wrapped around in a blanket and
there was a soft wind blowing, because it was getting on towards sunset,
and two young girl-cousins, a few years older than I, were dancing about
me on the grass. And I suddenly burst into tears, just like that, without
reason. And the sadness of that memory has, at intervals, haunted me
throughout the rest of my life.

But as I strolled down a quiet little road in the direction of the village,
with the station behind me, it suddenly struck me that while I remembered
nothing at all of the external features of my birth-place, there was
something else, something timeless and more vivid than memory, that
made me intimately acquainted with my surroundings even though I didn't
know where the path on which I was walking, that lay deep in white dust,
would lead to. In the stir of the noonday breeze was something anciently
familiar. And the patches of bluish-coloured grass, sifted around with
dunesand: were these not the things I had always known? And a sudden
fragrance, coming off from the warm earth and blending with the subtle
odour of black wattle, overwhelmed me for a moment, almost, as though I
had left Kuils River only yesterday.

Far from requiring Table Mountain any longer as a comforting
landmark, I now began to feel that I could show other people the way

around, here in this village. Even though I had to enquire of passing strangers the way to the main street, where the village stores were, and the post-office, and the local pub.

And because life in Kuils River is very leisurely, with the pace of things smooth and unhurried, I found many people who were glad to hold converse with a visitor from Johannesburg, and they told me many things, and at great length, about my home town from which I had emigrated at the age of four. And from numerous enquiries I made, putting my questions judiciously and in all sorts of roundabout ways, I elicited the fact that nobody in Kuils River had ever heard of me.

At least, the first lot of enquiries I made were of a tentative nature. I would ask, clearing my throat somewhat self-consciously, whether Kuils River did not perhaps have a few literary traditions, kind of; whether there was any local knowledge of anybody, distinguished, sort of, having been in Kuils River during the present century, sort of – in the literary like? All sorts of diffident, indirect questions like that. That was how I started off. But afterwards I just began asking them straight out. And the replies were always, monotonously, the same. There was Dr. F.C.L. Bosman, they said, of Cape Town University. Well, he was a writer, of course. And he was born in Kuils River. And C.H. Kuhn ('Mikro'), the author of the Afrikaans best-seller *Toiings*, had come to settle in Kuils River some years ago, to write, and everybody in the village was very proud to have him there, of course. And it was well-known that the local dominee had been contributing morally uplifting stories to the Afrikaans religious press for a good number of years. That was the sum total of Kuils River's literary associations, but for a small place like that it wasn't at all bad, they said.

'No, it isn't at all bad,' I agreed, each time.

Taken all round, it seemed to me that there could be such a thing, in Kuils River, as overdoing the old truth about a prophet not being without honour.

I enquired, later in the afternoon, as to whether there were any histori-cal monuments in Kuils River – any ancient, time-worn edifices, any noble and inspiring ruins. And they said yes, there was. They said there was Colonel Creswell. They said he lived at the top end of Kuils River, on an estate barricaded with palisades and with savage dogs roaming the grounds. They said that several English families had settled in Kuils River and that they all went in for tall stake-fences and fierce mastiffs.

I dashed off in the direction of where they indicated to me Colonel Creswell's house was, after they had again cautioned me about the Hounds of the Baskervilles loping about the wooded grounds with slavering jaws. Colonel Creswell. I couldn't believe it. What volumes of water had not flowed under Vaal River bridge, in dry seasons and all, since I had last seen Colonel Creswell's name in a newspaper.

I found the place, huge, rambling, closed in with pointed poles like what Harold's army erected before Hastings. I located the gate with some difficulty. It was a good distance up the driveway to the house, and I had to kick a big dog out of the way that was lying asleep in the sun. He disappeared into the undergrowth with a yelp. I was still considerably out of breath when, having been admitted by a servant into the drawing-room, I sat down to wait for Colonel Creswell to appear.

But I was glad I had come. I stayed there all afternoon. Towards evening we went and sat on the stoep. In appearance Colonel Creswell was more like the cartoons of him that had appeared in anti-Pact newspapers in those far-off days than he resembled a studio photograph of himself in the drawing-room. But that was all the years had done to him. His mind was as bright as ever. He was a fund of enthralling reminiscences. Intimate little stories about Merriman and Botha and Hertzog. And when he said that Smuts had never forgiven him he wiped his left eye, which was water-ing. He spoke about his birth-place, Malta or Gibraltar – I forget which he said – and about the first mine he worked on on the Rand, the Durban-Roodepoort, and about his having had to sever his connection with the Chamber of Mines in rather a big way, on account of some Chinamen he had kicked out.

'Don't you go back to the Rand sometimes?' I asked, 'to go and have a look at the Durban-Roodepoort again, for instance – all the old scenes?'

But Colonel Creswell said that he was already 85, and that while he would like to visit the Rand some day, there was hardly anybody there that still knew him. So he preferred Kuils River. It seemed very sad, somehow.

And so I told Colonel Creswell – and he was the only person in the village in whom I had confided this fact – that I was born in Kuils River – and that there was not a soul in my birth-place that knew me. We sat for a good while after that in silence.

The wind of early evening, sweeping across from the dunes, stirred through the tangled undergrowth. And it seemed chillier than the wind that blew from over the dunes when I was a child.

Veld Story

There is a fascination about old cemeteries of the kind that are dotted about the South African veld, family graveyards at the foot of koppies; small plots for burial grounds that were laid out during the past century, in the old days when amongst the harnesses and riems and trek-chains in the wagon-house, or by the side of the sacks of mealies in the grain shed there was always, on every farm, ready for use in emergency, a coffin.

One such old cemetery – a comparatively large one – is at Warmbaths, the headstones bearing dates going back to the 1840's. A number of Voortrekkers were buried there, not those who were leaders of any treks, but obscure persons, men and women and children, whose memories have been obliterated with the erasing of their names and the dates of their birth from the headstones. And when you look at the little mounds of sun bleached stones (do they search the veld specially for stones of the white sort when a mound is raised over a grave, or does the sun make the stones white with the years? – the sun and the rain?), a century does not seem so very long, somehow.

They must lie lightly on a grave, the stones that have not sunk so very deeply into the earth at the end of a hundred years.

And what is of more particular interest to a passer-by is an old cemetery somewhere on a lonely part of the veld, overgrown with tangled grass and oleanders and shut in with barbed wire fence, the rusted strands put very close together – and all traces lost long ago of the following generations of that family that had laid its dead to rest in a piece of ground closed in with barbed wire that is clothed with half a century of rust.

Such a graveyard I came across at the weekend on a farm that is within easy reach of Johannesburg. The farm has changed hands a good number of times in recent years. The new owners, I found, did not know very much about the original family of van Heerdens, whose names are engraved on the headstones in the cemetery.

There is still a stretch of rising ground in the neighbourhood that is known as van Heerden's Bult. But nobody named van Heerden has lived in those pans for as long as most people can recall.

I could not, of course, resist the temptation to climb over that fence. The oleander – Selon's-roos it is called in Marico – at one time the most popular flowering tree in certain parts of the country, because it is hardy and stands up well to drought conditions, had grown tall and shaggy, through not having been pruned (for how long, I wondered?), but the colour of its flowers tinted in well with the yellow of the grass and the sunlight and the pallid yellow of the mood evoked by the surroundings, and the upper part of the graveyard reposed in the cool of the oleander's shade.

At a place where the rusted wire had sagged slightly I climbed over into the enclosure.

From force of custom I looked first at the jars that had once held flowers. As always, in a graveyard on the veld, there were a number of vases and urns, of glass and porcelain, that held a peculiar fascination because they belonged to the irrevocable past.

I have seen, on veld graveyards in the Transvaal, cut glass vases that must have come from stately Cape homes; ornamental earthenware vessels, graceful in shade and lovely in their colouring, of a quality and craftsmanship that has enabled them to re-main, after half a century of weathering, still without crack or blemish.

It is also a not unusual circumstance to come across, in these isolated burial-places, bottles of antique design, some of them black with short necks and heavily-bellied, as though they had once contained some potent liquor, others delicately-shaped and in variegated patterns – made in far-off days to be receptacles of perfumes and unguents.

There were several interesting vases in this cemetery under the oleander. There was also a green bowl of cut glass, designed to hold fruit rather than flowers, exquisitely shaped and fitted with delicate silver handles. It had no doubt graced the sideboard of a dining-room some three-quarters of a century before. The green bowl was in superb condition, almost as though the mud with which it had been periodically splattered by one rain to be washed off by the next had also served to polish the smooth external surfaces, lingering a while in the inner curves.

On another mound were two Dresden figurines, hollowed out at the top for flowers. One of the figures was slightly chipped, but it looked good for another couple of centuries.

The names on the tombstones were all van Heerdens, or women with other surnames who had been born van Heerden. I looked at the dates. The last interment had taken place in the early years of the present century. It must have been after that date that the van Heerden family had trekked away.

Then I noticed a singular circumstance. The last six or seven tombstones all bore the same date, that of a year in the early part of this century. They were all van Heerdens. And they had all been buried between the 14th and the 30th days of September. Seven members of the family had all died within the same fortnight. The names and dates were still clearly legible. I made a closer study of the inscriptions. There were six children, three girls and three boys, the youngest eight, the oldest nineteen. And also the mother. At intervals from each other of a day or two a whole family had died and had been buried. During the month of September in a year in the early part of this century.

I wondered what had happened. How had they all come to die? It must have caused a stir in those parts, many years ago, an entire family dying off like that, within so short a period of time. It was something that must still be talked about, on winter evenings when, the day's work done, people sat around the open fireplaces in the kitchen and talked of strange things.

I went from one farm to the next to find out how it had all happened. And eventually I came across an old woman who had been born on a farm near where the van Heerdens had lived. And as a young woman, who was then on the point of being married, she had attended the funerals of several of the children and of the mother. And this woman told me, simply, that the whole family had died of enteric. That was all there was to it. Just a simple story of the veld. And after that the father had trekked away. To Rustenburg, some said.

I thought, when I went away, what a wonderful theme the story of the deaths of the van Heerdens could furnish for a novel. Each of these children and the mother. The little girl of fourteen on the threshold of womanhood, arriving at the age where she would furtively examine herself in the mirror, sloping the looking-glass downwards. And the young man of nineteen, who had passed through the sturm und drang period of adolescence – something that would not happen to a city-bred youth for another ten years – and was already beginning to assume the responsibilities of manhood. And so with the rest of the family, with their problems and conflicts and frustrations… the dreams and griefs and bitterness of childhood, and the dark strugglings of adolescence. And I feel that Mrs. van Heerden was in many ways a remarkable woman. And then all these problems suddenly solved. Just when the stage is set for the development of character, for the unwrapping of the future, for the intricacies of the unfolding of the lives of all these people – suddenly, it all stops. The story is indeed ended before it has begun. The problems are all solved before they have been fairly stated. All the loose ends tied up before they have become properly unravelled. Only life can create a story like that, so tremendous in its sweep, so intriguing in its possibilities – and so simple in the telling.

On the way back I re-passed the graveyard. I also found the place where I judged the van Heerdens' homestead had been. And some distance away was a spring, choked with gaudily-coloured weeds and long, thick grass of a brilliant green. A donga dense with all sorts of vegetation, blue lobelia and river reeds and rushes and kweekgras and yellow gazanias. And in this muddy water, slowly flowing towards the dam where there were wild ducks, must have been bred the enteric germs which half a century ago caused seven new mounds to be raised in the barbed wire enclosure beside the unpruned oleander.

Red and pink buphane also grows by the side of the donga that leads from the spring to the dam.

Marico Revisited

A month ago I revisited the Marico Bushveld, a district in the Transvaal to which I was sent, a long time ago, as a schoolteacher, and about which part of the country I have written, in the years that followed, a number of simple stories which I believe, in all modesty, are not without a certain degree of literary merit.

There were features about the Marico Bushveld that were almost too gaudy. That part of the country had been practically derelict since the Boer War and the rinderpest. Many of the farms north of the Dwarsberge had been occupied little more than ten years before by farmers who had trekked into the Marico from the Northern Cape and the Western Transvaal. The farmers there were real Boers. I am told that I have a deep insight into the character of the Afrikaner who lives his life on the platteland. I acquired this knowledge in the Marico, where I was sent when my mind was most open to impressions.

Then there was the bush. Thorn-trees. Withaaks and kameeldorings. The kremetartboom. Swarthaak and blinkblaar and wag-'n-bietjie. Moepels and marulas. The sunbaked vlakte and the thorn-tree and South Africa. Trees are more than vegetation and more than symbols and more than pallid sentimentality, of the order of 'Woodman, spare that tree,' or 'Poems are made by fools like me'. Nevertheless, what the oak and the ash and the cypress are to Europe, the thorn-tree is to South Africa. And if laurel and myrtle and bay are for chaplet and wreath, thorns are for a crown.

The bush was populated with kudus and cows and duikers and steenbokkies and oxen and gemsbok and donkeys and occasional leopards. There were also ribbokke in the krantzes and green and brown mambas, of which hair-raising stories were told, and mules that were used to pull cars because it was an unhealthy area for horses. Mules were also used for telling hair-raising stories about.

And the sunsets in the Marico Bushveld are incredible things, heavily striped like prison bars and flamboyant like their kafir blankets.

Then there were boreholes, hundreds of feet deep, from which water had to be pumped by hand into the cattle-troughs in times of drought. And there was a Bechuana chief who had once been to London, where he had been received in audience by His Majesty, George V, a former English king; and when, on departing from Buckingham Palace, he had been questioned by the High Commissioner as to what form the conversation had taken, he had replied, very simply, this Bechuana chief, 'We kings know what to discuss.'

There were occasional visits from Dutch Reformed Church Predikants. And a few meetings of the Dwarsberg Debatsvereniging. And there were several local feuds. For I was to find that while the bush was of infinite extent, and the farms very many miles apart, the paths through the thorn-trees were narrow.

It was to this part of the country, the northern section of the Marico Bushveld, where the Transvaal ends and the Bechuanaland Protectorate begins, that I returned for a brief visit after an absence of many years. And I found, what I should have known all along, of course, that it was the present that was haunted, and that the past was not full of ghosts. The phantoms are what you carry around with you, in your head, like you carry dreams under your arm.

And when you revisit old scenes it is yourself, as you were in the past, that you encounter, and if you are in love with yourself – as everybody should be in love with himself, since it is only in that way, as Christ pointed out, that a man can love his neighbour – then there is a sweet sadness in a meeting of this description. There is the gentle melancholy of the twilight, dark eyes in faces upturned in a trancelike pallor. And fragrances. And thoughts like soft rain falling on old tombstones.

And on the train that night on my way back to the Bushveld, I came across a soldier who said to me, 'As soon as I am out of this uniform I am going back to cattle-smuggling.'

These words thrilled me. A number of my stories have dealt with the time-honoured Marico custom of smuggling cattle across the frontier of the Bechuanaland Protectorate. So I asked whether cattle-smuggling still went on. 'More than ever,' the soldier informed me. He looked out of the train window into the dark. 'And I'll tell you that at this moment, as I am sitting here talking to you, there is somebody bringing in cattle through the wire.'

I was very glad to hear this. I was glad to find that the only part of my stories that could have dated had not done so. It is only things indirectly connected with economics that can change. Droughts and human nature don't.

Next morning we were in Mafeking. Mafeking is outside the Transvaal. It is about twenty miles inside the border of the Northern Cape. And to proceed to Ramoutsa, a native village in the Bechuanaland Protectorate which is the nearest point on the railway line to the part of the Groot Marico to which we wanted to go, we had first to get a permit from the immigration official in Mafeking. All this seemed very confusing, somehow. We merely wanted to travel from Johannesburg to an area in the North-Western Transvaal, and in order to get there it turned out that we had first to cross into the Cape Province, and that from the Cape we had to travel through the Bechuanaland Protectorate, which is a Crown Colony, and which you can't enter until an immigration official has first telephoned Pretoria about it.

We reached Ramoutsa late in the afternoon.

From there we travelled to the Marico by car. Within the hour we had crossed the border into the Transvaal. We were once more on the Transvaal soil, for which we were, naturally, homesick, having been exiles in foreign parts from since early morning. So the moment we crossed the barbed wire fence separating the Bechuanaland Protectorate from the Marico we stopped the car and got out on to the veld. We said it was fine to set foot on Transvaal soil once more. And we also said that while it was a good thing to travel through foreign countries, which we had been doing since six o'clock that morning, and that foreign travel had a broadening effect on the mind, we were glad that our heads had not been turned by these experiences, and that we had not permitted ourselves to be influenced by alien modes of life and thought.

We travelled on through the bush over stony paths that were little more than tracks going in between the trees and underneath their branches, the thorns tearing at the windscreen and the hood of the car in the same way as they had done years ago, when I had first visited the Marico. I was glad to find that nothing had changed.

Dusk found us in the shadow of the Dwarsberge, not far from our destination, and we came across a spot on the veld that I recognised. It was one of the stations at which the bi-weekly Government lorry from Zeerust stopped on its way up towards the Limpopo. How the lorry drivers knew that this place was a station, years ago, was through the presence of a large anthill, into the crest of which a pair of kudu antlers had been thrust. That spot had not changed. The anthill was still surmounted by what looked like that same pair of kudu horns. The station had not grown perceptibly in the intervening years. The only sign of progress was that, in addition to the horns on its summit, the anthill was further decorated with a rusty milkcan from which the bottom had been knocked out.

And so I arrived back in that part of the country to which the Transvaal Education Department in its wisdom had sent me years before. There is no other place I know that is so heavy with atmosphere, so strangely and darkly impregnated with that stuff of life that bears the authentic stamp of South Africa.

When I first went to the Marico it was in that season when the moepels were nearly ripening. And when I returned, years later, it was to find that the moepels in the Marico were beginning to ripen again.

The Affair at Ysterspruit

It was in the Second Boer War, at the skirmish of Ysterspruit near Klerksdorp, in February, 1902, that Johannes Engelbrecht, eldest son of Ouma Engelbrecht, widow, received a considerable number of bullet wounds, from which he subsequently died. And when she spoke about the death of her son in battle, Ouma Engelbrecht dwelt heavily on the fact that Johannes had fought bravely. She would enumerate his wounds, and, if you were interested, she would trace in detail the direction that each bullet took through the body of her son.

If you liked stories of the past, and led her on, Ouma Engelbrecht would also mention, after a while, that she had a photograph of Johannes in her bedroom. It was with great difficulty that a stranger could get her to bring out that photograph. But she usually showed it, in the end. And then she would talk very fast about people not being able to understand the feelings that went on in a mother's heart.

'People put the photograph away from them,' she would say, 'and they turn it face downwards on the rusbank. And all the time I say to them, no, Johannes died bravely. I say to them that they don't know how a mother feels. One bullet came in from in front, just to the right of his heart, and it went through his gall-bladder and then struck a bone in his spine and passed out through his hip. And another bullet ...'

So she would go on while the stranger studied the photograph of her son, Johannes, who died of wounds received in the skirmish at Ysterspruit.

When the talk came round to the old days, leading up to and including the Second Boer War, I was always interested when they had a photograph that I could examine, at some farmhouse in that part of the Groot Marico District that faces towards the Kalahari. And when they showed me, hanging framed against a wall of the voorkamer – or having brought it from an adjoining room – a photograph of a burgher of the South African Republic, father or son or husband or lover, then it was always with a thrill of pride in my land and my people that I looked on a likeness of a hero of the Boer War.

70

I would be equally interested if it was the portrait of a bearded kommandant or of a youngster of fifteen. Or of a newly-appointed veldkornet, looking important, seated on a riempies-stoel with his Mauser held upright so that it would come into the photograph, but also turned slightly to the side, for fear that the muzzle should cover up part of the veldkornet's face, or a piece of his manly chest. And I would think that that veldkornet never sat so stiffly on his horse – certainly not on the morning when the commando set out for the Natal border. And he would have looked less important, although perhaps more solemn, on a night when the empty bully-beef tins rattled against the barbed wire in front of a block-house, and the English Lee-Metfords spat flame.

I was a schoolteacher, many years ago, at a little school in the Marico bushveld, near the border of the Bechuanaland Protectorate. The Transvaal Education Department expected me to visit the parents of the school-children in the area at intervals. But even if this huisbesoek was not part of my after-school duties, I would have gone and visited the parents in any case. And when I discovered, after one or two casual calls, that the older parents were a fund of first-class story material, that they could hold the listener enthralled with tales of the past, with embroidered reminiscences of Transvaal life in the old days, then I became very conscientious about huisbesoek.

'What happened after that, Oom?' I would say, calling on a parent for about the third week in succession, 'when you were trekking through the kloof that night, I mean, and you had muzzled both the black calf with the dappled belly and your daughter, so that Mojaja's kafirs would not be able to hear anything?'

And then the Oom would knock out the ash from his pipe on to his veldskoen and he would proceed to relate – his words a slow and steady rumble and with the red dust of the road in their sound, almost – a tale of terror or of high romance or of soft laughter. It was quite by accident that I came across Ouma Engelbrecht in a two-roomed, mud-walled dwelling some little distance off the Government road and a few hundred yards away from the homestead of her son-in-law, Stoffel Brink, on whom I had called earlier in the afternoon. I had not been in the Marico very long, then, and my interview with Stoffel Brink had been, on the whole, unsatisfactory. I wanted to know how deep the Boer trenches were dug into the foot of the koppies at Magersfontein, where Stoffel Brink had fought. Stoffel Brink, on the other hand, was anxious to learn whether, in regard to what I taught the children, I would follow the guidance of the local school committee, of which he was chairman, or whether I was one of that new kind of schoolteacher who went by a little printed book of subjects supplied by the Education Department. He added that this latter class of schoolmaster was causing a lot of unpleasantness in the bushveld through teaching the children that the earth moved round the sun, and through broaching similar questions of a political nature.

I replied evasively, with the result that Stoffel Brink launched forth for almost an hour on the merits of the old-fashioned Hollander schoolmaster, who could teach the children all he knew himself in eighteen months, because he taught them only facts.

'If a child stays at school longer than that,' Stoffel Brink added, 'then for the rest of the time he can only learn lies.'

I left about then, and on my way back, a little distance from the road and half-concealed by tall bush, I found the two-roomed dwelling of Ouma Engelbrecht.

It was good, there.

I could see that Ouma Engelbrecht did not have much time for her son-in-law, Stoffel Brink. For when I mentioned his references to education, when I had merely sought to learn some details about the Boer trenches at Magersfontein, she said that maybe he could learn all there was to know in eighteen months, but he had not learnt how to be ordinarily courteous to a stranger who came to his door – a stranger, moreover, who was a schoolmaster asking information about the Boer War.

Then, of course, she spoke about her son, Johannes, who didn't have to hide in a Magersfontein trench, but was sitting straight up on his horse when all those bullets went through him at Ysterspruit, and who died of his wounds some time later. Johannes had always been such a well-behaved boy, Ouma Engelbrecht told me, and he was gentle and kind-hearted.

She told me many stories of his childhood and early youth. She spoke about a time when the span of red Afrikaner oxen got stuck with the wagon in the drift, and her husband and the kafirs, with long whip and short sjambok could not move them – and then Johannes had come along and he had spoken softly to the red Afrikaner oxen, and he had called on each of them by name, and the team had made one last mighty effort, and had pulled the wagon through to the other side.

'And yet they never understood him in these parts,' Ouma Engelbrecht continued. 'They say things about him, and I hardly ever talk of him any more. And when I show them his portrait, they hardly even look at it, and they put the picture away from them, and when they are sitting on that rusbank where you are sitting now, they place the portrait of Johannes face-downwards beside them.'

I told Ouma Engelbrecht, laughing reassuringly the while, that I stood above the pettiness of local intrigue. I told her that I had noticed that there were all kinds of queer undercurrents below the placid surface of life in the Groot Marico. There was the example of what had happened that very afternoon, when her son-in-law, Stoffel Brink, had conceived a nameless prejudice against me, simply because I was not prepared to teach the schoolchildren that the earth was flat. I told her that it was ridiculous to imagine that a man in my position, a man of education and wide tolerance, should allow himself to be influenced by local Dwarsberge gossip.

Ouma Engelbrecht spoke freely, then, and the fight at Ysterspruit lived for me again – Kemp and de la Rey and the captured English convoy, the ambush and the booty of a million rounds of ammunition. It was almost as though the affair at Ysterspruit was being related to me, not by a lonely woman whose son received his death-wounds on the vlaktes near Klerksdorp, but by a burgher who had taken a prominent part in the battle.

And so, naturally, I wanted to see the photograph of her son, Johannes Engelbrecht.

When it came to the Boer War (although I did not say that to Ouma Engelbrecht) I didn't care if a Boer commander was not very competent or very cunning in his strategy, or if a burgher was not particularly brave. It was enough for me that he had fought. And to me General Snyman, for instance, in spite of the history books' somewhat unflattering assessment of his military qualities, was a hero, nonetheless. I had seen General Snyman's photograph, somewhere: that face that was like Transvaal blouklip; those eyes that had no fire in them, but a stubborn and elemental strength. You still see Boers on the backveld with that look today. In my mind I had contrasted the portraits of General Snyman and Comte de Villebois Mareuil, the Frenchman who had come all the way from Europe to shoulder a Mauser for the Transvaal Republic. De Villebois, poet and romantic, last-ditch champion of the forlorn hope and the heroic lost cause ... Oh, they were very different, these two men, de Villebois Mareuil, the French nobleman and Snyman, the Boer. But I had an equal admiration for them both.

Anyway, it was well on towards evening when Ouma Engelbrecht, yielding at last to my cajoleries and entreaties, got up slowly from her chair and went into the adjoining room. She returned with a photograph enclosed in a heavy black frame. I waited, tense with curiosity, to see the portrait of that son of hers who had died of wounds at Ysterspruit, and whose reputation the loose prattle of the neighbourhood had invested with a dishonour as dark as the frame about his photograph.

Flicking a few specks of dust from the portrait, Ouma Engelbrecht handed over the picture to me.

And she was still talking about the things that went on in a mother's heart, things of pride and sorrow that the world did not understand, when, in an unconscious reaction, hardly aware of what I was doing, I placed beside me on the rusbank, face downwards, the photograph of a young man whose hat brim was cocked on the right side, jauntily, and whose jacket with narrow lapels was buttoned up high. With a queer jumble of inarticulate feelings I realised that, in the affair at Ysterspruit, they were all Mauser bullets that had passed through the youthful body of Johannes Engelbrecht, National Scout.

Mafeking Road

When people ask me – as they often do – how it is that I can tell the best stories of anybody in the Transvaal (Oom Schalk Lourens said, modestly), then I explain to them that I just learn through observing the way that the world has with men and women. When I say this they nod their heads wisely, and say that they understand, and I nod my head wisely also, and that seems to satisfy them. But the thing I say to them is a lie, of course.

For it is not the story that counts. What matters is the way you tell it. The important thing is to know just at what moment you must knock out your pipe on your veldskoen, and at what stage of the story you must start talking about the School Committee at Drogevlei. Another necessary thing is to know what part of the story to leave out.

And you can never learn these things.

Look at Floris, the last of the Van Barnevelts. There is no doubt that he had a good story, and he should have been able to get people to listen to it. And yet nobody took any notice of him or of the things he had to say. Just because he couldn't tell the story properly.

Accordingly, it made me sad whenever I listened to him talk. For I could tell just where he went wrong. He never knew the moment at which to knock the ash out of his pipe. He always mentioned his opinion of the Drogevlei School Committee in the wrong place. And, what was still worse, he didn't know what part of the story to leave out.

And it was no use my trying to teach him, because as I have said, this is the thing that you can never learn. And so, each time he had told his story, I would see him turn away from me, with a look of doom on his face, and walk slowly down the road, stoop-shouldered, the last of the Van Barnevelts.

On the wall of Floris's voorkamer is a long family tree of the Van Barnevelts. You can see it there for yourself. It goes back for over two hundred years, to the Van Barnevelts of Amsterdam. At one time it went even further back, but that was before the white ants started on the top part of it and ate away quite a lot of Van Barnevelts. Nevertheless, if you look at this list, you will notice that at the bottom under Floris's own name, there is the last entry, 'Stephanus'. And behind the name 'Stephanus', between two bent strokes, you will read the words: '*Obiit Mafeking.*'

At the outbreak of the Second Boer War Floris van Barnevelt was a widower, with one son, Stephanus, who was aged seventeen. The commando from our part of the Transvaal set off very cheerfully. We made a fine show with our horses and our wide hats, and our bandoliers, and with the sun shining on the barrels of our Mausers.

Young Stephanus van Barnevelt was the gayest of us all. But he said there was one thing he didn't like about the war, and that was that, in the end, we would have to go over the sea. He said that, after we had invaded the whole of the Cape, our commando would have to go on a ship and invade England also.

But we didn't go overseas, just then. Instead, our veldkornet told us that the burghers from our part had been ordered to join the big commando that was lying at Mafeking. We had to go and shoot a man there called Baden-Powell.

We rode steadily on into the west. After a while we noticed that our veldkornet frequently got off his horse and engaged in conversation with passing kafirs, leading them some distance from the roadside and speaking earnestly to them. Of course, it was right that our veldkornet should explain to the kafirs that it was wartime now, and that the Republic expected every kafir to stop smoking so much dagga and think seriously about what was going on. But we noticed that each time at the end of the conversation the kafir would point towards something, and that our veldkornet would take much pains to follow the direction of the kafir's finger.

Of course, we understood then, what it was all about. Our veldkornet was a young fellow, and he was shy to let us see that he didn't know the way to Mafeking.

Somehow, after that, we did not have so much confidence in our veldkornet.

After a few days we got to Mafeking. We stayed there a long while, until the English troops came up and relieved the place. We left then. We left quickly. The English troops had brought a lot of artillery with them. And if we had difficulty in finding the road to Mafeking, we had no difficulty in finding the road away from Mafeking. And this time our veldkornets did not need kafirs, either, to point with their fingers where we had to go. Even though we did a lot of travelling in the night.

Long afterwards I spoke to an Englishman about this. He said it gave him a queer feeling to hear about the other side of the story of Mafeking. He said there had been very great rejoicings in England when Mafeking was relieved, and it was strange to think of the other aspect of it – of a defeated country and of broken columns blundering through the dark.

I remember many things that happened on the way back from Mafeking. There was no moon. And the stars shone down fitfully on the road that was full of guns and frightened horses and desperate men. The veld throbbed with the hoof-beats of baffled commandos. The stars looked down on scenes that told sombrely of a nation's ruin; they looked on the muzzles of the Mausers that had failed the Transvaal for the first time.

Of course, as a burgher of the Republic, I knew what my duty was. And that was to get as far away as I could from the place where, in the sunset, I had last seen English artillery. The other burghers knew their duty also. Our kommandants and veldkornets had to give very few orders. Nevertheless, although I rode very fast, there was one young man who rode still faster. He kept ahead of me all the time. He rode, as a burgher should ride when there may be stray bullets flying, with his head well down and with his arms almost round the horse's neck.

He was Stephanus, the young son of Floris van Barnevelt.

There was much grumbling and dissatisfaction some time afterwards, when our leaders started making an effort to get the commandos in order again. In the end they managed to get us to halt. But most of us felt that this was a foolish thing to do. Especially as there was still a lot of firing going on all over the place, in haphazard fashion, and we couldn't tell how far the English had followed us in the dark. Furthermore, the commandos had scattered in so many different directions that it seemed hopeless to try and get them together again until after the war. Stephanus and I dismounted and stood by our horses. Soon there was a large body of men around us. Their figures looked strange and shadowy in the starlight. Some of them stood by their horses. Others sat on the grass by the roadside.

'Vas staan, Burghers, vas staan,' came the commands of our officers. And all the time we could still hear what sounded a lot like lyddite. It seemed foolish to be waiting there.

'The next they'll want,' Stephanus Barnevelt said, 'is for us to go back to Mafeking. Perhaps our kommandant has left his tobacco pouch behind, there.'

Some of us laughed at this remark, but Floris, who had not dismounted, said that Stephanus ought to be ashamed of himself for talking like that. From what we could see of Floris in the gloom, he looked quite impressive, sitting very straight in the saddle, with the stars shining on his beard and rifle.

'If the veldkornet told me to go back to Mafeking,' Floris said, 'I would go back.'

'That's how a burgher should talk,' the veldkornet said, feeling flattered. For he had had little authority since the time we found out what he was talking to the kafirs for.

'I wouldn't go back to Mafeking for anybody,' Stephanus replied, 'unless, maybe, it's to hand myself over to the English.'

'We can shoot you for doing that,' the veldkornet said. 'It's contrary to military law.'

'I wish I knew something about military law,' Stephanus answered. 'Then I would draw up a peace treaty between Stephanus Barnevelt and England.'

Some of the men laughed again. But Floris shook his head sadly. He said the Van Barnevelts had fought bravely against Spain in a war that lasted 80 years.

Suddenly, out of the darkness there came a sharp rattle of musketry, and our men started getting uneasy again. But the sound of the firing decided Stephanus. He jumped on his horse quickly.

'I am turning back,' he said, 'I am going to hands-up to the English.'

'No, don't go,' the veldkornet called to him lamely, 'or at least, wait until the morning. They may shoot you in the dark by mistake.' As I have said, the veldkornet had very little authority.

Two days passed before we again saw Floris van Barnevelt. He was in a very worn and troubled state, and he said that it had been very hard for him to find his way back to us.

'You should have asked the kafirs,' one of our number said with a laugh. 'All the kafirs know our veldkornet.'

But Floris did not speak about what happened that night, when we saw him riding out under the starlight, following after his son and shouting to him to be a man and to fight for his country. Also, Floris did not mention Stephanus again, his son who was not worthy to be a Van Barnevelt.

After that we got separated. Our veldkornet was the first to be taken prisoner. And I often felt that he must feel very lonely on St. Helena. Because there were no kafirs from whom he could ask the way out of the barbed wire camp.

Then, at last, our leaders came together at Vereeniging, and peace was made. And we returned to our farms, relieved that the war was over, but with heavy hearts at the thought that it had all been for nothing and that over the Transvaal the Vierkleur would not wave again.

And Floris van Barnevelt put back in its place, on the wall of the voorkamer, the copy of his family tree that had been carried with him in his knapsack throughout the war. Then a new schoolmaster came to this part of the Marico, and after a long talk with Floris, the schoolmaster wrote behind Stephanus's name, between two curved lines, the two words that you can still read there: 'Obiit Mafeking.'

Consequently, if you ask any person hereabouts what 'obiit' means, he is able to tell you right away, that it is a foreign word, and that it means to ride up to the English, holding your Mauser in the air, with a white flag tied to it, near the muzzle.

But it was long afterwards that Floris van Barnevelt started telling his story.

And then they took no notice of him. And they wouldn't allow him to be nominated for the Drogevlei School Committee on the grounds that a man must be wrong in the head to talk in such an irresponsible fashion.

But I knew that Floris had a good story, and that its only fault was that he told it badly. He mentioned the Drogevlei School Committee too soon. And he knocked the ash out of his pipe in the wrong place. And he always insisted on telling that part of the story that he should have left out.

The Traitor's Wife

We did not like the sound of the wind that morning, as we cantered over a veld trail that we had made much use of, during the past year, when there were English forces in the neighbourhood.

The wind blew short wisps of yellow grass in quick flurries over the veld and the smoke from the fire in front of a row of kafir huts hung low in the air. From that we knew that the third winter of the Boer War was at hand. Our small group of burghers dismounted at the edge of a clump of camel-thorns to rest our horses.

'It's going to be an early winter,' Jan Vermeulen said, and from force of habit he put his hand up to his throat in order to close his jacket collar over in front. We all laughed, then. We realised that Jan Vermeulen had forgotten how he had come to leave his jacket behind when the English had surprised us at the spruit a few days before. And instead of a jacket, he was now wearing a mealie sack with holes cut in it for his head and arms. You could not just close over in front of your throat, airily, the lapels cut in a grain bag.

'Anyway, Jan, you're all right for clothes,' Kobus Ferreira said, 'but look at me.'

Kobus Ferreira was wearing a missionary's frock coat that he had found outside Kronendal, where it had been hung on a clothes-line to air.

'This frock coat is cut so tight across my middle and shoulders that I have to sit very stiff and awkward in my saddle, just like the missionary sits on a chair when he is visiting at a farmhouse,' Kobus Ferreira added. 'Several times my horse has taken me for an Englishman, in consequence of the way I sit. I am only afraid that when a bugle blows my horse will carry me over the rant into the English camp.'

At Kobus Ferreira's remarks the early winter wind seemed to take on a keener edge.

For our thoughts went immediately to Leendert Roux, who had been with us on commando a long while and who had been spoken of as a likely man to be veldkornet – and who had gone out scouting, one night, and not come back with a report.

There were, of course, other Boers who had also joined the English. But there was not one of them that we had respected as much as we had done Leendert Roux.

Shortly afterwards we were on the move again.

In the late afternoon we emerged through the Crocodile Poort that brought us in sight of Leendert Roux's farmhouse. Next to the dam was a patch of mealies that Leendert Roux's wife had got the kafirs to cultivate.

'Anyway, we'll camp on Leendert Roux's farm and eat roast mealies, tonight,' our veldkornet, Apie Theron, observed.

'Let us first rather burn his house down,' Kobus Ferreira said. And in a strange way it seemed as though his violent language was not out of place, in a missionary's frock coat. 'I would like to roast mealies in the thatch of Leendert Roux's house.'

Many of us were in agreement with Kobus.

But our veldkornet, Apie Theron, counselled us against that form of vengeance.

'Leendert Roux's having his wife and farmstead here will yet lead to his undoing,' the veldkornet said. 'One day he will risk coming out here on a visit, when he hasn't got Kitchener's whole army at his back. That will be when we will settle our reckoning with him.'

We did not guess that that day would be soon.

The road we were following led past Leendert Roux's homestead. The noise of our horses' hoofs brought Leendert Roux's wife, Serfina, to the door. She stood in the open doorway and watched us riding by. Serfina was pretty, taller than most women, and slender, and there was no expression in her eyes that you could read, and her face was very white.

It was strange, I thought, as we rode past the homestead, that the sight of Serfina Roux did not fill us with bitterness.

82

Afterwards, when we had dismounted in the mealie-lands, Jan Vermeulen made a remark at which we laughed.

'For me it was the worst moment in the Boer War,' Jan Vermeulen said. 'Having to ride past a pretty girl, and me wearing just a sack. I was glad there was Kobus Ferreira's frock coat for me to hide behind.'

Jurie Bekker said there was something about Serfina Roux that reminded him of the Transvaal. He did not know how it was, but he repeated that, with the wind of early winter fluttering her dress about her ankles, that was how it seemed to him.

Then Kobus Ferreira said that he had wanted to shout out something to her when we rode past the door, to let Serfina know how we, who were fighting in the last ditch – and in unsuitable clothing – felt about the wife of a traitor. 'But she stood there so still,' Kobus Ferreira said, 'that I just couldn't say anything. I felt I would like to visit her, even.'

That remark of Kobus Ferreira's fitted in with his frock coat also. It would not be the first time a man in ecclesiastical dress called on a woman while her husband was away.

Then, once again, a remark of Jan Vermeulen's made us realise that there was a war on. Jan Vermeulen had taken the mealie sack off his body and had threaded a length of baling-wire above the places where the holes were. He was now restoring the grain bag to the use it had been meant for, and I suppose that, in consequence, his views generally also got sensible.

'Just because Serfina Roux is pretty,' Jan Vermeulen said, flinging mealie heads into the sack, 'let us not forget who and what she is. Perhaps it is not safe for us to camp tonight on this farm. She is sure to be in touch with the English. She may tell them where we are. Especially now that we have taken her mealies.'

But our veldkornet said that it wasn't important if the English knew where we were. Indeed, any kafir in the neighbourhood could go and report our position to them. But what did matter was that we should know where the English were. And he reminded us that in two years he had never made a serious mistake that way.

'What about the affair at the spruit, though?' Jan Vermeulen asked him. 'And my pipe and tinder-box were in the jacket, too.'

By sunset the wind had gone down. But there was a chill in the air. We had pitched our camp in the tamboekie grass on the far side of Leendert Roux's farm. And I was glad, lying in my blankets, to think that it was the turn of the veldkornet and Jurie Bekker to stand guard.

Far away a jackal howled. Then there was silence again. A little later the stillness was disturbed by sterner sounds of the veld at night. And those sounds did not come from very far away, either. They were sounds Jurie Bekker made – first, when he fell over a beacon, and then when he gave his opinion of Leendert Roux for setting up a beacon in the middle of a stretch of dubbeltjie thorns. The blankets felt very snug, pulled over my shoulders, when I reflected on those thorns.

And because I was young, there came into my thoughts, at Jurie Bekker's mention of Leendert Roux, the picture of Serfina as she had stood in front of her door.

The dream I had of Serfina Roux was that she came to me, tall and graceful, beside a white beacon on her husband's farm. It was that haunting kind of dream, in which you half know all the time, that you are dreaming. And she was very beautiful in my dream. And it was as though her hair was hanging half out of my dream and reaching down into the wind when she came closer to me. And I knew what she wanted to tell me. But I did not wish to hear it. I knew that if Serfina spoke that thing I would wake up from my dream. And in that moment, like it always happens in a dream, Serfina did speak.

'Opskud, kêrels!' I heard.

But it was not Serfina who gave that command. It was Apie Theron, the veldkornet. He came running into the camp with his rifle at the trail. And Serfina was gone. In a few minutes we had saddled our horses and were ready to gallop away. Many times during the past couple of years our scouts had roused us thus when an English column was approaching.

We were already in the saddle when Apie Theron let us know what was toward. He had received information, he said, that Leendert Roux had that very night ventured back to his homestead. If we hurried we might trap him in his own house. The veldkornet warned us to take no chances, reminding us that when Leendert Roux had still stood on our side he had been a fearless and resourceful fighter.

So we rode back during the night along the same way we had come in the afternoon. We tethered our horses in a clump of trees near the mealie-lands and started to surround the farmhouse. When we saw a figure running for the stable at the side of the house, we realised that Leendert Roux had been almost too quick for us.

In the cold, thin wind that springs up just before the dawn we surprised Leendert Roux at the door of his stable. But when he made no resistance it was almost as though it was Leendert Roux who had taken us by surprise. Leendert Roux's calm acceptance of his fate made it seem almost as though he had never turned traitor, but that he was laying down his life for the Transvaal.

In answer to the veldkornet's question, Leendert Roux said that he would be glad if Kobus Ferreira – he having noticed that Kobus was wear-ing the frock coat of a man of religion – would read Psalm 110 over his grave. He also said that he did not want his eyes bandaged. And he asked to be allowed to say goodbye to his wife.

Serfina was sent for. At the side of the stable, in the wind of early morning, Leendert and Serfina Roux, husband and wife, bade each other farewell.

Serfina looked even more shadowy than she had done in my dream when she set off back to the homestead along the footpath through the thorns. The sun was just beginning to rise. And I understood how right Jurie Bekker had been when he said that she was just like the Transvaal, with the dawn wind fluttering her skirts about her ankles as it rippled the grass. And I remembered that it was the Boer women that kept on when their menfolk recoiled before the steepness of the Drakensberge and spoke of turning back.

I also thought of how strange it was that Serfina should have come walking over to our camp, in the middle of the night, just as she had done in my dream. But where my dream was different was that she had reported not to me but to our veldkornet where Leendert Roux was.

Peaches Ripening in the Sun

The way Ben Myburg lost his memory (Oom Schalk Lourens said) made a deep impression on all of us. We reasoned that that was the sort of thing that a sudden shock could do to you. There were those in our small section of General du Toit's commando who could recall similar stories of how people in a moment could forget everything about the past, just because of a single dreadful happening.

A shock like that can have the same effect on you even if you are prepared for it. Maybe it can be worse, even. And in this connection I often think of what it says in the Good Book, about that which you most feared having now at last caught up with you.

Our commando went as far as the border by train. And when the engine came to a stop on a piece of open veld, and it wasn't for water, this time, and the engine-driver and fireman didn't step down with spanners and use bad language, then we understood that the train stopping there was the beginning of the Second Boer War.

We were wearing new clothes and we had new equipment, and the sun was shining on the barrels of our Mausers. Our new clothes had been requisitioned for us by our veldkornets at stores along the way. All the veldkornet had to do was to sign his name on a piece of paper for whatever his men purchased.

In most cases, after we had patronised a store in that manner, the shopkeeper would put up his shutters for the day. And three years would pass and the Boer War would be over before the shopkeeper would display any sort of inclination to take the shutters down again.

Maybe he should have put them up before we came.

Only one 'seksie' of General du Toit's commando entered Natal looking considerably dilapidated. This 'seksie' looked as though it was already the end of the Boer War, and not just the beginning. Afterwards we found out that their veldkornet had never learnt to write his name. We were glad that in the first big battle these men kept well to the rear, apparently conscious of how sinful they looked. For, to make matters worse, a regiment of Indian troops was fighting on that front, and we were not anxious that an Eastern race should see white men at such a disadvantage.

'You don't seem to remember me, Schalk,' a young fellow came up and said to me. I admitted that I didn't recognise him, straight away, as Ben Myburg. He did look different in those smart light-green riding pants and that new hat with the ostrich feather stuck in it. You could see he had patronised some mine concession store before the owner got his shutters down.

'But I would know you anywhere, Schalk,' Ben Myburg went on. 'Just from the quick way you hid that soap under your saddle a couple of minutes ago. I remembered where I had last seen something so quick. It was two years ago, at the Nagmaal in Nylstroom.'

I told Ben Myburg that if it was that jar of brandy he meant, then he must realise that there had also been a good deal of misunderstanding about it. Moreover, it was not even a full jar, I said.

But I congratulated him on his powers of memory, which I said I was sure would yet stand the Republic in good stead.

And I was right. For afterwards, when the war of the big commandos was over, and we were in constant retreat, it would be Ben Myburg who, next day, would lead us back to the donga in which we had hidden some mealie-meal and a tin of cooking fat. And if the tin of cooking fat was empty, he would be able to tell us right away if it was kafirs or baboons. A kafir had a different way of eating cooking fat out of a tin from what a baboon had, Ben Myburg said.

Ben Myburg had been recently married to Mimi van Blerk, who came from Schweizer-Reneke, a district that was known as far as the Limpopo for its attractive girls. I remembered Mimi van Blerk well. She had full red lips and thick yellow hair. Ben Myburg always looked forward very eagerly to getting letters from his pretty young wife. He would also read out to us extracts from her letters, in which she encouraged us to drive the English into the blue grass – which was the name we gave to the sea in those days. For the English we had other names.

One of Mimi's letters was accompanied by a wooden candle-box filled with dried peaches. Ben Myburg was most proud to share out the dried fruit among our company, for he had several times spoken of the orchard of yellow cling peaches that he had laid out at the side of his house.

'We've already got dried peaches,' Jurie Bekker said. Then he added, making free with our projected invasion of Natal: 'In a few weeks' time we will be picking bananas.'

It was in this spirit, as I have said, that we set out to meet the enemy. But nobody knew better than ourselves how much of this fine talk was to hide what we really felt. And I know, speaking for myself, that when we got the command 'Opsaal', and we were crossing the border between the Transvaal and Natal, I was less happy at the thought that my horse was such a mettlesome animal. For it seemed to me that my horse was far more anxious to invade Natal than I was. I had to rein him in a good deal on the way to Spioenkop and Colenso. And I told myself that it was because I did not want him to go too fast downhill.

Eighteen months later saw the armed forces of the Republic in a worse case than I should imagine any army has ever been in, and that army still fighting. We were spread all over the country in small groups. We were in rags.

Many burghers had been taken prisoner. Others had yielded themselves up to British magistrates, holding not their rifles in their hands but their hats. There were a number of Boers, also, who had gone and joined the English.

For the Transvaal Republic it was near the end of a tale that you tell, sitting around the kitchen fire on a cold night. The story of the Transvaal Republic was at that place where you clear your throat before saying which of the two men the girl finally married. Or whether it was the cattle-smuggler or the Sunday school superintendent who stole the money. Or whether it was a real ghost or just her uncle with a sheet round him that Lettie van Zyl saw at the drift.

One night, when we were camped just outside Nietverdiend, and it was Ben Myburg's and my turn to go on guard, he told me that he knew that part well.

'You see that rant there, Schalk?' he asked. 'Well, I have often stood on the other side of it, under the stars, just like now. You know, I've got a lot of peach-trees on my farm. Well, I have stood there, under the ripening peaches, just after dark, with Mimi at my side. There is no smell like the smell of young peach-trees in the evening, Schalk, when the fruit is ripening. I can almost imagine I am back there now. And it is just the time for it, too.'

I tried to explain to Ben Myburg, in a roundabout way, that although everything might be exactly the same on this side of the rant, he would have to be prepared for certain changes on the other side, seeing that it was war.

Ben Myburg agreed that I was probably right. Nevertheless, he began to talk to me at length about his courtship days. He spoke of Mimi with her full red lips and her yellow hair.

'I can still remember the evening when Mimi promised that she would marry me, Schalk,' Ben Myburg said. 'It was in Zeerust. We were there for the Nagmaal. When I walked back to my tent on the kerk-plein I was so happy that I just kicked the first three kafirs I saw.'

I could see that, talking to me while we stood on guard, Ben Myburg was living through that time all over again. I was glad, for their sakes, that no kafirs came past at that moment. For Ben Myburg was again very happy.

I was pleased, too, for Ben Myburg's own sake, that he did at least have that hour of deep joy in which he could recall the past so vividly. For it was after that that his memory went.

By the following evening we had crossed the rant and had arrived at Ben Myburg's farm. We camped among the smoke-blackened walls of his former homestead, erecting a rough shelter with some sheets of corrugated iron that we could still use. And although he must have known only too well what to expect, what Ben Myburg saw there came as so much of a shock to his senses that from that moment all he could remember from the past vanished forever.

It was pitiful to see the change that had come over him. If his farm had been laid to ruins, the devastation that had taken place in Ben Myburg's mind was no less dreadful.

Perhaps it was that, in truth, there was nothing more left in the past to remember.

We noticed, also, that in singular ways, certain fragments of the by-gone would come into Ben Myburg's mind; and that he would almost – but not quite – succeed in fitting these pieces together.

We observed that almost immediately. For instance, we remained camped on his farm for several days. And one morning, when the fire for our mealie-pap was crackling under one of the few remaining fruit-trees that had once been an orchard, Ben Myburg reached up and picked a peach that was, in advance of its season, ripe and yellow.

'It's funny,' Ben Myburg said, 'but I seem to remember, from long ago, reaching up and picking a yellow peach, just like this one. I don't quite remember where.'

We did not tell him.

Some time later our 'seksie' was captured in a night attack.

For us the Boer War was over. We were going to St. Helena. We were driven to Nylstroom, the nearest railhead, in a mule-wagon. It was a strange experience for us to be driving along the main road, in broad daylight, for all the world to see us. From years of wartime habit, our eyes still went to the horizon. A bitter thing about our captivity was that among our guards were men of our own people.

Outside Nylstroom we alighted from the mule-wagon and the English sergeant in charge of our escort got us to form fours by the roadside. It was queer – our having to learn to be soldiers at the end of a war instead of at the beginning.

Eventually we got into some sort of formation, the veldkornet, Jurie Bekker, Ben Myburg and I making up the first four. It was already evening. From a distance we could see the lights in the town. The way to the main street of Nylstroom led by the cemetery. Although it was dark, we could yet distinguish several rows of newly made mounds. We did not need to be told that they were concentration camp graves. We took off our battered hats and tramped on in a great silence.

Soon we were in the main street. We saw, then, what those lights were. There was a dance at the hotel. Paraffin lamps were hanging under the hotel's low, wide verandah. There was much laughter. We saw girls and English officers. In our unaccustomed fours we slouched past in the dark.

Several of the girls went inside then. But a few of the women-folk remained on the verandah, not looking in our direction. Among them I noticed particularly a girl leaning on an English officer's shoulder. She looked very pretty, with the light from a paraffin lamp shining on her full lips and yellow hair. When we had turned the corner, and the darkness was wrapping us round again, I heard Ben Myburg speak.

'It's funny,' I heard Ben Myburg say, 'but I seem to remember, from long ago, a girl with yellow hair, just like that one. I don't quite remember where.'

And this time, too, we did not tell him.

Birth Certificate

It was when At Naudé told us what he had read in the newspaper about a man who had thought all his life he was White, and had then discovered that he was Coloured, that the story of Flippus Biljon was called to mind. I mean, we all knew the story of Flippus Biljon. But because it was still early afternoon we did not immediately make mention of Flippus. Instead, we discussed, at considerable length, other instances that were within our knowledge of people who had grown up as one sort of person and had discovered in later life that they were in actual fact quite a different sort of person.

Many of these stories that we recalled in Jurie Steyn's voorkamer as the shadows of the thorn-trees lengthened were based only on hearsay. It was the kind of story that you had heard, as a child, at your grandmother's knee. But your grandmother would never admit, of course, that she had heard that story at her grandmother's knee. Oh, no. She could remember very clearly how it all happened, just like it was yesterday. And she could tell you the name of the farm. And the name of the landdrost who was summoned to take note of the extraordinary occurrence, when it had to do with a more unusual sort of changeling, that is. And she would recall the solemn manner in which the landdrost took off his hat when he said that there were many things that were beyond human understanding.

Similarly now, in the voorkamer, when he recalled stories of White children that had been carried off by a Bushman or a baboon or a werewolf, even, and had been brought up in the wilds and without any proper religious instruction, then we also did not think it necessary to explain where we had heard those stories. We spoke as though we had been actually present at some stage of the affair – more usually at the last scene, where the child, now grown to manhood and needing trousers and a pair of braces and a hat, gets restored to his parents, and the magistrate, after studying the birth certificate, says that there are things in this world that baffle the human mind.

And while the shadows under the thorn-trees grew longer, the stories we told in Jurie Steyn's voorkamer grew, if not longer, then, at least, taller.

'But this isn't the point of what I have been trying to explain,' At Naudé interrupted a story of Gysbert van Tonder's that was getting a bit confused in parts, through Gysbert van Tonder not being quite clear as to what a werewolf was. 'When I read that bit in the newspaper I started wondering how must a man feel, after he has grown up with adopted parents and he discovers, quite late in life, through seeing his birth certificate for the first time, that he isn't White, after all. That is what I am trying to get at. Supposing Gysbert were to find out suddenly – '

At Naudé pulled himself up short. Maybe there were one or two things about a werewolf that Gysbert van Tonder wasn't too sure about, and he would allow himself to be corrected by Oupa Bekker on such points. But there were certain things he wouldn't stand for.

'All right,' At Naudé said hastily, 'I don't mean Gysbert van Tonder, specially. What I am trying to get at is, how would any one of us feel? How would any White man feel, if he has passed as White all his life, and he sees for the first time, from his birth certificate, that his grandfather was Coloured? I mean, how would he *feel*? Think of that awful moment when he looks in the palm of his hand and he sees ...'

'He can have that awful moment,' Gysbert van Tonder said. 'I've looked at the palm of my hand. It's a White man's palm. And my finger-nails have also got proper halfmoons.'

At Naudé said he had never doubted that. No, there was no need for Gysbert van Tonder to come any closer and show him. He could see quite well enough just from where he was sitting. After Chris Welman had pulled Gysbert van Tonder back on to the rusbank by his jacket, counselling him not to do anything foolish, since At Naudé did not mean *him*, Oupa Bekker started talking about a White child in Schweizer-Reneke that had been stolen out of its cradle by a family of baboons.

'I haven't seen that cradle myself,' Oupa Bekker acknowledged, modestly. 'But I met many people who have. After the child had been stolen, neighbours from as far as the Orange River came to look at that cradle. And when they looked at it they admired the particular way that Heilart Nortje – that was the child's father – had set about making his household furniture, with glued *klinkpenne* in the joints, and all. But the real interest about the cradle was that it was empty, proving that the child had been stolen by baboons. I remember how one neighbour, who was not on very good terms with Heilart Nortjé, went about the district saying that it could only have *been* baboons.

'But it was many years before Heilart Nortjé and his wife saw their child again. By *saw*, I mean getting near enough to be able to talk to him and ask him how he was getting on. For he was always too quick, from the way the baboons had brought him up. At intervals Heilart Nortjé and his wife would see the tribe of baboons sitting on a rant, and their son, young Heilart, would be in the company of the baboons. And once, through his field-glasses, Heilart had been able to observe his son for quite a few moments. His son was then engaged in picking up a stone and laying hold of a scorpion that was underneath it. The speed with which his son pulled off the scorpion's sting and proceeded to eat up the rest of the scorpion whole filled the father's heart of Heilart Nortjé with a deep sense of pride.

'I remember how Heilart talked about it. 'Real intelligence', Heilart announced with his chest stuck out. 'A real baboon couldn't have done it quicker or better. I called my wife, but she was a bit too late. All she could see was him looking as pleased as anything and scratching himself. And my wife and I held hands and we smiled at each other and we asked each other, where does he get it all from?

'But then there were times again when that tribe of baboons would leave the Schweizer-Reneke area and go deep into the Kalahari, and Heilart Nortjé and his wife would know nothing about what was happening to their son, except through reports from farmers near whose homesteads the baboons had passed. Those farmers had a lot to say about what happened to some of their sheep, not to talk of their mealies and water-melons. And Heilart would be very bitter about those farmers. Begrudging his son a few prickly pears, he said.

'And it wasn't as though he hadn't made every effort to get his son back, Heilart said, so that he could go to catechism classes, since he was almost of age to be confirmed. He had set all sorts of traps for his son, Heilart said, and he had also thought of shooting the baboons, so that it would be easier, after that, to get his son back. But there was always the danger, firing into a pack like that, of his shooting his own son.

'The neighbour that I have spoken of before,' Oupa Bekker continued, 'who was not very well disposed towards Heilart Nortjé, said that the real reason Heilart didn't shoot was because he didn't always know – actually know – which was his son and which was one of the more flatheaded kees-baboons.'

It seemed that this was going to be a very long story. Several of us started getting restive … So Johnny Coen asked Oupa Bekker, in a polite sort of a way, to tell us how it all ended.

'Well, Heilart Nortjé caught his son, afterwards,' Oupa Bekker said. 'But I am not sure if Heilart was altogether pleased about it. His son was so hard to tame. And then the way he caught him. It was with the simplest sort of baboon trap of all … Yes, that one. A calabash with a hole in it just big enough for you to put your hand in, empty, but that you can't get your hand out of again when you're clutching a fistful of mealies that was put at the bottom of the calabash. Heilart Nortjé never got over that, really. He felt it was a very shameful thing that had happened to him. The thought that his son, in whom he had taken so much pride, should have allowed himself to be caught in the simplest form of monkey-trap.'

When Oupa Bekker paused, Jurie Steyn said that it was indeed a sad story, and it was no doubt perfectly true. There was just a certain tone in Jurie Steyn's voice that made Oupa Bekker continue.

'True in every particular,' Oupa Bekker declared, nodding his head a good number of times. 'The landdrost came over to see about it, too. They sent for the landdrost so that he could make a report about it. I was there, that afternoon, in Heilart Nortjé's voorkamer, when the landdrost came. And there were a good number of other people, also. And Heilart Nortjé's son, half-tamed in some ways but still baboon-wild in others, was there also. The landdrost studied the birth certificate very carefully. Then the landdrost said that what he had just been present at surpassed ordinary human understanding. And the landdrost took off his hat in a very solemn fashion.

'We all felt very embarrassed when Heilart Nortjé's son grabbed the hat out of the landdrost's hand and started biting pieces out of the crown.'

When Oupa Bekker said those words it seemed to us like the end of a story. Consequently, we were disappointed when At Naudé started making further mention of that piece of news he had read in the daily paper. So there was nothing else for it but that we had to talk about Flippus Biljon. For Flippus Biljon's case was just the opposite of the case of the man that At Naudé's newspaper wrote about.

Because he had been adopted by a Coloured family, Flippus Biljon had always regarded himself as a Coloured man. And then one day, quite by accident, Flippus Biljon saw his birth certificate. And from that birth certificate it was clear that Flippus Biljon was as White as you or I. You can imagine how Flippus Biljon must have felt about it. Especially after he had gone to see the magistrate at Bekkersdal, and the magistrate, after studying the birth certificate, confirmed the fact that Flippus Biljon was a White man.

'Thank you, *baas*,' Flippus Biljon said. 'Thank you very much, *my basie*.'

The Picture of Gysbert Jonker

This tobacco-bag, now (Oom Schalk Lourens said, producing a four-ounce linen bag with the picture on it of a leaping blesbuck – the trademark of a well-known tobacco company) well, it is very unusual, the way this tobacco-bag picture fits into the life story of Gysbert Jonker.

I had occasion to think of that only the other day, when at the Zeerust bioscope during the last Nagmaal they showed a film about an English lord who had his portrait painted. And it seemed that after that only the portrait changed, with the years, as the lord grew older and more sinful.

Some of the young people, when they got back from the bioscope, came and called on me, on the kerk-plein, and told me what a good film it was. A few of them hinted that I ought also to go to the bioscope, now and again – say, once in two years, or so – to get new ideas for my stories.

Koos Steyn's younger son, Frikkie, even went so far as to say, straight out, that I should go oftener than just once every two years. A good deal oftener. And that I shouldn't see the same film through more than once, either.

'Important things are happening in the world, Oom Schalk,' young Frikkie said. 'You know, culture and all that. That's why you should go to a film like the one we have just seen. A film with artists in it, and all.'

'Yes, artists, another young fellow said. 'Like an artist that got pointed out to me last time I was in Johannesburg. With his wide hat and his corduroy trousers, he looked just like a Marico farmer, except that his beard was too wild. We don't grow our beards so long in these parts, any more, since that new threshing-machine with the wide hopper came in. That machine is so quick.'

'That is the trouble with your stories, Oom Schalk,' Frikkie Steyn continued. 'The Boers in them all grew their beards too long. And the uppers of their veldskoens have got an old-fashioned look. Why can't you bring into your next story a young man with a pair of brown shop boots on, and' – hitching his pants up and looking down – 'yellow and pink striped socks with a – '

'And a waistcoat with long points coming over the top part of the trousers,' another young man interrupted him. 'And braces with clips that you can make longer or shorter, just as you like.'

Anyway, after Theunis Malan had demonstrated to me the difference between a loose and an attached collar, and then couldn't find his stud, and after an ouderling had come past just when another young man was using bad language because he couldn't get his head out through his shirt again – through somebody else having thoughtfully tied the shirt-tails together while the young man was explaining about a new kind of underwear – well, there wasn't much about their new Nagmaal clothes that these young men wanted me to leave out of my next story. And the ouderling, without knowing what was going on, and without trying to find out, even, merely shook his head solemnly as he went past.

And, of course, Frikkie Steyn, just to make sure I had it right, told the bioscope story of the English lord all over again – all the time that I was filling my pipe from a quarter-pound bag of Magaliesberg tobacco; the sort with the picture of the high-bounding blesbuck on it.

So I thought, well, maybe Gysbert was not an English lord. But I could remember the time when his portrait, painted in the most beautiful colours, hung in his voorkamer. And I also thought of the way in which Gysbert's portrait was on display on every railway platform and in every Indian shop in the country. And almost until the very end the portrait remained unchanged. It was only Gysbert Jonker who, despite all his efforts, altered with the years. But when the portrait did eventually change, it was a much more incredible transformation than anything that could have happened to the portrait of that lord in the bioscope story.

It was while we were sitting in the Indian store at Ramoutsa drinking coffee and waiting for the afternoon to get cool enough for us to be able to drive back home by mule and donkey-cart, that we first noticed the resemblance.

Our conversation was, as usual, of an edifying character. We spoke about how sensible we were to go on sitting in the Indian store, hour after hour, like that, and drinking coffee, instead of driving out in the hot sun and running the risk of getting sunstroke. Later on when some clouds came up, we were even more glad that we had not ventured out in our open carts, because everybody knows that the worst kind of sunstroke is what you get when the sun shines on to the back of your head through the clouds.

Of course, there were other forms of conveyance, such as Cape carts, we said. But that sort of thing only undermined you. Naturally, we did not wish to be undermined. We spoke about how the younger generation was losing its self-reliance through – and we started naming some of the things we saw on the shelves around us. Gramophones, we said. And paraffin candles in packets, we said, instead of making our own. And tubes with white grease that you squeeze at the end to polish your plates and spoons with, one of us said. No, it was to brush your teeth with, somebody else interrupted him. And we said that, well, whatever it was for, it was undermining. And we said that our own generation was being sapped, also.

After we had asked the Indian behind the counter to stand to one side, so that we could see better how we were being undermined, Hans Bekker pointed to a shelf holding tins of coffee. 'Formerly we burnt and ground our own coffee,' Hans Bekker said. 'Today – '

'Before I could walk,' Andries Claassens said, 'I used to shred my own tobacco from a black roll. I could cut up plug tobacco for my pipe before I could sharpen a slate-pencil. But now I have to sit with this little bag –'

I don't know who made the following observation, but we laughed at it for a long time. We looked from Andries Claassens's tobacco bag to the shelf on which dozens of similar bags were displayed. On each was the picture of a farmer with a black beard and a red-and-yellow checked shirt; and in his right hand, which was raised level with his shoulders, he held, elegantly if somewhat stiffly, a pipe. Perhaps you remember that picture, which did not appear only on the tobacco bags, but was reproduced, also, in the newspapers, and stood on oblong metal sheets, enamelled in bright colours, in front of every store.

When our attention had been drawn to it, we saw the resemblance very clearly. In respect of both his features and his expression, the farmer on the tobacco bag was almost the exact image of Gysbert Jonker. Gysbert's beard was not so neatly trimmed, and his eyebrows were straighter; also, his mouth considerably larger than the man's on the picture. But in every other way – taking into consideration the difference in their dress – the likeness was astonishing.

Gysbert Jonker was there, in the Indian store, with us, when we made the discovery. He seemed very much interested.

'You will now have to push your ears in under the sweatband of your hat, in the city fashion,' Hans Bekker said to Gysbert. 'You can't have them bent anymore.'

'And you will now have to hold your pipe up in the air, near to your shoulder, when you walk behind the plough,' Andries Claassens added, 'in your riding-breeches and leggings.'

We were more than a little surprised at Gysbert's answer.

'It is absurd to think that I could do farm-work in that rigout,' he replied. 'But on Sundays, and some evenings after work, I shall wear riding-pants and top-boots. And it's a queer thing, but I have always wanted a shirt with red-and-yellow checks. In any case, it's the least I can do, in view of the fact that this tobacco company has honoured the Marico by making use of the portrait of the district's most progressive cattle farmer in this way. I suppose the tobacco firm selected me for this purpose because of the improvements I made to my cement-dip last year.'

Gysbert Jonker added that next year he intended erecting another barbed wire camp on the other side of the dam, and that he would bring this to the notice of the tobacco company as well.

We suddenly found that we had nothing more to say. And we were so taken aback at the way Gysbert responded to the purely accidental circumstance of his resembling the man in the picture that we were quite unable to laugh about it, even.

And I am sure that I was not the only Marico farmer, driving back home later that afternoon over the dusty road through the camelthorns, who reflected earnestly on the nature (and dangers) of sunstroke.

After a while, however, we got used to the change that had taken place in Gysbert Jonker's soul.

Consequently, with the passage of time, there was less and less said about the gorgeously-coloured shirts that Gysbert Jonker wore on Sundays, when he strolled about the front part of his homestead in riding-breeches and gaiters, apparently carefree and at ease, except that he held his pipe high up near his shoulder, somewhat stiffly. In time, too, the ouderling ceased calling on Gysbert in order to dissuade him from going about dressed as a tobacco advertisement on Sundays – a practice that the ouderling regarded as a desecration of the Sabbath.

In spite of everything, we had to admit that Gysbert Jonker had succeeded to a remarkable degree in imitating his portrait – especially when he started shaving the sides of his eyebrows to make them look more curved, and when he had cultivated a smile that wrinkled up his left cheek, half-way to his ear. And he used to smile carefully, almost as though he was afraid that some of the enamel would chip off him.

Jonker on one occasion announced to a number of acquaintances at a meeting of the Dwarsberg debating society, 'Look at this shirt I have got on, for instance. Just feel the quality of it, and then compare it with the shirt on your tobacco-bag. I had my photo taken last month in Zeerust, in these clothes. I sent the photograph to the head office of the tobacco company in Johannesburg – and would you believe it? The tobacco people sent me, by the following railway-lorry, one of those life-sized enamelled pictures of myself painted on a sheet of iron. You know, the kind that you see on stations and in front of shops. I nailed it to the wall of my voorkamer.'

Gysbert kept up this foolishness for a number of years. And it was, of course, this particular characteristic of his that we admired. We could see from this that he was a real Afrikaner, as obstinate as the Transvaal turfsoil. Even when, with the years, it became difficult for him to compete successfully with his portrait that did not age, so that he had to resort to artificial aids to keep his hair and beard black – then we did not laugh about it. We even sympathised with him in his hopeless struggle against the onslaughts of time. And we noticed that, the older Gysbert Jonker got, the more youthful his shirt seemed.

In the end, Gysbert Jonker had to hands-up of course. But he gave in only after his portrait had changed. And it was so stupendous a change that it was beyond the capacity even of Gysbert to try to follow suit. One day suddenly – without any kind of warning from the tobacco firm – we noticed, when we were again in the Indian store at Ramoutsa, that the picture of the farmer in riding-pants had disappeared from the tobacco-bags. Just like that. The farmer was replaced with the picture of the leaping blesbuck that you see on this bag, here. Afterwards, the blesbuck took the place of the riding pants farmer on the enamelled iron sheets as well.

Meanwhile, however, when it dawned on us that the tobacco company was busy changing its advertisement, we made many carefully considered remarks about Gysbert Jonker. We said that he would now, in his old age, have to start practising the high jump, in order to be able to resemble his new portrait. We also said that he would now have to paint his belly white, like the blesbuck's. We also expressed the hope that a leopard wouldn't catch Gysbert Jonker when he walked about the veld on a Sunday morning, dressed up like his new portrait.

Nevertheless, I had the feeling that Gysbert Jonker did not altogether regret the fact that his portrait had been unrecognisably changed. For one thing, he was now relieved of the strain of having all the time to live up to the opinion that the tobacco company had formed of him.

And although he removed the enamelled portrait from the wall of his voorkamer, and used it to repair a hole in the pigsty, and although he wore his gaudily-coloured shirts every day, now, and while doing the roughest kind of work, just so as to get rid of them – yet there were times, when I looked at Gysbert Jonker, that my thoughts were carried right back to the past. Most often this would happen when he was smoking. To the end, he retained something of his enamelled way by holding his pipe, his hand raised almost level with his shoulder, elegantly, but just a shade stiffly.

Some years later, when Gysbert Jonker was engaged in wearing out the last of his red-and-yellow checked shirts, I came across him at the back of his pigsty. He was standing near the spot where he had replaced a damaged sheet of corrugated iron with his tobacco-advertisement portrait.

And it struck me that in some mysterious way, Gysbert Jonker had again caught up with his portrait. For they looked equally shabby and dilapidated, then, the portrait and Gysbert Jonker. They seemed to have become equally sullied – through the years and through sin. And so I turned away quickly from that rusted sheet of iron, with the picture on it of that farmer with his battered pipe, and his beard that was now greying and unkempt. And his shirt that looked as patched as Gysbert Jonker's own. And his eyes that had grown as wistful.

My First Love

It was when I visited the de Bruyns of Drogedal that I saw Lettie de Bruyn for the first time: in the sense that I saw her properly, I mean. I was then nearly twenty, and Lettie must have been somewhere between sixteen and seventeen. It was long since I had last visited the Drogedal area, for this region was not situated on the main road to Zeerust, but was connected with the outside world by a dusty little side-road that wound along the side of Paradys Kop. Thus I noticed a few changes that had taken place there since my last visit.

I drove the new teacher to Drogedal in the mule-cart so that he could visit the de Bruyn and Bekker families who lived somewhat isolatedly below the Paradys Kop. A considerable number of children from Drogedal attended the Heimweeberg School where the Transvaal Education Department had just appointed Mr. Herklaas Huysmans as the new head-master. Although he was only a year or two older than I was, I always addressed him as 'Mr. Huysmans'. There was something dignified about his appearance that prevented me from calling him bluntly 'neef Herklaas'. (Months later I thought out a whole lot of other names for him.)

The official position filled by Mr. Huysmans was of a highly responsible nature, for he was not only the principal of that little bushveld school, he was the whole school staff as well. He boarded with us on our farm, and my father was very pleased about this and urged me to spend as much time as possible in his company. My father maintained that it was of great educational value to me to associate with a school principal, seeing that I had only a little book learning.

I thought that my father, who during his whole life had only been to school for six months, would derive more benefit than I from Mr. Huysmans's company. However, I did not express my opinion. For I still lived with my parents, and my father was a man with the highest learning in the Marico as regards the handling of a short piece of undressed ox-hide.

One Saturday, after we had eaten our midday meal and before we had pushed our chairs back, Mr. Huysmans informed us that he should like that afternoon to visit the Bekkers and de Bruyns. They were the only families with children at Heimweeberg School whom he had not yet visited.

'The Education Department requires that I visit each pupil at his home once a term,' the principal explained, while he looked straight at me to suggest that it was time for me to run out and harness the mules.

'Yes, my son Schalk can take you over there,' said my father in his obliging way. 'It will be of educational value for Schalk, as well as, perhaps, dusty and hot on that road at this time of the day.'

'But we're having a shooting contest at Derdepoort this afternoon ...' I began to explain. But just at that moment my father made a gruff noise, which helped me immediately to see that my father was right, and that it was necessary for me to acquire further book knowledge. As a result the mules were harnessed and Mr. Huysmans and I were on the way to Drogedal in no time.

'Did the headmaster who was here before me visit the Drogedal families regularly?' Mr. Huysmans wanted to know after we had been on the road for about an hour and a half in the open mule-cart, while the sun burnt steadily down on our necks.

'No, not exactly,' I answered.

'I can well believe that,' said Mr. Huysmans meaningfully while perspiration poured from him.

For the last few miles the schoolmaster complained continuously about the dust and the heat and the horse-flies. Nevertheless I preferred that to the instructive sort of talk he was sometimes in the habit of giving. Since he was the cause of my not being able to attend the shooting contest at Derdepoort, it would have been unbearable to me if on top of that I still had to listen to any educational little talk about how many square Cape roods there are in a morgen.

At last we reached our destination.

'There are several Bekker and de Bruyn families living out here in the backveld,' I explained as the cart turned the last bend. 'Yes, and look, here now is Gys Bekker's place. That mud-coloured bit of wall sticking out between those two heaps. As you know, the Bekkers and de Bruyns have quite a number of children who go to school, but the people here are just slightly – how should I say? – conservative. Ah! now you can see Gys Bekker's house better. That is his dining-room – look, where that plump young Friesland bullock is coming out. And that woman with the wash-rag who is now coming after that bullock is Gys Bekker's ...'

Just then the schoolmaster interrupted me with the proposal that we should rather go and look up a few de Bruyn families. The Bekkers seemed, after all, slightly too conservative, the schoolmaster explained.

So it happened that later that afternoon we sat and drank coffee in Arnoldus de Bruyn's voorkamer. I have mentioned already the changes that were to be seen there. Arnoldus de Bruyn had, for example, fitted the voorkamer with a wooden ceiling. He had also laid out a front stoep of blue slate-stone, and had put up a wire fence with a green gate, with the result that even the stupidest son of fat calf would have to think twice before taking Arnoldus's voorkamer for the place where there was the manger with the cut-up sheaves.

I began to chat with Arnoldus de Bruyn about the improvements he had brought about. I sat on the riempies-bottomed bench next to Mr. Huysmans. Oom Arnoldus sat opposite us and puffed clouds of blue smoke up towards the ceiling – of which you could see he was very proud. His wife and a few older children also sat with us in the voorhuis.

I felt that a compliment was called for.

'Oom Arnoldus, you've really altered your house nicely,' I said. 'At least your house no longer looks so very much like a stable. What I mean is, who ever saw a cowshed with striped curtains in front of the window?'

Although I should have preferred to have expressed myself more skilfully, Arnoldus was highly pleased with my little speech and smiled in a satisfied son of way. My reference to Arnoldus de Bruyn's place gave rise, at any rate, to a detailed discussion by the schoolmaster of the subject 'The Dwellings of the Peoples of Distant Lands'. He ended with a description of the houses of the Eskimos which they build of ice. Arnoldus de Bruyn shook his head thoughtfully over this and said: 'Well, well – what won't people think of next!'

In the meantime I had taken a proper look at Lettie de Bruyn. She was another one of the changes I have spoken of. At any rate, she seemed to be very different from when we were children together. What especially surprised me was that she seemed so calm now. She had also grown tall: something I noticed when she approached the riempie bench to serve me and the schoolmaster with coffee. When I helped myself to sugar I spilled half my coffee in my saucer.

I wanted to chat a little with Lettie de Bruyn about our childhood years, but my tongue wouldn't come loose. Even in taking my second cup of coffee – which I also partly spilled, this time over the schoolmaster's trouser-leg – I couldn't find any words.

The following Saturday I again drove Mr. Huysmans over to Drogedal. He said that it was his duty to visit the families there, seeing that they had become so conservative simply because they had not had enough elevating company. Nevertheless, it was peculiar to me that on every one of the following Saturdays, when I drove Mr. Huysmans to Drogedal, he only visited the home of Arnoldus de Bruyn. He closed his eyes completely to the other de Bruyn families, and as far as the Bekkers were concerned, it was clear that he wouldn't have been much perturbed if they had grown more conservative by the day.

Naturally I did not mind. I could never scrape up enough courage to address a word directly to Lettie de Bruyn, but did progress so far as to lay my hand lightly on hers (after I had first put my cup down) each time she came and stood in front of me with the tray. She always blushed. It moved me to think how much the two of us could say to each other, Lettie de Bruyn and I, without using words – and without even needing much learning for it either.

Mr. Huysmans spoke in his most elevating manner about how envious other teachers were of him, because he was so talented.

'A colleague of mine even said out of jealousy,' Mr. Huysmans declared, 'that the Department sent me here because I am useless.'

I winked at Lettie when the teacher spoke like that. She smiled back.

So you can imagine how shocked I was on the morning Mr. Huysmans, all-innocently, announced to my parents that he would no longer impose on them at our house over the weekends, since he intended henceforth to ride on the school wagon to Drogedal every Friday afternoon and stay over until Monday morning at the de Bruyns'.

From then on until the end of the school-term we no longer saw Mr. Huysmans at our farm during the weekends. And I could think of no excuse for visiting Drogedal. There was no way by which I could communicate with Lettie de Bruyn.

I am certain that none of the pupils of Heimweeberg School could have longed for the end of the schoolterm as much as I, whose schooldays were already so far behind me.

But at last the schools did break up. Mr. Huysmans went to Pretoria to spend the holidays there with his parents. The Marico Boers inspanned their ox-wagons and took the road to Zeerust in order to attend the Nagmaal. And thus I knew where I would again meet Lettie de Bruyn.

It was with the inevitability of something that happens in a dream that Lettie de Bruyn came to me, in a night of summer fragrances, when the stars glistened hugely.

This time, also, we still did not speak. By an arrangement which we had made without the use of words, she slipped out of the veld-tent that Arnoldus de Bruyn had pitched on the church square, to come and meet me. She was wearing a long white dress, and when she came near to me I saw how tall and thin she was, and how pale her cheeks were – white, like her dress. When I stretched out my arms she withdrew herself playfully. I chased her. But when I caught up with her and laughing took her into my arms, she suddenly turned her face away. Before I could grasp what was happening, I let her slip out of my arms again. It all had the feeling of a dream. The suddenness of her movements took me by surprise, and before I could collect myself again she suddenly pressed her mouth against my cheek. Then she ran into the shadows, to the tent where her parents and brothers and sisters were sleeping.

I knew that she would come to me again the next night.

What troubled me was the realisation that lately Lettie de Bruyn had learnt too much. Undoubtedly she had been learning during the school-term that had just ended. I walked through the deserted streets of Zeerust; I walked under the stars, overwhelmed by the age-old sorrow of first love.

The Brothers

It is a true saying that man may plan, but that God has the last word (Oom Schalk Lourens said).

And it was no different with Krisjan Lategan. He had one aim, and that was to make sure that his farm should remain the home of Lategans from one generation to the next until the end of the world. This would be in about two hundred years, according to the way in which a church elder, who was skilled in Biblical prophecy, had worked it out. It would be on a Sunday morning.

Krisjan Lategan wanted his whole family and all his descendants around him, so that on the Last Day they could all stand up together in an orderly fashion. There was to be no unseemly rushing around to look for Lategans who had wandered off into distant parts. Especially with the Last Day being a Sunday and all. Krisjan Lategan was particular that a solemn occasion should not be marred by the bad language that always went with rounding up stray oxen on a morning when you had to trek.

Afterwards, when they brought the telegraph up to Nietverdiend, and they showed the church elder how they could tap out messages from as far away as Cape Town, the elder shook his head and said that he did not give the world a full two hundred years any more. And when in Zeerust he heard a talking machine that could sing songs and speak words just through your turning a handle, the elder said that the end of the world was now quite near.

And he said it almost as though he was glad.

It was then that Krisjan Lategan set about the construction of the family vault at the end of his farm. It was the kind of vault that you see on some farms in the Cape. There was a low wall around it like the kind you build for a sheep fold, and the vault was only a few feet below the level of the ground, and you walked down steps to a wooden door fastened with a chain. Inside were tamboetie wood trestles for the coffins to go on. The trestles were painted with tar, to keep away the white ants.

It was a fine vault. Farmers came from many miles away to admire it.

And, as always happens in such cases, after their first feelings of awe had worn off, the visitors would make remarks which, in the parts of the Marico near the Bechuanaland border, regularly aroused guffaws.

They said, yes, it was quite a nice house, but where was the chimney? They also said that if you got up in the middle of the night and reached your hand under the bed – well, the vault wasn't a properly fixed up kind of vault at all.

The remark Hans van Tonder made was also regarded as very clever. Pointing to the tar on the trestles, he said he couldn't understand why old Krisjan should be so concerned about keeping the white ants out. 'When you lie in your coffin, it's not by *ants* that you get eaten up,' Hans van Tonder said. 'You get ants in your shirt, maybe, but not in your shroud.'

Krisjan Lategan's neighbours had a lot of things of this nature to say about his vault when it was newly-constructed. All the same, not one of them would have been anxious to go to the vault alone at night after Krisjan Lategan had been laid to rest in it.

And yet all Krisjan Lategan's plans came to nothing. Shortly after his death certain events occurred on his farm, as a result of which one of his two sons came to an untimely end, and his corpse was placed in the vault in a coffin that was much too long. And the other son fled so far out of the Marico that it would certainly not be possible to find him again before the Last Day. And even then, on the Day of Judgement, he would not be likely to push himself forward to any extent.

Everybody in the bushveld knew of the bitterness that there was between old Krisjan Lategan's two sons, Doors and Lodewyk, who were in all things so unlike each other. At their father's death the two brothers were in their twenties. Neither was married. Doors was a few years older than Lodewyk.

Lodewyk, the younger brother, was tall and good-looking, and his nature was adventurous. The elder brother, Doors, was a hunchback. He had short legs and unnaturally broad shoulders. He was credited with great strength. Because of his grotesque shape, the kafirs told stories about him that had to do with witchcraft, and that could not be true.

At his father's funeral, Doors, with his short stature and the shapeless hump on his back, looked particularly ungainly among the other pall-bearers, all straight and upstanding men of the veld. During the simple service before the open doors of the vault a child burst out crying. It was something of a scandal that the child wept out of terror of Doors Lategan's hunched figure, and not because of sorrow for the departed. When the child got home his parents gave him something else to cry about.

Soon afterwards Lodewyk Lategan left the farm for the diamond diggings at Doornpan. Before that the brothers had quarrelled violently in the mealie-lands. The kafirs said that quarrel had been about what cattle Lodewyk could take with him to the diggings. When Lodewyk went it was with the new wagon and the best span of oxen. And Doors said that if he ever returned to the farm he would kill him.

In that spirit the brothers parted. Tant Alie, old Krisjan Lategan's widow, remained on the farm with her elder son, Doors. She was an aging woman with no force of character. She came of a Cape family of which quite a few members were known to be 'simpel', although nobody, of course, thought any the less of them on that account. They belonged to a sheep district, Tant Alie's family, and we of the Marico, who were cattle farmers, said that for a sheep farmer it was even a help if he was a bit soft in the head.

But whatever Tant Alie might have thought and felt about the estrangement that was between her sons, she did not ever discuss the matter.

Lodewyk left for the diamond fields in the company of Flippie Geel, who had a piece of government land at Koedoesrand that he was supposed to improve. About all he had done in that direction, so far, was to sell the galvanised iron water-tank that he had found on the place. Flippie Geel was a good deal older than Lodewyk Lategan. For that reason it seems all the more surprising that he should have helped Lodewyk in his subsequent foolish actions. Perhaps Flippie Geel found that going with Lodewyk was easier than work.

From what came out afterwards, it would appear that Lodewyk Lategan and Flippie Geel did not dig much on their claim. But they put in a lot of time in the bar, drinking wine that Lodewyk paid for through selling his trek oxen, a pair at a time.

Lodewyk Lategan was not the first Marico farmer who had gone to the diggings and had there been able to see the wonder of his red Afrikaner cattle being turned into red wine in front of his eyes – and not by means of looking-glasses, either, such as they say the conjuror uses for his tricks in the Zeerust hall at Nagmaal.

And when he was in his cups Lodewyk would think out many schemes for getting even with his brother, Doors, who, he said, had defrauded him of his share of the inheritance.

One day Lodewyk got hold of a plan that he decided to carry out. From this you can get some idea of how crack-brained the plans must have been that he didn't act on. Anyway, he got Flippie Geel to write to Doors that his brother Lodewyk had been killed in an accident on the diggings, and that his body was being sent home in a coffin by transport wagon. And a few days later a coffin, which Lodewyk had made to his size, arrived at the Lategan farm. Inside the coffin, instead of a corpse, was a mealie-sack that Lodewyk and Flippie Geel had filled with gravel.

I can picture Lodewyk and Flippie getting blisters on their hands from filling the sack – since that was perhaps the only time, on the diggings, that the two of them had got down to working with a shovel.

It is difficult to know what plan Lodewyk Lategan had with the coffin. Of course, he was drunk nearly always during that period. And if, as he claimed, he had not inherited his due portion of the family property, it is nevertheless likely that he inherited a full share of his mother's weakness of mind. But he must surely have expected Doors to unscrew the lid of the coffin, if for no other reason than to make certain that his brother really was dead.

Lodewyk could surely not have foreseen Doors acting the way he did when the coffin was delivered on the front stoep of the Lategan homestead. Without getting up from the riempies chair on which he was sitting – well forward because of his hump – Doors shouted for the farm kafirs to come and fetch away the coffin.

'Take this box to the vault and put it on a trestle,' Doors said. 'And don't put the lock back.'

He silenced his mother when she asked to be allowed to gaze for the last time on the face of her dead son.

The transport driver, who had helped to carry the coffin on to the stoep, and had stood bare-headed beside it in reverence for the dead, felt there was something out of place in the figure he cut. He pushed his hat firmly on to his head. Then he walked back to his team, a very amazed man.

There are some who say that Doors Lategan had second sight. Or if it wasn't second sight it was a depth of cunning that was as good as second sight. And he had guessed that his brother Lodewyk's body was not in the coffin.

At the time, however, the farmers of the neighbourhood naturally had no suspicions of this nature. And they said it was not right that Doors should be so unfeeling. They said that the least Doors could have done was to put a black mourning band round his arm when he went to the poort to pump water for his cattle. They said he could also, when he went to load the pigs into the crates for the market, have worn a piece of crepe trimming in his hat. There was no harm in showing respect, people said.

A few weeks later it was known that Lodewyk's ghost was haunting the Lategan farm. Several kafirs swore to having seen the ghost of Baas Lodewyk on moonlight nights. They had seen Baas Lodewyk's ghost by the vault. Baas Lodewyk's ghost was sitting on the low wall, they said. And if they hadn't known that it couldn't be, they would even have thought that what Baas Lodewyk's ghost was holding in its hand was a black bottle. There was another kafir who said that he had heard Baas Lodewyk's ghost singing. He didn't stay long enough to make sure what song it was, the kafir added.

But what were even better established were the times when Lodewyk's ghost was seen driving along the high road in the back of Flippie Geel's mule-cart that had a half-hood over the back seat. For even white people had seen Lodewyk's ghost riding in the back seat of Flippie Geel's mule-cart. It was known that Flippie Geel had recently returned to the Marico to improve his government land some more. He was now trying to sell a mealie-planter with green handles that he had also found on the place.

Because in life Lodewyk Lategan had been Flippie Geel's bosom friend, it was not considered surprising that Lodewyk's ghost should have been seen haunting the back seat of Flippie Geel's mule-can. But they were glad for Flippie's sake that Flippie hadn't turned round. Lodewyk's ghost looked too awful, the people said who saw it. It was almost as though it was trying to hide itself away against the half-hood of the cart.

It was when Hans van Tonder, fighting down his fears, crept up to Flippie Geel's window, one night, that the truth came out. Hans van Tonder was prepared for almost any dreadful sight when he looked through the window of the rondavel. But what met his gaze was something more unholy than he could ever have imagined. He saw Lodewyk sitting with his feet on the table and a look of contentment on his face, eating ostrich biltong. Next day everybody in the Marico knew that Lodewyk Lategan was not dead – not unless the ostrich biltong had killed him in between, that was.

Shortly afterwards came the night when Doors's kafirs reported to him that they had seen Baas Lodewyk climbing through the barbed wire with a gun in his hands. Doors took down his Mauser from the wall and went into the veld.

Next morning, in the Lategan family vault, a sack of gravel had been replaced by a body, and the coffin-lid had been screwed on again. During the night one brother had been murdered. The other had fled. He was never caught.

Several days passed before the veldkornet came to the Lategan farm. And then Tant Alie would not give him permission to open the coffin. And she was unexpectedly firm about it.

'One of my sons is in the vault and the other is a fugitive over the face of the earth,' Tant Alie said. 'I don't want to know which is which.'

Nevertheless, Tant Alie had to give way when the veldkornet came back with an official paper. To reach the coffin the veldkornet had to pass by the sack of gravel, which had burst open at the top. He kicked the gravel about a few times on the not very hopeful off-chance of turning up a diamond. Then he unscrewed the lid. In the coffin that was much too long for him – although it was cramped for breadth – lay Doors, the hunchback brother, with a bullet in his heart.

But even before the veldkornet opened the coffin it was known in the Marico that it was Doors, the elder brother that had been murdered. For when the younger brother, Lodewyk Lategan, fled from the district he drove off in Flippie Geel's mule-cart. Several people had seen Lodewyk driving along the highway in the night. And those people said that for Lodewyk's own sake they were glad that Lodewyk did not look round.

It was well for Lodewyk Lategan, they said, that he should drive off and not know that there was a passenger in the back seat. The passenger had broad shoulders and the starlight shone through his ungainly hump.

The Wind in the Trees

There were dark patches on the washed-out blue of Gerrit van Biljon's shirt (Oom Schalk Lourens said), when I saw him on that morning, kneeling before a hole that he had been chopping in the stony ground in front of his house. Those patches were damp marks of sweat. Gerrit van Biljon was kneeling down in front of the hole, on that forenoon of a summer's day when I saw him, and he was scraping out fragments of loosened earth and stones with his hands.

The ground was very hard, and Gerrit was digging the hole with a long cold-chisel and a heavy hammer, which were more serviceable than the pickaxe with which he had evidently commenced digging, and which was now lying some distance away from the hole. About twenty yards away, to be exact. It was apparent to me that that was how far Gerrit van Biljon had thrown the pick at the moment when he had decided to go to the toolshed for the hammer and cold-chisel.

'You are digging, Neef Gerrit,' I observed.

I was curious why a farmer of the Marico bushveld should be down on his knees, like the way Gerrit was, in the heat of the forenoon, with the sweat coming out through his shirt in dark patches, and the sun striking on the back of his neck, in the space between the wide brim of his hat and the top of his faded shirt-collar.

Gerrit van Biljon did not answer. Instead he reached still deeper into the hole and started feeling for more bits of loose ground. The sun beat full on to the back of his neck, which would have been very red by now if he had been an Englishman. As it was, no amount of sun could do much more to the colour of the back of Gerrit's neck, which was already almost as brown as the earth lying beside the hole. The worst that could happen to Gerrit would be sunstroke. And you know, the most suitable conditions under which you can get sunstroke in the Marico are when the rays of the midday sun strike on the back of your neck through a thin haze of cloud.

Therefore, when for the second time Gerrit van Biljon had not answered my question, I looked hopefully upwards. But from one horizon to the other the heavens were a deep and intense blue. Bush and koppie, withaak and kremetart and kameeldoring were dreaming languidly under a cloudless sky. I realised that there was not much prospect of Gerrit getting sunstroke, but I nevertheless consoled myself with the thought that having the full blaze on his neck like that must be very unpleasant for him.

I also realised that it was no use my asking Gerrit van Biljon any more direct questions. So I tried sideways, in the manner in which de Wet, after studying the ground, brought his commando round to that part of Sanna's Post where the English general did not want any Mauser bullets to come from.

'Have the Bechuanas on your farm trekked somewhere else, Neef Gerrit,' I asked, casually, 'back to the Protectorate?'

Thus I succeeded, for the first time, in getting Gerrit van Biljon to talk.

'No, they have not left,' he replied. And then, a little later, after he had struck the cold-chisel about another half-dozen times, he asked, very reluctantly, 'Why?'

'Because, if the Bechuanas have not left,' I answered, 'why is it that you, a Marico Boer, should so far have forgotten about farming, as to be here, on your hands and knees, digging a hole in the ground and in the hot sun, with the sweat making all those damp patches on your shirt?'

And after I had scanned Gerrit van Biljon's back carefully, from his battered hat to those patched veldskoens, I added, 'Like a kafir.'

When Gerrit stood up, at that point, and dusted some of the worst pieces of loose earth from the knees of his khaki trousers, I noticed that his digging the hole had not done his hands much good. I don't mean the scraping-out part of the digging. That part had been all right: his hands were tough enough for that. But I could see that there had been a few occasions when Gerrit had missed the head of the cold-chisel. I could see that from his left hand. And it also seemed that he had swung his hammer quite powerfully on those occasions when he had missed.

'I am digging,' Gerrit van Biljon said to me, and he spoke with a grave thoughtfulness, as though he wanted to make quite sure that he used the right words, 'a hole.'

I said that I had thought as much. I told him that I believed that he had first used the pick and found that it was not much good. And that he had then gone to fetch the cold-chisel.

'It doesn't look as though that is much good, either,' I added.

Gerrit van Biljon put his left hand behind his back with what he apparently thought was an unobtrusive gesture.

'No,' he said, 'I am getting on all right.'

'And after you have finished digging the hole?' I enquired, trying to sound unconcerned, and as though I was really thinking about something else.

'Then,' Gerrit said solemnly, 'I am going to dig another hole.'

That was how difficult it was for me to find out, on that hot forenoon that was already lengthening into midday, why Gerrit van Biljon was digging holes in the stony ground in front of his house.

So I sat down on the ground under a nearby thorn-tree. I lit my pipe, and while the blue smoke curled away among the green foliage I reflected on the strange way in which the mind of the human being works, and how the human being can't always distinguish, very readily, between what is important and what is unimportant. Thus, I had set out from my farm early that morning on foot to search for my mules that had strayed out of the camp two days before. And when in the course of my wanderings through the bush I had at various times come across four kafirs, each of whom had, in reply to my questioning, pointed in a different direction, I knew that the mules could not be far off. Mules are like that.

But my search for the mules had led me as far as Gerrit van Biljon's homestead, and the moment I saw Gerrit crouched over that hole in the ground I knew right away, without having to think, even, that it was more important for me to satisfy my curiosity in regard to what Gerrit van Biljon was doing than to find the mules. So I had to stay.

When the sun was directly overhead Gerrit's wife Sarie came and called us for dinner. Gerrit and Sarie had several young children who would not be back from school until the afternoon. Accordingly, the three of us arranged ourselves about the table in the voorkamer. While we ate we talked at first only of trivial things. I said that what brought me here was that I was looking for my mules, which had strayed.

'It seems to me that it is not only your mules that have strayed,' Gerrit van Biljon said, without looking up from his plate. 'If you stay away from your farm much longer it will be your mules that will be starting to look for you.'

This remark of Gerrit's made me feel rather uncomfortable. Therefore, to relieve the tension, I began relating what I thought was an amusing little story about Koos Venter who had at one time farmed at Derdepoort, and who had started digging holes on his farm because of something a kafir witch-doctor had told him about buried treasure.

'His pick was very blunt by the time they took it away from him,' I said. 'And when they put him on the lorry for Pretoria, and he was singing, nobody knew for sure whether he was mad before he started digging those holes, or whether he went mad, at a later stage, from sunstroke. But the next time you go near Derdepoort you must have a look at that farm where Koos Venter stayed. It has got so many holes in it that the man who is on it now says that he is wondering if he can't use it as some sort of sieve. He thinks the Government might be able to make use of his farm for sifting something in a big way. But he can't think what, exactly. Yes, it is lucky that it doesn't rain very often in this part of the Marico. Because in the wet weather that farm leaks very badly.

'You will probably be able to see that farm quite soon, now, Neef Gerrit,' I finished up significantly. 'The lorry for Pretoria passes that way.'

I would have said still more. But at that moment I caught Sarie's eye. Gerrit van Biljon's wife Sarie was a pleasant-looking woman. When she smiled her eyes had a pretty trick of getting long and narrow, so that she looked like a little girl, and there came with her smile a soft and alluring curve to her lips. But Sarie's eyes got narrow now in a manner I did not like. And what curves there were on her lips went all the wrong way.

So I said that I was only joking. And that I had best be going. And that I didn't think I would really wait for coffee. And that perhaps the mules were quite near, somewhere, waiting for me, maybe, and that if I didn't leave at once I might miss them.

And so it came about, just because I no longer had any curiosity in that direction, that Gerrit van Biljon explained to me what it was that he was doing. While he talked his wife Sarie came into the voorkamer several times with coffee. Sometimes she lingered a little while, and I noticed that whenever she glanced in her husband's direction, while he talked, there was a light in her eyes which made me realise what risks I had been running in jesting about Gerrit. And when she walked about the room, driving out the flies with quick little movements, I knew that the cloth she was waving around was not a piece of wedding dress.

It was a simple story that Gerrit van Biljon told me, and he took a long time over it, and when he had finished with the telling it was no story at all. And that was one of the reasons why I liked his story.

'I am planting blue-gum trees,' Gerrit van Biljon said, 'in those holes I am digging. For shade.'

I was speechless. For a moment I wondered if Gerrit van Biljon's condition was not perhaps even worse than the state of mind of Koos Venter, the other man who had dug holes on his farm.

'But trees,' I said. 'Neef Gerrit, trees. Surely the whole Marico is full of trees. I mean, there is nothing here but trees. We can't even grow mealies. Why you had to chop down hundreds of trees to clear a space for your homestead and the cattle-kraal. And they are all shady trees, too.'

Gerrit van Biljon shook his head. And he told me the story of how he met his wife Sarie on her father's farm in Schweizer-Reineke, in front of the farmhouse under a tall blue-gum. It was a simple story of a boy and girl who fell in love. Of initials carved on a white trunk. Of a smile in the dusk. And hands touching and a quick kiss. And tears. Oh, it was a very simple story that Gerrit van Biljon told me. And as he spoke I could see that it was a story that would go on for ever. Two lovers in the evening and a pale wind in a tall tree. And Sarie's red lips. And two hearts haunted for ever by the fragrance of blue-gum trees. No, there was nothing at all in that story.

121

It was the sort of thing that happens every day. It was just something foolish about the human heart.

'And if it had been any other but a blue-gum tree,' Gerrit van Biljon said, 'it would not have been the same thing.'

1 knew better, of course, but I did not tell him so.

Then Gerrit explained that he was going to plant a row of blue-gums in front of his house.

'I have ordered the plants from the Government Test Station in Potchefstroom,' he went on. 'I am getting only the best plants. It takes a blue-gum only twenty years to grow to its full height. For the first couple of years the trees will grow hardly at all, because of the stones. But after a few years, when the roots have found their way into the deeper parts of the soil, the trunks will shoot up very quickly. And in the late afternoons I shall sit under the tallest blue-gum, with my wife beside me and our children playing about. The wind stirring through a blue-gum makes a different sound from when it blows through any other kind of shadow. At least, that is how it is for me.'

Gerrit van Biljon said he didn't care if a pig occasionally wandered away from the trough at the back of the house, at feeding time, and scratched himself on the trunk of one of the trees. That was how tolerant the thought of the blue-gums made him feel.

'Only –,' he added, rather quickly, 'I only hope the pig doesn't overdo it. I don't want him to make a habit of it, of course.'

'Perhaps I will even read a book under one of the trees, some day,' Gerrit said, finally. 'You see, outside of the Bible I have never read a book. Just bits of newspaper and things. Yes, perhaps I will even read a book. But mostly – well, mostly I will just rest.'

So that was Gerrit van Biljon's story.

As he had prophesied, the blue-gums, after not seeming to want to grow at all, at first, suddenly started to shoot up, and they grew almost to their full height in something over eight years. And I often saw Sarie sitting under the tallest tree, with her youngest child playing on the grass beside her, and I was sure that Gerrit van Biljon rested as peacefully under the withaak by the foot of the koppie at the far end of the farm as he would have done in the blue-gum's shade.

The Clay-Pit

Although it happened so many years ago, anybody in Zeerust can still tell you the story of Diederik Uys and Johanna Greyling and old Bertus Pienaar. And when they mention certain events that happened at the clay-pit where Bertus was making bricks for the new house that he never built, people in Zeerust will declare that they can still go and point out that same spot to you – as though it is all just something of yesterday. They don't explain that earth and stones have been washed into that depression by many rains, and that tall weeds cover the site of the clay-pit, like a grave on a farm that has passed into the hands of strangers.

And whoever tells you the story will always add, at the end of it, that even though Diederik Uys was guilty he should never have been hanged. You will also be told that what actually hanged Diederik Uys was a strand of Johanna Greyling's hair, that was of a wanton colour, yellow, not unlike the colour of a hangman's rope if you were to tease out the ends.

Whereas the truth is that her hair was not always light.

Anyway, you can see from this that the incidents linking together the fortunes of the young bywoner, Diederik Uys, and of the girl, Johanna Greyling, and of the aging Bertus Pienaar made a good story, that was told over and over again. Otherwise each person who tells this story would not be able to bring in that touch about the hangman's rope so confidently. A high-school girl, home for the holidays, would otherwise not be able to talk of the strings in a hangman's noose as familiarly as though it were crochet thread.

Bertus Pienaar and his wife were both past middle age and childless when they adopted a girl of ten from the Church orphanage in Kimberley. This action of theirs aroused a good deal of discussion at the time. It was not unreasonable that Bertus Pienaar and his wife should have decided to adopt a child who would continue, on their bushveld farm, from where they would one day have to leave off. But then you would have expected them to adopt a man-child, still young enough to be bent in the way he should grow. He would need to have a strong voice and sturdy legs: which were more important than broad shoulders, since these would develop naturally with the responsibilities that went with a 6,000-morgen farm. His features, also, must not be too sharp; nor his eyes too thoughtful. Else he might grow of a sudden restive, some morning when there would be a low wind in the maroelas.

No doubt Bertus Pienaar and his wife knew exactly, when they went to the orphanage, what was the kind of child that they desired to adopt. But because their lives had been in more than one way barren they were perhaps not surprised, in the moment of making their choice, to find that they had picked, instead, a small, dark-haired girl who had a ready smile, and about whose parents the matron could tell them nothing.

Some years later Bertus Pienaar's wife died.

And not long after that people in the bushveld began to shake their heads at the way Bertus was treating his adopted daughter.

Since Bertus Pienaar was known to be a God-fearing man, a good deal could be overlooked about the manner in which he saw fit to discipline Johanna Greyling after she had left school and was passing from the stage of childhood into young womanhood.

It was said of old Bertus Pienaar, also, that in his dealings with his neighbours he was a hard man. That was one reason why, for instance, his singular action after Johanna Greyling's confirmation did not make more talk. At her catechism Johanna wore a white frock that was so showy that it might almost have been made of silk. Only, everybody knows, of course, that silk is black. And Johanna looked so comely in that white frock that the predikant did not even notice when she gave the wrong answer to the first question, 'Whence do you know your wretchedness?' Whereas every member of the confirmation class knew that the answer was, 'Out of the word of God.'

Yet, when she came back to the farm, Bertus made Johanna take off that frock, that must have cost him the price of quite a number of sheep-skins. And he straight-away went and thrust the dress into the flames of the bread-oven at the side of the house.

A neighbour, Oupa van Tonder, a man who used few words but those usually the right ones, commented on Bertus Pienaar's action thus:

'Bertus has got a queer idea of a wardrobe,' Oupa van Tonder said.

At that time everybody in the Marico knew that Johanna Greyling had no more than two frocks, which she wore on alternate weeks. It was also known that there were wash-days on which Bertus Pienaar would stride across to where Johanna was kneeling beside the bath-tub by the dam and would correct her with the end of a sjambok laid across her shoulders. Several Marico farmers, driving past the dam on their way to Ramoutsa, had actually seen Bertus Pienaar administering instruction to his daughter in that fashion.

It was only on account of the esteem, of a long-standing nature, in which Bertus Pienaar was held by the Dwarsberge community that some farmer did not pull up his mule-team and, having tied the reins to the off-wheel, go over to the dam and lay the doubled thongs of the sjambok across Bertus Pienaar's shoulder-blades, instead. Part of this esteem was due to Bertus's piety and deep love of religion. The other part of it arose from the fact that, although past middle life, he was still agile on his feet. And when teaching a kafir not to let the cattle stray into the lucerne lands Benus would always first draw back two paces and then charge forward with the whole weight of his body behind his fist. The doctor who came to attend the kafir said he did not think that even a charging rhinoceros could have taught the kafir as well as Bertus had done. The doctor said that after he had counted the number of stitches.

Consequently, when Johanna Greyling ran away from Bertus Pienaar to Diederik Uys, a bywoner in his early twenties living on an adjoining farm, there were many people in the Marico who were inclined to sympathise with the young couple.

In the end, however, Bertus Pienaar got Johanna Greyling back. Except that Bertus seemingly promised Diederik Uys that he would treat his adopted daughter less harshly in the future, little was known for sure as to what happened at that interview. Nevertheless, in places where farmers foregathered, many questions where asked, in the manner of one man speaking to another, as to why the young fellow Diederik Uys had let go of his girl so easily.

Shortly afterwards something else happened on Bertus Pienaar's farm that caused more discussion than ever. Bertus had had a clay-pit dug for bricks for his new house. And he made Johanna Greyling help tread the clay. The kafirs poured buckets of water into the hole. Bertus Pienaar stood on the side of the pit with a long whip, driving half a dozen head of oxen round and round in the wet earth. And along with the cattle, the skirts of her print dress raised high, Johanna Greyling tramped in the red clay of the Transvaal.

The murder, a few days later, of Bertus Pienaar, caused less stir in the Marico than the fact of his having made his adopted daughter tread clay.

It was at daybreak that the kafirs, coming to work with their buckets and spades, found their baas lying by the edge of the pit, with his face pressed deep into the hardening mud. Veldkornet Apie Nel, of the landdrost's office, was on the scene soon afterwards.

'They must have fought a long time in the night,' Apie Nel said, surveying the area of grass that had been flattened by heavy boots. 'They should rather have fought inside the clay-pit. They would then have kneaded up quite a lot of clay.'

Veldkornet Nel spoke lightly. He had not much sympathy with Bertus Pienaar. And that was how most people felt about the matter. Old Bertus had got what was coming to him, people said.

They also believed that that was why Apie Nel allowed several months to go by before he went over to the whitewashed rondavel of Diederik Uys, one afternoon, and discoursing on matters of no greater earnestness than the rust in late wheat sowings, took Diederik Uys into custody. But why Apie Nel had waited so long was because he had hoped that in some way Diederik Uys would betray his guilt. He was a deep one, Apie Nel, and he had much patience.

Meanwhile, Johanna Greyling had again run away. And this time there had been no one to fetch her back to the farm. It was learnt a little later that she had got as far as Kimberley, where she obtained employment of a sort.

She must have run pretty fast along the transport road to Kimberley, with just two dresses and no money, people said, trying to be funny. For they knew that a young and attractive girl like Johanna Greyling would not have to wear out much shoe-leather in getting to Kimberley, transport drivers being what they were. Moreover, it was agreed that it was not just her memories of the orphanage in Kimberley that had served to draw Johanna back to the diamond-mining town, with its dance-halls and saloons.

After Apie Nel had arrested Diederik Uys he searched his room, taking possession, among other things, of a tin locket that held a dark curl from Johanna Greyling's forehead. Afterwards Apie Nel returned the locket to his prisoner.

The veldkornet was in a difficult position. As things stood, there was so much public sympathy with Diederik Uys on account of Bertus Pienaar's unnatural usage of the girl, Johanna Greyling, that no Zeerust jury would bring in a verdict more stern than homicide, which would mean only a year or two of imprisonment. Such a verdict might have suited Diederik Uys. But it would not suit Veldkornet Apie Nel. A murder case came his way but rarely. Quite soon he would reach the age when he would have to retire. He would not be able to look back on his career with a proper kind of satisfaction if, at the end of it, he would have to admit that he had never succeeded in getting a white man hanged.

That was no doubt what caused the veldkornet to apply, through the public prosecutor, for a postponement of the trial of Diederik Uys until Johanna Greyling could be brought into court as a witness.

Johanna Greyling was subpoenaed. In court she said little. But when the coach that brought her back from Kimberley stopped in front of the Transvaal Hotel, half the population of Zeerust saw her alight on to the pavement. The fate of Diederik Uys was sealed.

A woman like that, people said. And if in court Johanna Greyling spoke but few words, the Zeerust public had a good deal to say outside of the courthouse – and inside, too, in whispers.

Immediately all sympathy switched to the late Bertus Pienaar. People remembered that he had lived an upright and joyless life. And they said it was cowardly of a young fellow to go and suffocate an old man in the clay-pit, like that. They spoke as though Bertus Pienaar was a man who would allow just any passing stranger to push his face in the mud, and choke him in it, quietly.

They recalled how, after his wife's death, Bertus had tried to be both father and mother to Johanna Greyling, so that they spoke almost wistfully of the sjambok with which he had sought to guide her along the right paths. And what was the thanks he got? – they asked.

For when Johanna Greyling stepped off the coach in Zeerust it was in the low-bosomed dress and the high heels of a harlot. And her cheeks were shamelessly painted the colour that old Bertus Pienaar's bricks would have been if he had had a chance to fire them in the kiln. And her hair was bleached the yellow of tamboekie grass in winter.

People had heard of abandoned women in the Kimberley dance-halls bleaching their hair. But this was the first time that Zeerust itself had been disgraced by the presence of such a woman. Everybody felt disgraced, including farmers who came from many miles away just to look at her.

And that was why the lawyers of Diederik Uys put up so half-hearted a defence for their client in court. They knew there would be no mercy for a man who could have associated with such a woman. In the brazen presence of Johanna Greyling no juryman could pause to reflect that Diederik Uys had, after all, loved not a painted strumpet but a girl who had only two print dresses which she washed until they were threadbare.

I have often wondered what Diederik Uys thought, too, when he saw Johanna Greyling in court. And how he felt afterwards, in the solitude of his cell. I wonder what he thought when he opened the tin locket and gazed on that poor strand of dark hair inside – and realised that it no longer matched the bleached tresses of the Jezebel who had leaned on the rail of the witness-box. But I feel that if he still remembered her as that farm girl who had once run away to him, then the hanging of Diederik Uys would, in the years to come, have been but a hollow triumph for Veldkornet Apie Nel.

Anyway, that is the story as it is to this day still told in Zeerust. One point, however, that everybody who tells the story seems to overlook is Bertus Pienaar's role in it, which was no less important for its having been so straightforward.

It is easy to see, in all Bertus Pienaar's actions, a thwarted passion for Johanna Greyling. And the fact that Diederik Uys did not at first seriously oppose Johanna's return to her adopted father's home shows that he had instinctively no fears in at least that respect. Diederik's letting her go like that was actually an insult to Bertus Pienaar.

Then there is Johanna Greyling. She must have had much of a sombre knowledge of life shut up inside her. Something as dark as that strand of hair enclosed in Diederik Uys's tin locket. Of course, Johanna Greyling knew at first hand that it was not she who had crossed Bertus Pienaar in his desire for her. She knew that it was his advancing age and not her virtue that stood between Bertus Pienaar and his passion. But it could not have brought ease to her smarting shoulder-blades – the knowledge that when her adopted father wielded the sjambok it was in the rage of impuissance.

One cannot pass by Johanna Greyling just lightly, somehow. Johanna Greyling, walking about the night-streets of Kimberley, blonde-headed and with her high heels clicking on the pavement. Lifting her steps high as she had done in former days in the clay-pit of her adopted father.

Cometh Comet

Hans Engelbrecht was the first farmer in the Schweizer-Reineke district to trek (Oom Schalk Lourens said). With his wife and daughter and what was left of his cattle he moved away to the northern slopes of the Dwarsberge, where the drought was less severe. Afterwards he was joined by other farmers from the same area. I can still remember how untidy the veld looked in those days, with rotting carcasses and sun-bleached bones lying about everywhere. Day after day we had stood at the bore-holes, pumping an ever-decreasing trickle of brackish water into the cattle troughs. We watched in vain for a sign of a cloud. And it seemed that if anything did fall out of that sky, it wouldn't do us much good: it would be a shower of brimstone, most likely.

Still, it was a fine time for the aasvoëls and the crows. That was at the beginning, of course. Afterwards, when all the carcasses had been picked bare, and the Boers had trekked, most of the birds of prey flew away, also.

We trekked away in different directions. Four or five families eventually came to a halt at the foot of the Dwarsberge, near the place where Hans Engelbrecht was outspanned. In a vast area of the Schweizer-Reneke district only one man had chosen to stay behind. He was Ocker Gieljan, a young bywoner who had worked for Hans Engelbrecht since his boyhood. Ocker Gieljan spoke rarely, and then his words did not always seem to us to make sense.

Hans Engelbrecht was only partly surprised when, on the morning that the ox-wagon was loaded and the long line of oxen that were skin and bone started stumbling along the road to the north, Ocker Gieljan made it clear that he was not leaving the farm. The native voorlooper had already gone to the head of the span and Hans Engelbrecht's wife and his eighteen-year-old daughter, Maria, were seated on the wagon, under the tent-sail, when Ocker Gieljan suddenly declared that he had decided to stay behind on the farm 'to look after things here.'

This was another instance of Ocker Gieljan's saying something that did not make sense. There could be nothing for him to look after, there, since in the whole district hardly even a lizard was left alive.

Hans Engelbrecht was in no mood to waste time in arguing with a daft bywoner. Accordingly, he got the kafirs to unload half a sack of mealie-meal and a quantity of biltong in front of Ocker Gieljan's mud-walled room.

During the past few years it had not rained much in the Marico bushveld, either. But there was at least water in the Malopo, and the grazing was fair. Several months passed. Every day, from our camp by the Malopo, we studied the skies, which were of an intense blue. There was no longer that yellow tinge in the air that we had got used to in the Schweizer-Reneke district. But there was never a rain cloud.

The time came, also, when Hans Engelbrecht was brought to understand that the Lord had visited still more trouble on himself and his family. A little while before we had trekked away from our farm, a young insurance agent had left the district suddenly for Cape Town. That was a long distance to run away, especially when you think of how bad the roads were in those days. And in some strange fashion it seemed to me as though that young insurance agent was actually our leader. For he stood, after all, with his light hat and short jacket at the head of our flight out of the Schweizer-Reneke area.

It became a commonplace, after a while, for Maria Engelbrecht to be seen seated in the grass beside her father's wagon, weeping. Few pitied her. She must have sat in the grass too often, with that insurance agent with the pointed, polished shoes, Lettie Grobler said to some of the women – forgetting that there had been no grass left in the Schweizer-Reneke veld at the time when Hans Engelbrecht's daughter was being courted.

It was easy for Maria to wipe the tears from her face, another woman said. Easier than to wipe away the shame, the woman meant.

Now and again, from some traveller who had passed through Schweizer-Reneke, we who had trekked out of that stricken region would hear a few useless things about it. We learnt nothing that we did not already know. Ocker Gieljan was still on the Engelbrecht farm, we heard. And the only other living creature in the whole district was a solitary crow. A passing traveller had seen Ocker Gieljan at the borehole. He was pumping water into a trough for the crow, the traveller said.

'When his mealie-meal gives out, Ocker will find his way here, right enough,' Hans Engelbrecht growled impatiently.

Then the night came when, from our encampment beside the Molopo, we first saw the comet, in the place above the Dwarsberge rante where the sun had gone down. We all began to wonder what that new star with the long tail meant. Would it bring rain? We didn't know. We could see, of course, that the star was an omen. Even an uneducated kafir would know that. But we did not know what sort of omen it was.

If the bark of the maroelas turned black before the polgras was in seed, we would know that it would be a long winter. And if a wind sprang up suddenly in the evening, blowing away from the sunset, we would next morning send the cattle out later to graze. We knew many things about the veld and the sky and the seasons. But even the oldest Free State farmer among us didn't know what effect a comet had on a mealie crop.

Hans Engelbrecht said that we should send for Rev. Losper, the missionary who ministered to the Bechuanas at Ramoutsa. But the rest of us ignored his suggestion.

During the following nights the comet became more clearly visible. A young policeman on patrol in those parts called on us one evening. When we spoke to him about the star, he said that he could do nothing about it, himself. It was a matter for the higher authorities, he said, laughing.

Nevertheless, he had made a few calculations, the policeman explained, and he had sent a report to Pretoria. He estimated that the star was twenty-seven and half miles in length, and that it was travelling faster than a railway train. He would not be surprised if the star reached Pretoria before his report got there. That would spoil his chances of promotion, he added.

We did not take much notice of the policeman's remarks, however. For one thing, he was young. And, for another, we did not have much respect for the police.

'If a policeman doesn't even know how to get on to the spoor of a couple of kafir oxen that I smuggle across the Bechuanaland border,' Thys

Bekker said, 'how does he expect to be able to follow the footprints of a star across the sky? That is big man's work.'

The appearance of the comet caused consternation among the Bechuanas in the village of Ramoutsa, where the mission station was. It did not take long for some of their stories about the star to reach our encampment on the other side of the Malopo. And although, at first, most of us professed to laugh at what we said were just ignorant kafir superstitions, yet in the end we also began to share something of the Bechuanas' fears.

'Have you heard what the kafirs say about the new star?' Arnoldus Grobler, husband of Lettie Grobler, asked of Thys Bekker. 'They say that it is a red beast with a fat belly like a very great chief, and it is going to come to eat up every blade of grass and every living thing.'

'In that case, I hope he lands in Schweizer-Reneke,' Thys Bekker said. 'If that red beast comes down on my farm, all that will happen is that in a short while there will be a whole lot more bones lying around to get white in the sun.'

Some of us felt that it was wrong of Thys Bekker to treat the matter so lightly. Moreover, this story only emanated from Ramoutsa, where there were a mission station and a post office. But a number of other stories, that were in every way much better, started soon afterwards to come out of the wilder pans of the bushveld, travelling on foot. It seemed that the farther a tribe of kafirs lived away from civilisation, the more detailed and dependable was the information they had about the comet.

I know that I began to feel that Hans Engelbrecht had made the right suggestion in the first place, when he had said that we should send for the missionary. And I sensed that a number of others in our camp shared my feelings. But not one of us wanted to make this admission openly.

In the end it was Hans Engelbrecht himself who sent to Ramoutsa for Rev. Losper. By that time the comet was – each night in its rising – higher in the heavens, and it soon got round that the new star portended the end of the world. Lettie Grobler went so far as to declare that she had seen the good Lord Himself riding in the tail of the comet. What convinced us that she had, indeed, seen the Lord, was when she said that He had on a hat of the same shape as the predikant in Zwartruggens wore.

Lettie Grobler also said that the Lord was coming down to punish all of us for the sins of Maria Engelbrecht. This thought disturbed us greatly. We began to resent Maria's presence in our midst.

It was then that Hans Engelbrecht had sent for the missionary.

Meanwhile, Rev. Losper had his hands full with the Bechuanas at Ramoutsa, who seemed on the point of panicking in earnest. The latest story about the comet had just reached them, and because it had come from somewhere out of the deepest part of Africa, where the natives wore arrows tipped with leopard fangs, stuck through their nostrils, like moustaches, it was easily the most terrifying story of all. The story had come to the village, thumped out on the tomtoms.

The Bechuana chief at Ramoutsa – so Rev. Losper told us afterwards – fell into such a terror at the message brought by the speaking drums, that he thrust a handful of earth into his mouth, without thinking. He would have swallowed it, too, the missionary said, if one of his indunas hadn't restrained him in time, pointing out to the chief that perhaps the drum-men had got the message wrong. For, since the post office had come to Ramoutsa, the kafirs whose work in the village it was to receive and send out messages on their tomtoms had got somewhat out of practice.

Consequently, because of the tumult at Ramoutsa, it happened that Ocker Gieljan arrived at the encampment before Rev. Losper got there.

Ocker Gieljan looked very tired and dusty on that afternoon when he walked up to Hans Engelbrecht's wagon. He took off his hat and, smiling somewhat vacantly, sat down without speaking in the shade of the veld-tent, inside which Maria Engelbrecht lay on a mattress. Neither Hans Engelbrecht nor his wife asked Ocker Gieljan any questions about his journey from the Schweizer-Reneke farm. They knew that he could have nothing to tell.

Shortly afterwards, Ocker Gieljan made a communication to Hans Engelbrecht, speaking diffidently. Thereupon Hans Engelbrecht went into the tent and spoke to his wife and daughter. A few minutes later he came out, looking pleased with himself.

'Sit down here on this riempies-stoel, Ocker,' Hans Engelbrecht said to his prospective son-in-law, 'and tell me how you came to leave the farm.'

'I got lonely,' Ocker Gieljan answered, thoughtfully. 'You see, the crow flew away. I was alone, after that. The crow was then already weak. He didn't fly straight, like crows do. His wings wobbled.'

When he told me about this, years later, Hans Engelbrecht said that something in Ocker Gieljan's tone brought him a sudden vision of the way his daughter, Maria, had also left the Schweizer-Reneke district. With broken wings.

I thought that Rev. Losper looked relieved to find, on his arrival at the camp, some time later, that all that was required of him, now, was the performance of a marriage ceremony.

On the next night but one, Maria Engelbrecht's child was born. All the adults in our little trekker-community came in the night and the rain – which had been falling steadily for many hours – with gifts for Maria and her child.

And when I saw the star again, during a temporary break in the rain clouds, it seemed to me that it was not such a new star, at all: that it was, indeed, a mighty old star.

Sold Down the River

We had, of course, heard of Andre Maritz's play and his company of play-actors long before they got to Zeerust (Oom Schalk Lourens said).

For they had travelled a long road. Some of the distance they went by train. Other parts of the way they travelled by mule-cart or ox-wagon. They visited all the dorps from the Cape – where they had started from – to Zeerust in the Transvaal, where Hannekie Roodt left the company. She had an important part in the play, as we knew even before we saw her name in big letters on the posters.

Andre Maritz had been somewhat thoughtless, that time, in his choice of a play for his company to act in. The result was that there were some places that he had to go away from at a pace rather faster than could be made by even a good mule-team. Naturally, this sort of thing led to Andre Maritz's name getting pretty well known throughout the country – and without his having to stick up posters, either.

The trouble did not lie with the acting. There was not very much wrong with that. But anybody could have told Andre Maritz that he should never have toured the country with that kind of a play. There was a negro in it, called Uncle Tom, who was supposed to be very good and kind-hearted. Andre Maritz, with his face blackened, took that part. And there was also a white man in the play, named Simon Legree. He was the kind of white man who, if he was your neighbour, would think it funny to lead the Government tax-collector to the aardvark hole that you were hiding in.

It seems that Andre Maritz had come across a play that had been popular on the other side of the sea; and he translated it into Afrikaans and adapted it to fit in with South African traditions. Andre Maritz's fault was that he hadn't adapted the play enough.

The company made this discovery in the very first Free State dorp they got to. For, when they left that town, Andre Maritz had one of his eyes blackened, and not just with burnt cork.

Andre Maritz adapted his play a good deal more, immediately after that. He made Uncle Tom into a much less kind-hearted negro. And he also made him steal chickens.

The only member of the company that the public of the backveld seemed to have any time for was the young man who acted Simon Legree.

Thus it came about that we heard of Andre Maritz's company when they were still far away, touring the highveld. Winding their play-actors' road northwards, past koppies and through vlaktes, and by blue-gums and willows.

After a few more misunderstandings with the public, Andre Maritz so far adapted the play to South African conditions as to make Uncle Tom threaten to hit Topsy with a brandy bottle.

The result was that, by the time the company came to Zeerust, even the Church elder, Theunis van Zyl, said that there was much in the story of Uncle Tom that could be considered instructive.

True, there were still one or two little things. Elder van Zyl declared, that did not perhaps altogether accord with what was best in our outlook. For instance, it was not right that we should be made to feel so sentimental about the slave-girl as played by Hannekie Roodt. The elder was referring to that powerful scene in which Hannekie Roodt got sold down the river by Simon Legree. We couldn't understand very clearly what it meant to be sold down the river. But from Hannekie Roodt's acting we could see that it must be the most awful fate that could overtake anybody.

She was so quiet. She did not speak in that scene. She just picked up the small bundle containing her belongings. Then she put her hand up to her coat collar and closed over the lapel in front, even though the weather was not cold.

Yet there were still some people in Zeerust who, after they had attended the play on the first night, thought that that scene could be improved on. They said that when Hannekie Roodt walked off the stage for the last time, sold down the river, and carrying the bundle of her poor possessions tied up in a red-spotted rag, a few of her mistress's knives and forks could have been made to drop out of the bundle. As I have said, Andre Maritz's company eventually arrived in Zeerust. They came by mule-cart from Slurry, where the railway ended in those days. They stayed at the Marico Hotel, which was a few doors from Elder van Zyl's house. It was thus that Andre Maritz met Deborah, the daughter of the elder. That was one thing that occasioned a good deal of talk. Especially as we believed that even if Hannekie Roodt was not actually married to Andre Maritz in the eyes of the law, the two of them were nevertheless as nearly husband and wife as it is possible for play-actors to be, since they are known to be very unenlightened in such matters.

The other things that gave rise to much talk had to do with what happened on the first night of the staging of the play in Zeerust. Andre Maritz hired the old hall adjoining the mill. The hall had last been used two years before.

The result was that, after the curtain had gone up for the first act of Andre Maritz's play, it was discovered that a wooden platform above the stage was piled high with fine flour that had sifted through the ceiling from the mill next door. The platform had been erected by the stage company that had given a performance in the hall two years previously. That other company had used the platform to throw down bits of paper from to look like snow, in a scene in which a girl gets thrust out into the world with her baby in her arms.

At the end of the first act, when the curtain was lowered, Andre Maritz had the platform swept. But until then, with all that flour coming down, it looked as though he and his company were moving about the stage in a Cape mist. Each time an actor took a step forward or spoke too loudly – down would come a shower of fine meal. Afterwards the players took to standing in one place as much as possible, to avoid shaking down the flour – and in fear of losing their way in the mist, too, by the look of things.

Naturally, all this confused the audience a good deal. For, with the flour sifting down on to the faces of the actors, it became difficult, after a little while, to tell which were the white people in the play and which the negroes. Towards the end of the first act Uncle Tom, with a layer of flour covering his make-up, looked just as white as Simon Legree.

During the time that the curtain was lowered, however, the flour was swept from the platform and the actors repaired their faces very neatly, so that when the next act began there was nothing any more to remind us of that first unhappy incident.

Later on I was to think that it was a pity that the consequences of that second unhappy incident, that of Andre Maritz's meeting with the daughter of Elder van Zyl, could not also have been brushed away so tidily.

The play was nevertheless very successful. And I am sure that in the crowded hall that night there were few dry eyes when Hannekie Roodt played her great farewell scene. When she picked up her bundle and got ready to leave, having been sold down the river, you could see by her stillness that her parting from her lover and her people would be for ever. No one who saw her act that night would ever forget the tragic moment when she put her hand up to her coat collar and closed over the lapels in front, even though – as I have said – the weather was not cold.

The applause at the end lasted for many minutes.

The play got the same enthusiastic reception night after night. Meanwhile, off the stage, there were many stories linking Deborah van Zyl's name with Andre Maritz's.

'They say that Deborah van Zyl is going to be an actress now,' Flip Welman said when several of us were standing smoking in the hardware store. 'She is supposed to be getting Hannekie Roodt's part.'

'We all know that Deborah van Zyl has been talking for a long while about going on the stage,' Koos Steyn said. 'And maybe this is the chance she has been waiting for. But I can't see her in Hannekie Roodt's part for very long. I think she will rather be like the girl in that other play we saw here a few years ago – the one with the baby.'

Knowing what play-actors were, I could readily picture Deborah van Zyl being pushed out into the world, carrying a child in her arms, and with white-paper snow fluttering about her.

As for Hannekie Roodt, she shortly afterwards left Andre Maritz's company of play-actors. She arranged with Koos Steyn to drive her, with her suitcases, to Slurry station. Koos explained to me that he was a married man and so he could not allow it to be said of him, afterwards, that he had driven alone in a cart with a play-actress. That was how it came about that I rode with them.

But Koos Steyn need have had no fears of the kind that he hinted at.

Hannekie Roodt spoke hardly a word. At close hand she looked different from what she had done on the stage. Her hair was scraggy. I also noticed that her teeth were uneven and that there was loose skin at her throat.

Yet, there was something about her looks that was not without a strange sort of beauty. And in her presence there was that which made me think of great cities. There were also marks on her face from which you could tell that she had travelled a long road. A road that was longer than just the thousand miles from the Cape to the Marico.

Hannekie Roodt was going away from Andre Maritz. And during the whole of that long journey by mule-cart she did not once weep. I could not help but think that it was true what people said about play-actors. They had no real human feelings. They could act on the stage and bring tears to your eyes, but they themselves had no emotions.

We arrived at Slurry station. Hannekie Roodt thanked Koos Steyn and paid him. There was no platform there in those days. So Hannekie had to climb up several steps to get on to the balcony of the carriage. It was almost as though she were getting on to the stage. We lifted up her suitcases for her.

Koos Steyn and I returned to the mule-cart. Something made me look back over my shoulder. That was my last glimpse of Hannekie Roodt. I saw her put her hand up to her coat collar. She closed over the lapels in front. The weather was not cold.

Dopper and Papist

It was a cold night (Oom Schalk Lourens said) on which we drove with Gert Bekker in his Cape cart to Zeerust. I sat in front, next to Gert, who was driving. In the back seat were the predikant, Rev. Vermooten, and his ouderling, Isak Erasmus, who were on their way to Pretoria for the meeting of the synod of the Dutch Reformed Church. The predikant was lean and hawk-faced; the ouderling was fat and had broad shoulders.

Gert Bekker and I did not speak. We had been transport drivers together in our time, and we had learnt that when it is two men alone, travelling over a long distance, it is best to use few words, and those well-chosen. Two men, alone in each other's company, understand each other better the less they speak.

The horses kept up a good, steady trot. The lantern, swinging from side to side with the jogging of the cart, lit up stray patches of the uneven road and made bulky shadows rise up among the thorn-trees. In the back seat the predikant and the ouderling were discussing theology.

'You never saw such a lot of brand-siek sheep in your life,' the predikant was saying, 'as what Chris Haasbroek brought along as tithe.'

We then came to a stony part of the road, and so I did not hear the ouderling's reply; but afterwards, above the rattling of the cartwheels, I caught other snatches of God-fearing conversation, to do with the raising of pew rents.

From there the predikant started discussing the proselytising activities being carried on among the local Bapedi kafirs by the Catholic mission at Vleisfontein. The predikant dwelt particularly on the ignorance of the Bapedi tribes and on the idolatrous form of the Papist Communion service, which was quite different from the Protestant Nagmaal, the predikant said, although to a Bapedi, walking with his buttocks sticking out, the two services might, perhaps, seem somewhat alike.

Rev. Vermooten was very eloquent when he came to denouncing the heresies of Catholicism. And he spoke loudly, so that we could hear him on the front seat. And I know that both Gert Bekker and I felt very good, then, deep inside us, to think that we were Protestants. The coldness of the night and the pale flickering of the lantern-light among the thorn-trees gave an added solemnity to the predikant's words.

I felt that it might perhaps be all right to be a Catholic if you were walking on a Zeerust side-walk in broad daylight, say. But it was a different matter to be driving through the middle of the bush on a dark night, with just a swinging lantern fastened to the side of a Cape can with baling-wire. If the lantern went out suddenly, and you were left in the loneliest part of the bush, striking matches, then it must be a very frightening thing to be a Catholic, I thought.

This led me to thinking of Piet Reilly and his family, who were Afrikaners, like you and me, except that they were Catholics. Piet Reilly even brought out his vote for General Lemmer at the last Volksraad election, which we thought would make it unlucky for our candidate. But General Lemmer said no, he didn't mind how many Catholics voted for him. A Catholic's vote was, naturally, not a good as a Dopper's, he said, but the little cross that had to be made behind a candidate's name cast out the evil that was of course otherwise lurking in a Catholic's ballot paper. And General Lemmer must have been right, because he got elected, that time.

While I was thinking on those lines, it suddenly struck me that Piet Reilly was now living on a farm about six miles on the bushveld side of Sephton's Nek, and that we would be passing his farmhouse, which was near the road, just before daybreak. It was comforting to think that we would have the predikant and the ouderling in the Cape-cart with us, when we passed the homestead of Piet Reilly, a Catholic, in the dark.

I tried to hear what the predikant was saying, in the back seat, to the ouderling. But the predikant was once more dealing with an abstruse point of religion and had lowered his voice accordingly. I could catch only fragments of the ouderling's replies.

'Yes, dominee,' I heard the ouderling affirm, 'you are quite right. If he again tries to overlook your son for the job of anthrax inspector, then you must make it clear to the Chairman of the Board that you have all that information about his private life ...'

I realised then that you could find much useful guidance for your everyday problems in the conversation of holy men.

The night got colder and darker.

The palm of my hand, pressed tight around the bowl of my pipe, was the only part of me that felt warm. My teeth began to chatter. I wished that, next time we stopped to let the horses blow, we could light a fire and boil coffee. But I knew that there was no coffee left in the chest under the back seat.

While I sat silent next to Gert Bekker, I continued to think of Piet Reilly and his wife and children. With Piet, of course, I could understand it. He himself had merely kept up the religion – if you could call what the Catholics believe in a religion – that he had inherited from his father and his grandfather. But there was Piet Reilly's wife, Gertruida, now. She had been brought up a respectable Dopper girl. She was one of the Drogedal Bekkers, and was, in fact, distantly related to Gert Bekker, who was sitting on the Cape-cart next to me. There was something for you to ponder about, I thought to myself, with the cold all the time looking for new places in my skin through which to strike into my bones.

The moment Gertruida met Piet Reilly she forgot all about the sacred truths she had learnt at her mother's knee. And on the day she got married she was saying prayers to the Virgin Mary on a string of beads, and was wearing a silver cross at her throat that was as soft and white as the roses she held pressed against her. Here was now a sweet Dopper girl turned Papist.

As I have said, I knew that there was no coffee left in the box under the back seat; but I did know that under the front seat there was a full bottle of raw peach brandy. In fact, I could see the neck of the bottle protruding from between Gert Bekker's ankles.

I also knew, through all the years of transport-driving that we had done together, that Gert Bekker had already, over many miles of road, been thinking how we could get the cork off the bottle without the predikant and the ouderling shaking their heads reprovingly. And the way he managed it in the end was, I thought, highly intelligent.

For, when he stopped the cart again to rest the horses, he alighted beside the road and held out the bottle to our full view.

'There is brandy in this bottle, dominee,' Gert Bekker said to the predikant, 'that I keep for the sake of the horses on cold nights, like now. It is an old Marico remedy for when horses are in danger of getting the floute. I take a few mouthfuls of the brandy, which I then blow into the nostrils of the horses, who don't feel the cold so much, after that. The brandy revives them.'

Gert commenced blowing brandy into the face of the horse on the near side, to show us.

Then he beckoned to me, and I also alighted and went and stood next to him, taking turns with him in blowing brandy into the eyes and nostrils of the offside horse. We did this several times.

The predikant asked various questions, to show how interested he was in this old-fashioned method of overcoming fatigue in draught-animals. But what the predikant said at the next stop made me perceive that he was more than a match for a dozen men like Gert Bekker in point of astuteness.

When we stopped the cart, the predikant held up his hand. 'Don't you and your friend trouble to get off this time,' the predikant called out when Gert Bekker was once more reaching for the bottle, 'the ouderling and I have decided to take turns with you in blowing brandy into the horses' faces. We don't want to put all the hard work on to your shoulders.'

We made several more halts after that, with the result that daybreak found us still a long way from Sephton's Nek. In the early dawn we saw the thatched roof of Piet Reilly's house through the thorn-trees some distance from the road. When the predikant suggested that we call at the homestead for coffee, we explained to him that the Reillys were Catholics.

'But isn't Piet Reilly's wife a relative of yours?' the predikant asked of Gert Bekker. 'Isn't she your second cousin, or something?'

'They are Catholics,' Gert answered.

'Coffee,' the predikant insisted.

'Catholics,' Gert Bekker repeated stolidly.

The upshot of it was, naturally enough, that we outspanned shortly afterwards in front of the Reilly homestead. That was the kind of man that the predikant was in an argument.

'The coffee will be ready soon,' the predikant said as we walked up to the front door. 'There is smoke coming out of the chimney.'

Almost before we had stopped knocking, Gertruida Reilly had opened both the top and bottom doors. She started slightly when she saw, standing in front of her, a minister of the Dutch Reformed Church. In spite of her look of agitation, Gertruida was still pretty, I thought, after ten years of being married to Piet Reilly.

When she stepped forward to kiss her cousin. Gert Bekker, I saw him turn away, sadly; and I realised something of the shame that she had brought on her whole family through her marriage to a Catholic.

'You looked startled when you saw me, Gertruida,' the predikant said, calling her by her first name, as though she was still a member of his congregation.

'Yes,' Gertruida answered. 'Yes – I was – surprised.'

'I suppose it was a Catholic priest that you wanted to come to your front door,' Gert Bekker said, sarcastically. Yet there was a tone in his voice that was not altogether unfriendly.

'Indeed, I was expecting a Catholic priest,' Gertruida said, leading us into the voorkamer. 'But if the Lord has sent the dominee and his ouderling, instead, I am sure it will be well, also.'

It was only then, after she had explained to us what had happened, that we understood why Gertruida was looking so troubled. Her eight-year-old daughter had been bitten by a snake; they couldn't tell from the fang-marks if it was a ringhals or a bakkop. Piet Reilly had driven off in the mule-cart to Vleisfontein, the Catholic Mission Station, for a priest.

They had cut open and cauterised the wound and had applied red permanganate. The rest was a matter for God. And that was why, when she saw the predikant and the ouderling at her front door, Gertruida believed that the Lord had sent them.

146

I was glad that Gert Bekker did not at that moment think of mentioning that we really came for coffee.

'Certainly, I shall pray for your little girl's recovery,' the predikant said to Gertruida. 'Take me to her.'

Gertruida hesitated.

'Will you – will you pray for her the Catholic way, dominee?' Gertruida asked.

Now it was the predikant's turn to draw back.

'But, Gertruida,' he said, 'you, you whom I myself confirmed in the Enkel-Gereformeerde Kerk in Zeerust – how can you now ask me such a thing? Did you not learn in the catechism that the Romish ritual is a mockery of the Holy Ghost?'

'I married Piet Reilly,' Gertruida answered simply, 'and his faith is my faith. Piet has been very good to me, Father. And I love him.'

We noticed that Gertruida called the predikant 'Father', now, and not 'Dominee'. During the silence that followed, I glanced at the candle burning before an image of the Mother Mary in a corner of the voorkamer. I looked away quickly from that unrighteousness.

The predikant's next words took us by complete surprise. 'Have you got some kind of a prayer-book,' the predikant asked, 'that sets out the – the Catholic form for a …'

'I'll fetch it from the other room,' Gertruida answered. When she had left, the predikant tried to put our minds at ease.

'I am only doing this to help a mother in distress,' he explained to the ouderling. 'It is something that the Lord will understand. Gertruida was brought up a Dopper girl. In some ways she is still one of us. She does not understand that I have no authority to conduct this Catholic service for the sick.'

The ouderling was going to say something.

But at that moment Gertruida returned with a little black book that you could almost have taken for a Dutch Reformed Church psalm-book. Only, I knew that what was printed inside it was as iniquitous as the candle burning in the corner.

Yet I also began to wonder if, in not knowing the difference, a Bapedi really was so very ignorant, even though he walked with his buttocks sticking out.

'My daughter is in this other room,' Gertruida said, and started in the direction of the door. The predikant followed her. Just before entering the bedroom he turned round and faced the ouderling.

'Will you enter with me, Brother Erasmus?' the predikant asked.

The ouderling did not answer. The veins stood out on his forehead. On his face you could read the conflict that went on inside him. For what seemed a very long time he stood quite motionless. Then he stooped down to the rusbank for his hat – which he did not need – and walked after the predikant into the bedroom.

Funeral Earth

We had a difficult task, that time (Oom Schalk Lourens said), teaching Sijefu's tribe of Mtosas to become civilised. But they did not show any appreciation. Even after we had set fire to their huts in a long row round the slopes of Abjaterskop, so that you could see the smoke almost as far as Nietverdiend, the Mtosas remained just about as unenlightened as ever. They would retreat into the mountains, where it was almost impossible for our commando to follow them on horseback. They remained hidden in the thick bush.

'I can sense these kafirs all around us,' Veldkornet Andries Joubert said to our 'seksie' of about a dozen burghers when we had come to a halt in a clearing amid the tall withaaks. 'I have been in so many kafir wars that I can almost smell when there are kafirs lying in wait for us with assegais. And yet all day long you never see a single Mtosa that you can put a lead bullet through.'

He also said that if this war went on much longer we would forget altogether how to handle a gun. And what would we do then, when we again had to fight England?

Young Fanie Louw, who liked saying funny things, threw back his head and pretended to be sniffing the air with discrimination. 'I can smell a whole row of assegais with broad blades and short handles,' Fanie Louw said. 'The stabbing assegai has got more of a selons-rose sort of smell about it than a throwing spear. The selons-rose that you come across in graveyards.'

The veldkornet did not think Fanie Louw's remark very funny, however. And he said we all knew that this was the first time Fanie Louw had ever been on commando. He also said that if a crowd of Mtosas were to leap out of the bush on to us suddenly, then you wouldn't be able to smell Fanie Louw for dust. The veldkornet also said another thing that was even better.

Our group of burghers laughed heartily. Maybe Veldkornet Joubert could not think out a lot of nonsense to say just on the spur of the moment, in the way that Fanie Louw could, but give our veldkornet a chance to reflect first and he would come out with the kind of remark that you just had to admire.

Indeed, from the very next thing Veldkornet Joubert said, you could see how deep was his insight. And he did not have to think much, either, then.

'Let us get out of here as quick as hell, men,' he said, speaking very distinctly. 'Perhaps the kafirs are hiding out in the open turf lands, where there are no trees. And none of this long tamboekie grass, either.'

When we emerged from that stretch of bush we were glad to discover that our veldkornet had been right, like always.

For another group of Transvaal burghers had hit on the same strategy.

'We were in the middle of the bush,' their leader, Combrinck, said to us, after we had exchanged greetings. 'A very thick part of the bush, with withaaks standing up like skeletons. And we suddenly thought the Mtosas might have gone into hiding out here in the open.'

You could see that Veldkornet Joubert was pleased to think that he had, on his own, worked out the same tactics as Combrinck, who was known as a skilful kafir-fighter. All the same, it seemed as though this was going to be a long war.

It was then that, again speaking out of his turn, Fanie Louw said that all we needed now was for the kommandant himself to arrive there in the middle of the turf lands with the main body of burghers. 'Maybe we should even go back to Pretoria to see if the Mtosas aren't perhaps hiding in the Volksraad,' he said. 'Passing laws and things. You know how cheeky a Mtosa is.'

'It can't be worse than some of the laws that the Volksraad is already passing now,' Combrinck said, gruffly. From that we could see that why he had not himself been appointed kommandant was because he had voted against the President in the last elections.

By that time the sun was sitting not more than about two Cape feet above a tall koppie on the horizon. Accordingly, we started looking about for a place to camp. It was muddy in the turf lands, and there was no fire-wood there, but we all said that we did not mind. We would not pamper ourselves by going to sleep in the thick bush, we told one another. It was war time, and we were on commando, and the mud of the turf lands was good enough for us, we said.

It was then that an unusual thing happened.

For we suddenly did see Mtosas. We saw them from a long way off. They came out of the bush and marched right out into the open. They made no attempt to hide. We saw in amazement that they were coming straight in our direction, advancing in single file. And we observed, even from that distance, that they were unarmed. Instead of assegais and shields they carried burdens on their heads. And almost in that same moment we realised, from the heavy look of those burdens, that the carriers must be women.

For that reason we took our guns in our hands and stood waiting. Since it was women, we were naturally prepared for the lowest form of treachery.

As the column drew nearer we saw that at the head of it was Ndambe, an old native whom we knew well. For years he had been Sijefu's chief counsellor. Ndambe held up his hand. The line of women halted. Ndambe spoke. He declared that we white men were kings among kings and elephants among elephants. He also said that we were ringhals snakes more poisonous and generally disgusting than any ringhals snake in the country.

We knew, of course, that Ndambe was only paying us compliments in his ignorant Mtosa fashion. And so we naturally felt highly gratified. I can still remember the way Jurie Bekker nudged me in the ribs and said, 'Did you hear that?'

When Ndambe went on, however, to say that we were filthier than the spittle of a green tree toad, several burghers grew restive. They felt that there was perhaps such a thing as carrying these tribal courtesies a bit too far.

It was then that Veldkornet Joubert, slipping his finger inside the trigger guard of his gun, requested Ndambe to come to the point. By the expression on our veldkornet's face, you could see that he had had enough of compliments for one day.

They had come to offer peace, Ndambe told us then.

What the women carried on their heads were presents.

At a sign from Ndambe the column knelt in the mud of the turf land.

151

They brought lion and zebra skins and elephant tusks, and beads and brass bangles and, on a long mat, the whole haunch of a red Afrikaner ox, hide and hoof and all. And several pigs cut in half. And clay pots filled to the brim with white beer. And also – and this we prized most – witch-doctor medicines that protected you against *goël* spirits at night and the evil eye. Ndambe gave another signal. A woman with a clay pot on her head rose up from the kneeling column and advanced towards us. We saw then that what she had in the pot was black earth. It was wet and almost like turf soil. We couldn't understand what they wanted to bring us that for. As though we didn't have enough of it, right there where we were standing and sticking to our veldskoens, and all. And yet Ndambe acted as though that was the most precious part of the peace offerings that his chief, Sijefu, had sent us.

It was when Ndambe spoke again that we saw how ignorant he and his chief and the whole Mtosa tribe were, really.

He took a handful of soil out of the pot and pressed it together between his fingers. Then he told us how honoured the Mtosa tribe was because we were waging war against them. In the past they had only had flat-faced Mshangaans with spiked knobkerries to fight against, he said, but now it was different. Our veldkornet took half a step forward, then, in case Ndambe was going to start flattering us again. So Ndambe said, simply, that the Mtosas would be glad if we came and made war against them later on, when the harvests had been gathered in. But in the meantime the tribe did not wish to continue fighting.

It was the time for sowing.

Ndambe let the soil run through his fingers, to show us how good it was. He also invited us to taste it. We declined.

We accepted his presents and peace was made. And I can still remember how Veldkornet Joubert shook his head and said, 'Can you beat the Mtosas for ignorance?'

And I can still remember what Jurie Bekker said, also. That was when something made him examine the haunch of beef more closely, and he found his own brand mark on it.

It was not long afterwards that the war came against England.

By the end of the second year of the war the Boer forces were in a very bad way. But we would not make peace. Veldkornet Joubert was now promoted to kommandant. Combrinck fell in the battle before Dalmanutha. Jurie Bekker was still with us, and so was Fanie Louw. And it was strange how attached we had grown to Fanie Louw during the years of hardship that we went through together in the field. But up to the end we had to admit that, while we had got used to his jokes, and we knew there was no harm in them, we would have preferred it that he should stop making them.

He did stop, and for ever, in a skirmish near a block-house. We buried him in the shade of a thorn-tree. We got ready to fill in his grave, after which the kommandant would say a few words and we would bare our heads and sing a psalm. As you know, it was customary at a funeral for each mourner to take up a handful of earth and fling it in the grave.

When Kommandant Joubert stooped down and picked up his handful of earth, a strange thing happened. And I remembered that other war, against the Mtosas. And we knew – although we would not say it – what was now that longing in the heart of each of us. For Kommandant Joubert did not straightaway drop the soil into Fanie Louw's grave. Instead he kneaded the damp ground between his fingers. It was as though he had forgotten that it was funeral earth. He seemed to be thinking not of death then, but of life.

We patterned after him, picking up handfuls of soil and pressing it together. We felt the deep loam in it, and saw how springy it was, and we let it trickle through our fingers. And we could remember only that it was the time for sowing.

I understood then how, in an earlier war, the Mtosas had felt, they who were also farmers.

Unto Dust

I have noticed that when a young man or woman dies, people get the feeling that there is something beautiful and touching in the event, and that it is different from the death of an old person. In the thought, say, of a girl of twenty sinking into an untimely grave, there is a sweet wistfulness that makes people talk all kinds of romantic words. She died, they say, young, she that was so full of life and so fair. She was a flower that withered before it bloomed, they say, and it all seems so fitting and beautiful that there is a good deal of resentment, at the funeral, over the crude questions that a couple of men in plain clothes from the landdrost's office are asking about cattle-dip.

But when you have grown old, nobody is very much interested in the manner of your dying. Nobody except you yourself, that is. And I think that your past life has got a lot to do with the way you feel when you get near the end of your days. I remember how, when he was lying on his deathbed, Andries Wessels kept on telling us that it was because of the blameless path he had trodden from his earliest years that he could compose himself in peace to lay down his burdens. And I certainly never saw a man breathe his last more tranquilly, seeing that right up to the end he kept on murmuring to us how happy he was, with heavenly hosts and invisible choirs of angels all around him.

Just before he died, he told us that the angels had even become visible. They were medium-sized angels, he said, and they had cloven hoofs and carried forks. It was obvious that Andries Wessels's ideas were getting a bit confused by then, but all the same I never saw a man die in a more hallowed sort of calm.

Once, during the malaria season in the Eastern Transvaal, it seemed to me, when I was in a high fever and like to die, that the whole world was a big burial-ground. I thought it was the earth itself that was a graveyard, and not just those little fenced-in bits of land dotted with tombstones, in the shade of a Western Province oak tree or by the side of a Transvaal koppie. This was a nightmare that worried me a great deal, and so I was very glad, when I recovered from the fever, to think that we Boers had

154

properly marked-out places on our farms for white people to be laid to rest in, in a civilised Christian way, instead of having to be buried just anyhow, along with a dead wild-cat, maybe, or a Bushman with a clay pot, and things.

When I mentioned this to my friend, Stoffel Oosthuizen, who was in the Low Country with me at the time, he agreed with me wholeheartedly. There were people who talked in a high-flown way of death as the great leveller, he said, and those high-flown people also declared that everyone was made kin by death. He would still like to see those things proved, Stoffel Oosthuizen said. After all, that was one of the reasons why the Boers trekked away into the Transvaal and the Free State, he said, because the British Government wanted to give the vote to any Cape Coloured person walking about with a *kroes* head and big cracks in his feet.

The first time he heard that sort of talk about death coming to all of us alike, and making us all equal, Stoffel Oosthuizen's suspicions were aroused. It sounded like out of a speech made by one of those liberal Cape politicians, he explained.

I found something very comforting in Stoffel Oosthuizen's words.

Then, to illustrate his contention, Stoffel Oosthuizen told me a story of an incident that took place in a bygone Transvaal Kafir War. I don't know whether he told the story incorrectly, or whether it was just that kind of story, but by the time he had finished, all my uncertainties had, I discovered, come back to me.

'You can go and look at Hans Welman's tombstone any time you are at Nietverdiend,' Stoffel Oosthuizen said. 'The slab of red sandstone is weathered by now, of course, seeing how long ago it all happened. But the inscription is still legible. I was with Hans Welman on the morning when he fell. Our commando had been ambushed by the kafirs and was retreating. I could do nothing for Hans Welman. Once, when I looked round, I saw a tall kafir bending over him and plunging an assegai into him. Shortly afterwards I saw the kafir stripping the clothes off Hans Welman. A yellow kafir dog was yelping excitedly around his black master. Although I was in grave danger myself, with several dozen kafirs making straight for me on foot through the bush, the fury I felt at the sight of what that tall kafir was doing made me hazard a last shot. Reining in my horse, and taking what aim I could under the circumstances, I pressed the trigger. My luck was in. I saw the kafir fall forward beside the naked body of Hans Welman. Then I set spurs to my horse and galloped off at full speed, with the foremost of my pursuers already almost upon me. The last I saw was that yellow dog bounding up to his master – whom I had wounded mortally, as we were to discover later.

'As you know, that kafir war dragged on for a long time. There were few pitched battles. Mainly, what took place were bush skirmishes, like the one in which Hans Welman lost his life.

'After about six months, quiet of a sort was restored to the Marico and Zoutpansberg districts. Then the day came when I went out, in company of a handful of other burghers, to fetch in the remains of Hans Welman, at his widow's request, for burial in the little cemetery plot on the farm. We took a coffin with us on a Cape-cart.

'We located the scene of the skirmish without difficulty. Indeed, Hans Welman had been killed not very far from his own farm, which had been temporarily abandoned, together with the other farms in that part, during the time that the trouble with the kafirs had lasted. We drove up to the spot where I remembered having seen Hans Welman lying dead on the ground, with the tall kafir next to him. From a distance I again saw that yellow dog. He slipped away into the bush at our approach. I could not help feeling that there was something rather stirring about that beast's fidelity, even though it was bestowed on a dead kafir.

'We were now confronted with a queer situation. We found that what was left of Hans Welman and the kafir consisted of little more than pieces of sun-dried flesh and the dismembered fragments of bleached skeletons. The sun and wild animals and birds of prey had done their work. There was a heap of human bones, with here and there leathery strips of blackened flesh. But we could not tell which was the white man and which the kafir. To make it still more confusing, a lot of bones were missing altogether, having no doubt been dragged away by wild animals into their lairs in the bush. Another thing was that Hans Welman and that kafir had been just about the same size.'

Stoffel Oosthuizen paused in his narrative, and I let my imagination dwell for a moment on that situation. And I realised just how those Boers must have felt about it: about the thought of bringing the remains of a Transvaal burgher home to his widow for Christian burial, and perhaps having a lot of kafir bones mixed up with the burgher – lying with him in the same tomb on which the mauve petals from the oleander overhead would fall.

'I remember one of our party saying that that was the worst of these kafir wars,' Stoffel Oosthuizen continued. 'If it had been a war against the English, and part of a dead Englishman had got lifted into that coffin by mistake, it wouldn't have mattered so much,' he said.

There seemed to me in this story to be something as strange as the African veld. Stoffel Oosthuizen said that the little party of Boers spent almost a whole afternoon with the remains in order to try to get the white man sorted out from the kafir. By the evening they had laid all they could find of what seemed like Hans Welman's bones in the coffin in the Cape cart. The rest of the bones and flesh they buried on the spot.

Stoffel Oosthuizen added that, no matter what the difference in the colour of their skin had been, it was impossible to say that the kafir's bones were less white than Hans Welman's. Nor was it possible to say that the kafir's sun-dried flesh was any blacker than the white man's. Alive, you couldn't go wrong in distinguishing between a white man and a kafir. Dead, you had great difficulty in telling them apart.

'Naturally, we burghers felt very bitter about the whole affair,' Stoffel Oosthuizen said, 'and our resentment was something that we couldn't explain, quite. Afterwards, several other men who were there that day told me that they had the same feelings of suppressed anger that I did. They wanted somebody – just once – to make a remark such as "in death they were not divided". Then you would have seen an outburst all right. Nobody did say anything like that, however. We all knew better. Two days later a funeral service was conducted in the little cemetery on the Welman farm, and shortly afterwards the sandstone memorial was erected that you can still see there.'

That was the story Stoffel Oosthuizen told me after I had recovered from the fever. It was a story that, as I have said, had in it features as strange as the African veld. But it brought me no peace in my broodings after that attack of malaria. Especially when Stoffel Oosthuizen spoke of how he had occasion, one clear night when the stars shone, to pass that quiet grave-yard on the Welman farm. Something leapt up from the mound beside the sandstone slab. It gave him quite a turn, Stoffel Oosthuizen said, for the third time – and in that way – to come across that yellow kafir dog.

Willem Prinsloo's Peach Brandy

No (Oom Schalk Lourens said) you don't get flowers in the Groot Marico. It is not a bad district for mealies, and I once grew quite good onions in a small garden I made next to the dam. But what you can really call flowers are rare things here. Perhaps it's the heat. Or the drought.

Yet whenever I talk about flowers, I think of Willem Prinsloo's farm on Abjaterskop, where the dance was, and I think of Fritz Pretorius, sitting pale and sick by the roadside, and I think of the white rose that I wore in my hat, jauntily. But most of all I think of Grieta.

If you walk over my farm to the hoogte, and look towards the north-west, you can see Abjaterskop behind the ridge of the Dwarsberge. People will tell you that there are ghosts at Abjaterskop, and that it was once the home of witches. I can believe that. I was at Abjaterskop only once. That was many years ago. And I never went there again. Still, it wasn't ghosts that kept me away; nor was it the witches.

Grieta Prinsloo was due to come back from the finishing school at Zeerust, where she had gone to learn English manners and diction and other high-class subjects. Therefore Willem Prinsloo her father, arranged a big dance on his farm at Abjaterskop to celebrate Grieta's return.

I was invited to the party. So was Fritz Pretorius. So was every white person in the district, from Derdepoort to Ramoutsa. What was more, practically everybody went. Of course, we were all somewhat nervous about meeting Grieta. With all the superior things she had learnt at the finishing school, we wouldn't be able to talk to her in a chatty sort of way, just as though she were an ordinary Boer girl. But what fetched us all to Abjaterskop in the end was our knowledge that Willem Prinsloo made the best peach brandy in the district.

Fritz Pretorius spoke to me of the difficulty brought about by Grieta's learning.

'Yes, jong,' he said, 'I am feeling pretty shaky about talking to her, I can tell you. I have been rubbing up my education a bit, though. Yesterday I took out my old slate that I last used when I left school seventeen years ago and I did a few sums. I did some addition and subtraction. I tried a little multiplication, too. But I have forgotten how it is done.'

I told Fritz that I would have liked to have helped him, but I had never learnt as far as multiplication.

The day of the dance arrived. The post-cart bearing Grieta to her father's house passed through Drogedal in the morning. In the afternoon I got dressed. I wore a black jacket, fawn trousers, and a pink shirt. I also put on the brown boots that I had bought about a year before, and that I had never had occasion to wear. For I would have looked silly walking about the farm in a pair of shop boots, when everybody else wore home-made veldskoens.

I believed, as I got on my horse, and set off down the Government Road, with my hat rakishly on one side, that I would be easily the best-dressed young man at that dance.

It was getting on towards sunset when I arrived at the foot of Abjaterskop, which I had to skirt in order to reach Willem Prinsloo's farm nestling in a hollow behind the hills. I felt, as I rode, that it was stupid for a man to live in a part that was reputed to be haunted. The trees grew taller and denser, as they always do on rising ground. And they also got a lot darker.

All over the place were queer, heavy shadows. I didn't like the look of them. I remembered stories I had heard of the witches of Abjaterskop, and what they did to travellers who lost their way in the dark. It seemed an easy thing to lose your way among those tall trees. Accordingly I spurred my horse on to a gallop, to get out of this gloomy region as quickly as possible. After all, a horse is sensitive about things like ghosts and witches, and it was my duty to see my horse was not frightened unnecessarily. Especially as a cold wind suddenly sprang up through the poort, and once or twice it sounded as though an evil voice were calling my name. I started riding fast then. But a few moments later I looked round and realised the position. It was Fritz Pretorius galloping along behind me.

'What was your hurry?' Fritz asked when I had slowed down to allow his overtaking me.

'I wished to get through those trees before it was too dark, I answered, 'I didn't want my horse to get frightened.'

'I suppose that's why you were riding with your arms round his neck,' Fritz observed, 'to soothe him.'

I did not reply. But what I did notice was that Fritz was also very stylishly dressed. True, I beat him as far as shirt and boots went, but he was dressed in a new grey suit, with his socks pulled up over the bottoms of his trousers. He also had a handkerchief which he ostentatiously took out of his pocket several times.

Of course I couldn't be jealous of a person like Fritz Pretorius. I was only annoyed at the thought that he was making himself ridiculous by going to a party with an outlandish thing like a handkerchief.

We arrived at Willem Prinsloo's house. There were so many ox-wagons drawn up on the veld that the place looked like a laager. Prinsloo met us at the door.

'Go right through, kêrels,' he said, 'the dancing is in the voorhuis. The peach brandy is in the kitchen.'

Although the voorhuis was big it was so crowded as to make it almost impossible to dance. But it was not as crowded as the kitchen. Nor was the music in the voorhuis – which was provided by a number of men with guitars and concertinas – as loud as the music in the kitchen, where there was no band, but each man sang for himself.

We knew from these signs that the party was a success.

When I had been in the kitchen for about half an hour I decided to go into the voorhuis. It seemed a long way, now, from the kitchen to the voorhuis, and I had to lean against the wall several times to think. I passed a number of other men who were also leaning against the wall like that, thinking. One man even found that he could think best by sitting on the floor with his head in his arms.

You could see that Willem Prinsloo made good peach brandy.

Then I saw Fritz Pretorius, and the sight of him brought me to my senses right away. Airily flapping his white handkerchief in time with the music, he was talking to a girl who smiled up at him with bright eyes and red lips and small white teeth.

I knew at once that it was Grieta.

She was tall and slender and very pretty, and her dark hair was braided with a wreath of white roses that you could see had been picked that same morning in Zeerust. And she didn't look the sort of girl, either, in whose presence you had to appear clever and educated. In fact, I felt I wouldn't really need the twelve times table which I had torn off the back of a school writing book, and had thrust into my jacket pocket before leaving home.

You can imagine that it was not too easy to get a word in with Grieta while Fritz was hanging around. But I managed it eventually, and while I was talking to her I had the satisfaction of seeing, out of the corner of my eye, the direction Fritz took. He went into the kitchen, flapping his hand-kerchief behind him – into the kitchen, where the laughter was, and the singing, and Willem Prinsloo's peach brandy.

I told Grieta that I was Schalk Lourens.

'Oh yes, I have heard of you,' she answered, 'from Fritz Pretorius.'

I knew what that meant. So I told her that Fritz was known all over the Marico for his lies. I told her other things about Fritz. Ten minutes later, when I was still talking about him, Grieta smiled and said that I could tell her the rest some other night.

'But I must tell you one more thing now,' I insisted. 'When he knew that he would be meeting you here at the dance, Fritz started doing homework.'

I told her about the sums, and Grieta laughed softly. It struck me again how pretty she was. And her eyes were radiant in the candlelight. And the roses looked very white against her dark hair. And all this time the dancers whirled around us, and the band in the voorhuis played lively dance tunes, and from the kitchen there issued sounds of jubilation.

The rest happened very quickly.

I can't even remember how it all came about. But what I do know is that when we were outside, under the tall trees, with the stars over us, I could easily believe that Grieta was not a girl at all, but one of the witches of Abjaterskop who wove strange spells.

Yet to listen to my talking nobody would have guessed the wild, thrilling things that were in my heart.

I told Grieta about last year's drought, and about the difficulty of keeping the white ants from eating through the door and window frames, and about the way my new brown boots tended to take the skin off my toes if I walked quickly.

Then I moved close up to her.

'Grieta,' I said, taking her hand, 'Grieta, there is something I want to tell you.'

She pulled away her hand. She did it very gently, though. Sorrowfully, almost.

'I know what you want to say,' she answered.

I was surprised at that.

'How do you know, Grieta?' I asked.

'Oh, I know lots of things,' she replied, laughing again, 'I haven't been to finishing school for nothing.'

'I don't mean that,' I answered at once, 'I wasn't going to talk about spelling or arithmetic. I was going to tell you that ...'

'Please don't say it, Schalk,' Grieta interrupted me. 'I – I don't know whether I am worthy of hearing it. I don't know, even ...'

'But you are so lovely,' I exclaimed. 'I have got to tell you how lovely you are.'

But at the very moment I stepped forward she retreated swiftly, eluding me. I couldn't understand how she had timed it so well. For, try as I might, I couldn't catch her. She sped lightly and gracefully amongst the trees, and I followed as best I could.

Yet it was not only my want of learning that handicapped me. There were also my new boots. And Willem Prinsloo's peach brandy. And the shaft of a mule-cart – the lower end of the shaft, where it rests in the grass.

I didn't fall very hard, though. The grass was long and thick there. But even as I fell a great happiness came into my heart. And I didn't care about anything else in the world.

Grieta had stopped running. She turned round. For an instant her body, slender and misty in the shadows, swayed towards me. Then her hand flew to her hair. Her fingers pulled at the wreath. And the next thing I knew was that there lay, within reach of my hand, a small white rose.

I shall always remember the thrill with which I picked up that rose, and how I trembled when I stuck it in my hat. I shall always remember the stir I caused when I walked into the kitchen. Everybody stopped drinking to look at the rose in my hat. The young men made jokes about it. The older men winked slyly and patted me on the back.

Although Fritz Pretorius was not in the kitchen to witness my triumph, I knew he would get to hear of it somehow. That would make him realise that it was impudence for a fellow like him to set up as Schalk Lourens's rival.

During the rest of the night I was a hero.

The men in the kitchen made me sit on the table. They plied me with brandy and drank to my health. And afterwards, when a dozen of them carried me outside, on to an ox-wagon, for fresh air, they fell with me only once. At daybreak I was still on that wagon.

I woke up feeling very sick – until I remembered about Grieta's rose. There was that white rose still stuck in my hat, for the whole world to know that Grieta Prinsloo had chosen me before all other men.

But what I didn't want people to know was that I had remained asleep on that ox-wagon after the other guests had gone. So I rode away very quietly, glad that nobody was astir to see me go.

My head was dizzy as I rode back, but in my heart it felt like green wings beating; and although it was day now, there was the same soft wind in the grass that had been there when Grieta flung the rose at me, standing under the stars.

I rode slowly through the trees on the slope of Abjaterskop, and had reached the place where the path turns south again, when I saw something that made me wonder if, at these fashionable finishing schools, they did not perhaps teach the girls too much.

First I saw Fritz Pretorius's horse by the roadside.

Then I saw Fritz. He was sitting up against a thorn-tree, with his chin resting on his knees. He looked very pale and sick. But what made me wonder much about those finishing schools was that in Fritz's hat, which had fallen on the ground some distance away from him, there was a small white rose.

Makapan's Cave

Kafirs? (said Oom Schalk Lourens). Yes, I know them. And they're all the same. I fear the Almighty, and I respect His works, but I could never understand why He made the kafir and the rinderpest. The Hottentot is a little better. The Hottentot will only steal the biltong hanging out on the line to dry. He won't steal the line as well. That is where the kafir is different.

Still, sometimes you come across a good kafir, who is faithful and upright and a true Christian and doesn't let the wild-dogs catch the sheep. I always think that it isn't right to kill that kind of kafir.

I remember about one kafir we had, by the name of Nongaas. How we got him was after this fashion. It was in the year of the big drought, when there was no grass, and the water in the pan had dried up. Our cattle died like flies. It was terrible. Every day ten or twelve or twenty died. So my father said we must pack everything on the wagons and trek up to the Dwarsberge, where he heard there had been good rains. I was six years old then, the youngest in the family. Most of the time I sat in the back of the wagon, with my mother and my two sisters. My brother Hendrik was seventeen, and he helped my father and the kafirs to drive on our cattle. That was how we trekked. Many more of our cattle died along the way, but after about two months we got into the Lowveld and my father said that God had been good to us. For the grass was green along the Dwarsberge.

One morning we came to some kafir huts, where my father bartered two sacks of mealies for a roll of tobacco. A picannin of about my own age was standing in front of a hut, and he looked at us all the time and grinned. But mostly he looked at my brother Hendrik. And that was not a wonder, either. Even in those days my brother Hendrik was careful about his appearance, and he always tried to be fashionably dressed. On Sunday he even wore socks. When we had loaded up the mealies, my father cut off a plug of Boer tobacco and gave it to the picannin, who grinned still more, so that we saw every one of his teeth, which were very white. He put the plug in his mouth and bit it. Then we laughed. The picannin looked just like a puppy that has swallowed a piece of meat, and turns his head sideways, to see how it tastes.

That was in the morning. We went right on until the afternoon, for my father wanted to reach Tweekoppiesfontein, where we were going to stand with our cattle for some time. It was late in the afternoon when we got there, and we started to outspan. Just as I was getting off the wagon, I looked round and saw something jumping quickly behind a bush. It looked like some animal, so I was afraid, and told my brother Hendrik, who took up his gun and walked slowly towards the bush. We saw, directly afterwards, that it was the picannin whom we had seen that morning in front of the hut. He must have been following behind our wagons for about ten miles. He looked dirty and tired, but when my brother went up to him he began to grin again, and seemed very happy. We did not know what to do with him, so Hendrik shouted to him to go home, and started throwing stones at him. But my father was a merciful man, and after he had heard Nongaas's story – for that was the name of the picannin – he said he could stay with us, but he must be good, and not tell lies and steal, like the other kafirs. Nongaas told us in the Bechuana language, which my father understood, that his father and mother had been killed by the lions, and that he was living with his uncle, whom he didn't like, but that he liked my brother Hendrik, and that was why he had followed our wagons.

Nongaas remained with us for many years. He grew up with us. He was a very good kafir, and as time went by he became much attached to all of us. But he worshipped my brother Hendrik. As he grew older, my father sometimes spoke to Nongaas about his soul, and explained to him about God. But although he told my father that he understood, I could see that whenever Nongaas thought of God, he was really only thinking of Hendrik.

It was just after my twenty-first birthday that we got news that Hermanus Potgieter and his whole family had been killed by a kafir tribe under Makapan. They also said that after killing him, the kafirs stripped off old Potgieters's skin and made wallets out of it in which to carry their dagga. It was very wicked of the kafirs to have done that, especially as dagga makes you mad and it is a sin to smoke it. A commando was called up from our district to go and attack the tribe and teach them to have respect for the white man's skin. My mother and sisters baked a great deal of harde beskuit which we packed up, together with mealie-meal and biltong. We also took out the lead mould and melted bullets. The next morning my brother and I set out on horseback for Makapan's kraal. We were accompanied by Nongaas, whom we took along with us to look after the horses and light the fires. My father stayed at home. He said that he was too old to go on commando, unless it was to fight the red-coats, if there were still any left.

But he gave us some good advice.

'Don't forget to read your Bible, my sons,' he called out as we rode away. 'Pray the Lord to help you, and when you shoot always aim for the stomach.' These remarks were typical of my father's deeply religious nature and he also knew that it was easier to hit a man in the stomach than in the head: and it is just as good, because no man can live long after his intestines have been shot away.

Well, we rode on, my brother and I, with Nongaas following a few yards behind us on the pack-horse. Now and again we fell in with other burghers, many of whom brought their wagons with them, until, on the third day, we reached Makapan's kraal, where the big commando had already gone into camp. We got there in the evening, and everywhere as far as we could see there were fires in a big circle. There were over two hundred wagons, and on their tents the fires shone red and yellow. We reported ourselves to the veldkornets, who showed us a place where we could camp, next to the four Van Rensburg brothers. Nongaas had just made the fire and boiled the coffee when one of the Van Rensburgs came up and invited us over to their wagon. They had shot a rietbok and were roasting pieces of it on the coals.

We shook hands and said it was good weather for the mealies if only the *ruspes* didn't eat them, and that it was time we had another president, and that rietbok tasted very fine when roasted on the coals. Then they told us what had happened about the kafirs. Makapan and his followers had seen the commandos coming from a distance, and after firing a few shots at them had all fled into the caves in the krantz. These caves stretched underground very far and with many turnings. So, as the Boers could not storm the kafirs without losing heavily, the kommandant gave instructions that the ridge was to be surrounded and the kafirs starved out. They were all inside the cave, the whole tribe, men, women and children. They had already been there six days, and as they couldn't have much food left, and as there was only a small dam with brackish water, we were hopeful of being able to kill off most of the kafirs without wasting ammunition.

Already, when the wind blew towards us from the mouth of the caves, the stink was terrible. We would have pitched our camp further back, only that we were afraid some of the kafirs would escape between the fires.

The following morning I saw for the first time why we couldn't drive the kafirs from their lairs, even though our commando was four hundred strong. All over, through the rocks and bushes, could see black openings in the krantz, that led right into the deep parts of the earth. Here and there we could see dead bodies lying. But there were still a lot of kafirs left that were not dead and them we could not see. But they had guns, which they had bought from the illicit traders and the missionaries, and they shot at us whenever we came within range. And all the time there was that stench of decaying bodies.

For another week the siege went on. Then we heard that our leaders, Marthinus Wessel Pretorius and Paul Kruger, had quarrelled. Kruger wanted to attack the kafirs immediately and finish the affair, but Pretorius said it was too dangerous and he didn't want any more burghers killed. He said that already the hand of the Lord lay heavy upon Makapan, and in another few weeks the kafirs would all be dead of starvation. But Paul Kruger said that it would even be better if the hand of the Lord lay still heavier upon the kafirs. Eventually Paul Kruger obtained permission to take fifty Volunteers and storm the caves from one side, while Kommandant Piet Potgieter was to advance from the other side with two hundred men, to distract the attention of the kafirs. Kruger was popular with all of us, and nearly everyone volunteered to go with him. So he picked fifty men, among whom were the Van Rensburgs and my brother. Therefore, as I did not want to stay behind and guard the camp, I had to join Piet Potgieter's commando.

All the preparations were made, and the following morning we got ready to attack. My brother Hendrik was very proud and happy at having been chosen for the more dangerous part. He oiled his gun very carefully and polished up his veldskoens.

Then Nongaas came up and I noticed that he looked very miserable. 'My baas,' he said to my brother Hendrik, 'you mustn't go and fight. They'll shoot you dead.'

My brother shook his head.

'Then let me go with you, baas,' Nongaas said; 'I will go in front and look after you.'

Hendrik only laughed.

'Look here, Nongaas,' he said, 'you can stay behind and cook the dinner. I will get back in time to eat it.'

The whole commando came together and we all knelt down and prayed. Then Marthinus Wessel Pretorius said we must sing Hymn Number 23, 'Rest my soul, thy God is king'. Furthermore, we sang another hymn and also a psalm. Most people would have thought that one hymn would be enough. But not so Pretorius. He always made quite sure of everything he did. Then we moved off to the attack. We fought bravely, but the kafirs were many, and they lay in the darkness of the caves and shot at us without our being able to see them. While the fighting lasted it was worse than the lyddite bombs at Paardeberg. And the stench was terrible. We tied handkerchiefs round the lower part of our face, but that did not help. Also, since we were not Englishmen, many of us had no handkerchiefs. Still we fought on, shooting at an enemy we could not see. We rushed right up to the mouth of one of the caves, and even got some distance into it, when our leader, Kommandant Piet Potgieter, flung up his hands and fell backwards, shot through the breast. We carried him out, but he was quite dead. So we lost heart and retired.

When we returned from the fight we found that the other attacking party had also been defeated. They had shot many kafirs, but there were still hundreds of them left, who fought all the more fiercely with hunger gnawing at their bellies.

I went back to our camp. There was only Nongaas, sitting forward on a stone, with his face on his arms. An awful fear clutched me as I asked him what was wrong.

'Baas Hendrik,' he replied, and as he looked at me in his eyes there was much sorrow. 'Baas Hendrik did not come back.'

I went out immediately and made enquiries, but nobody could tell me anything for sure. They remembered quite well seeing my brother Hendrik when they stormed the cave. He was right in amongst the foremost of the attackers. When I heard that, I felt a great pride in my brother, although I also knew that nothing else could be expected of the son of my father. But no man could tell me what had happened to him. All they knew was that when they got back he was not amongst them.

I spoke to Marthinus Wessel Pretorius and asked him to send out another party to seek for my brother. But Pretorius was angry.

'I will not allow one more man,' he replied. 'It was all Kruger's doing. I was against it from the start. Now Kommandant Potgieter has been killed, who was a better man than Kruger and all his Dopper clique put together. If any man goes back to the caves I shall discharge him from the commando.'

But I don't think it was right of Pretorius. Because Paul Kruger was only trying to do his duty, and afterwards, when he was nominated for president, I voted for him.

It was eleven o'clock when I again reached our part of the laager. Nongaas was still sitting on the flat stone, and I saw that he had carried out my brother Hendrik's instructions, and that the pot was boiling on the fire. The dinner was ready, but my brother was not there. That sight was too much for me, and I went and lay down alone under the Van Rensburgs' wagon.

I looked up again, about half an hour later, and I saw Nongaas walking away with a water-bottle and a small sack strapped to his back. He said nothing to me, but I knew he was going to look for my brother Hendrik. Nongaas knew that if his baas was still alive he would need him. I supposed it was his intention to lie in wait near one of the caves and then crawl inside when the night came. That was a very brave thing to do. If Makapan's kafirs saw him they would be sure to kill him, because he was helping the Boers against them, and also because he was a Bechuana.

The evening came, but neither my brother Hendrik nor Nongaas. All that night I sat with my face to the caves and never slept. Then in the morning I got up and loaded my gun. I said to myself that if Nongaas had been killed in the attempt there was only one thing left for me to do. I myself must go to my brother.

I walked out first into the veld in case one of the officers saw me and made me come back. Then I walked along the ridge and got under cover of the bushes. From there I crawled along, hiding in the long grass and behind the stones, so that I came to one part of Makapan's stronghold where things were more quiet. I got within about two hundred yards of a cave. There I lay very still, behind a big rock, to find out if there were any kafirs watching from that side. Occasionally I heard the sound of a shot being fired, but that was far away. Afterwards I fell asleep, for I was very weary with the anxiety and through not having slept the night before.

When I woke up the sun was right overhead. It was hot and there were no clouds in the sky. Only there were a few aasvoëls, which flew round and round very slowly, without ever seeming to flap their wings. Now and again one of them would fly down and settle on the ground, and it was very horrible. I thought of my brother Hendrik and shivered. I looked towards the cave. Inside it seemed as though there was something moving. A minute later I saw that it was a kafir coming stealthily towards the entrance. He appeared to be looking in my direction, and for fear that he should see me and call the other kafirs, I jumped up quickly and shot at him, aiming at the stomach. He fell over like a sack of potatoes and I was thankful for my father's advice. But I had to act quickly. If the other kafirs had heard the shot they would all come running up at once. And I didn't want that to happen. I didn't like the look of those aasvoëls. So I decided to take a great risk. Accordingly I ran as fast as I could towards the cave and rushed right into it, so that, even if the kafirs did come, they wouldn't see me amongst the shadows. For a long time I lay down and waited. But as no more kafirs came, I got up and walked slowly down a dark passage, looking round every time to see that nobody followed me, and to make sure that I would find my way back. For there were many twists and turnings, and the whole krantz seemed to be hollowed out.

I knew that my search would be very difficult. But there was something that seemed to tell me that my brother was near by. So I was strong in my faith, and I knew that the Lord would lead me aright. And I found my brother Hendrik, and he was alive. It was with a feeling of great joy that I came across him. I saw him in the dim light that came through a big slit in the roof. He was lying against a boulder, holding his leg and groaning. I saw afterwards that his leg was sprained and much swollen, but that was all that was wrong. So great was my brother Hendrik's surprise at seeing me that at first he could not talk. He just held my hand and laughed softly, and when I touched his forehead I knew that he was feverish. I gave him some brandy out of my flask, and in a few words he told me all that had happened. When they stormed the cave he was right in front and as the kafirs retreated he followed them up. But they all ran in different ways until my brother found himself alone. He tried to get back, but lost his way and fell down a dip. In that way he sprained his ankle so severely that he had been in agony all the time. He crawled into a far corner and remained there, with the danger and the darkness and his pain. But the worst of all was the stink of the rotting bodies.

'Then Nongaas came,' my brother Hendrik said.

'Nongaas?' I asked him.

'Yes,' he replied, 'He found me and gave me food and water, and carried me on his back. Then the water gave out and I was very thirsty. So Nongaas took the bottle to go and fill it at the pan. But it is very dangerous to get there, and I am so frightened they may kill him.'

'They will not kill him,' I said. 'Nongaas will come back.' I said that, but in my heart I was afraid. For the caves were many and dark, and the kafirs were blood-mad. It would not do to wait. So I lifted Hendrik on my shoulder and carried him towards the entrance. He was in much pain.

'You know,' he whispered, 'Nongaas was crying when he found me. He thought I was dead. He has been very good to me – so very good. Do you remember that day when he followed behind our wagons? He looked so very trustful and so little, and yet I – I threw stones at him. I wish I did not do that. I only hope that he comes back safe. He was crying and stroking my hair.'

As I said, my brother Hendrik was feverish.

'Of course he will come back,' I answered him. But this time I knew that I lied. For as I came through the mouth of the cave I kicked against the kafir I had shot there. The body sagged over to one side and I saw the face.

Drieka and the Moon

There is a queer witchery about the moon when it is full – Oom Schalk Lourens remarked – especially the moon that hangs over the valley of the Dwarsberge in the summer time. It does strange things to your mind, the Marico moon, and in your heart are wild and fragrant fancies, and your thoughts go very far away. Then, if you have been sitting on your front stoep, thinking these thoughts, you sigh and murmur something about the way of the world, and carry your chair inside.

I have seen the moon in other places besides the Marico. But it is not the same there.

Braam Venter, the man who fell off the Government lorry once, near Nietverdiend, says that the Marico moon is like a woman laying green flowers on a grave. Braam Venter often says things like that. Particularly since the time he fell off the lorry. He fell on his head, they say.

Always when the moon shines full like that it does something to our hearts that we wonder very much about and that we never understand. Always it awakens memories. And it is singular how different these memories are with each one of us.

Johannes Oberholzer says that the full moon always reminds him of one occasion when he was smuggling cattle over the Bechuanaland border. He says he never sees a full moon without thinking of the way it shone on the steel wire-cutters that he was holding in his hand when two mounted policemen rode up to him. And the next night Johannes Oberholzer again had a good view of the full moon; he saw it through the window of the place he was in. He says the moon was very large and very yellow, except for the black stripes in front of it.

And it was in the light of the full moon that hung over the thorn-trees that I saw Drieka Breytenbach. Drieka was tall and slender. She had fair hair and blue eyes, and lots of people considered that she was the prettiest woman in the Marico. I thought so, too, that night I met her under the full moon by the thorn-trees. She had not been in the Bushveld very long. Her husband, Petrus Breytenbach, had met her and married her in the Schweizer-Reneke district, where he had trekked with his cattle for a while during the big drought.

Afterwards, when Petrus Breytenbach was shot dead with his own Mauser by a kafir working on his farm, Drieka went back to Schweizer-Reneke, leaving the Marico as strangely and as silently as she had come to it.

And it seemed to me that the Marico was a different place because Drieka Breytenbach had gone. And I thought of the moon, and the tricks it plays with your senses, and the stormy witchery that it flings at your soul. And I remembered what Braam Venter said, that the full moon is like a woman laying green flowers on a grave. And it seemed to me that Braam Venter's words were not so much nonsense, after all, and that worse things could happen to a man than that he should fall off a lorry on his head. And I thought of other matters.

But all this happened only afterwards.

When I saw Drieka that night she was leaning against a thorn-tree beside the road where it goes down to the drift. But I didn't recognise her at first. All I saw was a figure dressed in white with long hair hanging down loose over its shoulders. It seemed very unusual that a figure should be there like that at such a time of night. I remembered certain stories I had heard about white ghosts. I also remembered that a few miles back I had seen a boulder lying in the middle of the road. It was a fair-sized boulder and it might be dangerous for passing mule-carts. So I decided to turn back at once and move it out of the way.

I decided very quickly about the boulder. And I made up my mind so firmly that the saddle-girth broke from the sudden way in which I jerked my horse back on his haunches. Then the figure came forward and spoke, and I saw it was Drieka Breytenbach.

'Good evening,' I said in answer to her greeting, 'I was just going back because I had remembered about something.'

'About ghosts?' she asked.

'No,' I replied truthfully, 'about a stone in the road.'

Drieka laughed at that. So I laughed too. And then Drieka laughed again. And then I laughed. In fact, we did quite a lot of laughing between us. I got off my horse and stood beside Drieka in the moonlight. And if somebody had come along at that moment and said that the Predikant's mule-cart had been capsized by the boulder in the road I would have laughed still more.

That is the sort of thing the moon in the Marico does to you when it is full.

I didn't think of asking Drieka how she came to be there, or why her hair was hanging down loose, or who it was that she had been waiting for under the thorn-tree. It was enough that the moon was there, big and yellow over the veld, and that the wind blew softly through the trees and across the grass and against Drieka's white dress and against the mad singing of the stars.

Before I knew what was happening we were seated on the grass under the thorn-tree whose branches leant over the road. And I remember that for quite a while we remained there without talking, sitting side by side on the grass with our feet in the soft sand. And Drieka smiled at me with a misty sort of look in her eyes, and I saw that she was lovely.

I felt that it was not enough that we should go on sitting there in silence. I knew that a woman – even a moon-woman like Drieka – expected a man to be more than just good-humoured and honest. I knew that a woman wanted a man also to be an entertaining companion for her. So I beguiled the passing moments for Drieka with interesting conversation.

I explained to her how a few days before a pebble had worked itself into my veldskoen and had rubbed some skin off the top of one of my toes. I took off my veldskoen and showed her the place. I also told her about the rinderpest and about the way two of my cows had died of the miltsiek. I also knew a lot about blue-tongue in sheep, and about gallamsiekte and the haarwurm, and I talked to her airily about these things, just as easily as I am talking to you.

But, of course, it was the moonlight that did it. I never knew before that I was so good in this idle, butterfly kind of talk. And the whole thing was so innocent, too. I felt that if Drieka Breytenbach's husband, Petrus, were to come along and find us sitting side by side, he would not be able to say much about it. At least, not very much.

After a while I stopped talking. Drieka put her hand in mine.

'Oh, Schalk,' she whispered, and the moon and that misty look were in her blue eyes.

'Do tell me some more.' I shook my head.

'I am sorry, Drieka,' I answered, 'I don't know any more.'

'But you must, Schalk,' she said very softly. 'Talk to me about – about other things.'

I thought steadily for some moments.

'Yes, Drieka,' I said at length, 'I have remembered something. There is one more thing I haven't told you about the blue-tongue in sheep …'

'No, no, not that,' she interrupted, 'talk to me about other things. About the moon, say.'

So I told her two things that Braam Venter had said about the moon. I told her the green flower one and the other one.

'Braam Venter knows lots more things like that about the moon,' I explained, 'you'll see him next time you go to Zeerust for the Nagmaal. He is a short fellow with a bump on his head from where he fell …'

'Oh, no, Schalk,' Drieka said again, shaking her head, so that a wisp of her fair head brushed against my face, 'I don't want to know about Braam Venter. Only about you. You think out something on your own about the moon and tell it to me.'

I understood what she meant.

'Well, Drieka,' I said thoughtfully. 'The moon – the moon is all right.'

'Oh, Schalk!' Drieka cried. 'That's much finer than anything Braam Venter could ever say – even with that bump on his head.'

Of course, I told her that it was nothing and that I could perhaps say something even better if I tried. But I was very proud, all the same. And somehow it seemed that my words brought us close together. I felt that a handful of words, spoken under the full moon, had made a new and witch thing come into the life of Drieka and me.

We were holding hands then, sitting on the grass with our feet in the road, and Drieka leant her head on my shoulder, and her long hair stirred softly against my face, but I looked only at her feet. And I thought for a moment that I loved her. And I did not love her because her body was beautiful, or because she had red lips, or because her eyes were blue. In that moment I did not understand about her body or her lips or her eyes. I loved her for her feet; and because her feet were in the road next to mine. And yet all the time I felt, far away at the back of my mind, that it was the moon that was doing these things to me.

'You have got good feet for walking on,' I said to Drieka.

'Braam Venter would have said that I have got good feet for dancing on,' Drieka answered, laughing. And I began to grow jealous of Braam Venter.

The next thing I knew was that Drieka had thrown herself into my arms.

'Do you think I am very beautiful, Schalk?' Drieka asked.

'You are very beautiful, Drieka,' I answered slowly, 'very beautiful.'

'Will you do something for me, Schalk?' Drieka asked again, and her red lips were very close to my cheek. 'Will you do something for me if I love you very much?'

'What do you want me to do, Drieka?'

She drew my head down to her lips and whispered hot words in my ear.

And so it came about that I thrust her from me, suddenly. I jumped unsteadily to my feet; I found my horse and rode away. I left Drieka Breytenbach where I had found her, under the thorn-tree by the roadside, with her hot whisperings still ringing in my ears, and before I reached home the moon had set behind the Dwarsberge.

Well, there is not much left for me to tell you. In the days that followed, Drieka Breytenbach was always in my thoughts. Her long, loose hair and her red lips and her feet that had been in the roadside sand with mine. But if she really was the ghost that I had at first taken her to be, I could not have been more afraid of her.

And it seemed singular that, while it had been my words spoken in the moonlight, that helped to bring Drieka and me closer together, it was Drieka's hot breath, whispering wild words in my ear, that sent me so suddenly from her side.

Once or twice I even felt sorry for having left in that fashion

And later on when I heard that Drieka Breytenbach had gone back to Schweizer-Reneke, and that her husband had been shot dead with his own Mauser by one of the farm kafirs, I was not surprised. In fact, I had expected it. Only it did not seem right somehow, that Drieka should have got a kafir to do the thing that I had refused to do.

Veld Maiden

I know what it is – Oom Schalk Lourens said – when you talk that way about the veld. I have known people who sit like you do and dream about the veld, and talk strange things, and start believing in what they call the soul of the veld, until in the end the veld means a different thing to them from what it does to me.

I only know that the veld can be used for growing mealies on, and it isn't very good for that, either. Also, it means very hard work for me, growing mealies. There is the ploughing, for instance. I used to get aches in my back and shoulders from sitting on a stone all day long on the edge of the lands, watching the kafirs and the oxen and the plough going up and down, making furrows. Hans Coetzee, who was a Boer War prisoner at St. Helena, told me how he got sick at sea from watching the ship going up and down, up and down, all the time.

And it's the same with ploughing. The only real cure for this ploughing sickness is to sit quietly on a riempies bench on the stoep, with one's legs raised slightly, drinking coffee until the ploughing season is over. Most of the farmers in the Marico Bushveld have adopted this remedy, as you have no doubt observed by this time.

But there the veld is. And it is not good to think too much about it. For then it can lead you in strange ways. And sometimes – sometimes when the veld has led you very far – there comes into your eyes a look that God did not put there.

It was in the early summer, shortly after the rains, that I first came across John de Swardt. He was sitting next to a tent that he had pitched behind the maroelas at the far end of my farm, where it adjoins Frans Welman's lands. He had been there several days and I had not known about it, because I sat much on my stoep then, on account of what I have already explained to you about the ploughing.

He was a young fellow with long black hair. When I got nearer I saw what he was doing. He had a piece of white buck-sail on a stand in front of him and he was painting my farm. He seemed to have picked out all the useless bits for his pictures – a krantz and a few stones and some clumps of khaki-bos.

'Young man,' I said to him, after we had introduced ourselves, 'when people in Johannesburg see that picture they will laugh and say that Schalk Lourens lives on a barren piece of rock, like a lizard does. Why don't you rather paint the fertile parts? Look at that vlei there, and the dam. And put in that new cattle-dip that I have just built up with reinforced concrete. Then, if Piet Grobler or General Kemp sees this picture, he will know at once that Schalk Lourens has been making improvements on the farm.'

The young painter shook his head.

'No,' he said, 'I want to paint only the veld. I hate the idea of painting boreholes and cattle-dips and houses and concrete – especially concrete. I want only the veld. Its loneliness. Its mystery. When this picture is finished I'll be proud to put my name to it.'

'Oh, well, that is different,' I replied, 'as long as you don't put my name to it. Better still,' I said, 'put Frans Welman's name on it. Write underneath that this is Frans Welman's farm.'

I said that because I still remembered that Frans Welman had voted against me at the last election of the Drogekop School Committee.

John de Swardt then took me into his tent and showed me some other pictures he had painted at different places along the Dwarsberge. They were all the same sort of pictures, barren and stony. I thought it would be a good idea if the Government put up a lot of pictures like that on the Kalahari border for the locusts to see. Because that would keep the locusts out of the Marico.

Then John de Swardt showed me another picture he had painted and when I saw that I got a different opinion about this thing that he said was art. I looked from De Swardt to the picture and then back again to De Swardt.

'I'd never have thought it of you,' I said, 'and you look such a quiet sort, too.'

'I call it the "Veld Maiden",' John de Swardt said.

'If the Predikant saw it he'd call it by other names,' I replied. 'But I am a broad-minded man. I have been once in the bar in Zeerust and twice in the bioscope when I should have been attending Nagmaal. So I don't hold it against a young man for having ideas like this. But you mustn't let anybody here see this Veld Maiden unless you paint a few more clothes on her.'

'I couldn't,' De Swardt answered, 'that's just how I see her. That's just how I dream about her. For many years now she has come to me so in my dreams.'

'With her arms stretched out like that?' I asked.

'Yes.'

'And with ...'

'Yes, yes, just like that,' De Swardt said very quickly. Then he blushed and I could see how very young he was. It seemed a pity that a nice young fellow like that should be so mad.

'Anyway, if ever you want a painting job,' I said when I left, 'you can come and white-wash the back of my sheep-kraal.'

I often say funny things like that to people.

I saw a good deal of John de Swardt after that, and I grew to like him. I was satisfied – in spite of his wasting his time in painting bare stones and weeds – that there was no real evil in him. I was sure that he only talked silly things about visions and the spirit of the veld because of what they had done to him at the school in Johannesburg where they taught him all that nonsense about art, and I felt sorry for him. Afterwards I wondered for a little while if I shouldn't rather have felt sorry for the art school. But when I had thought it all out carefully I knew that John de Swardt was only very young and innocent, and that what happened to him later on was the sort of thing that does happen to those who are simple of heart.

On several Sundays in succession I took De Swardt over the rant to the house of Frans Welman. I hadn't a very high regard for Frans' judgment since the time he voted for the wrong man at the School Committee. But I had no other neighbour within walking distance, and I had to go some-where on a Sunday.

We talked of all sorts of things. Frans's wife Sannie was young and pretty, but very shy. She wasn't naturally like that. It was only that she was afraid to talk in case she said something of which her husband might disapprove. So most of the time Sannie sat silent in the corner, getting up now and again to make more coffee for us.

Frans Welman was in some respect what people might call a hard man. For instance, it was something of a mild scandal the way he treated his wife and the kafirs on his farm. But then, on the other hand, he looked very well after his cattle and pigs. And I have always believed that this is more important in a farmer than that he should be kind to his wife and his kafirs.

Well, we talked about the mealies and the drought of the year before last and the subsidies, and I could see that in a short while the conversation would come round to the Volksraad, and as I wasn't anxious to hear how Frans was going to vote at the General Election – believing that so irresponsible a person should not be allowed to vote at all – I quickly asked John de Swardt to tell us about his paintings.

Immediately he started off about his Veld Maiden.

'Not that one,' I said, kicking his shin, 'I meant your other paintings. The kind that frighten the locusts.'

I felt that this Veld Maiden thing was not a fit subject to talk about, especially with a woman present. Moreover, it was Sunday.

Nevertheless, that kick came too late. De Swardt rubbed his shin a few times and started on his subject, and although Frans and I cleared our throats awkwardly at different parts, and Sannie looked on the floor with her pretty cheeks very red, the young painter explained everything about that picture and what it meant to him.

'It's a dream I have had for a long time, now,' he said at the end, 'and always she comes to me, and when I put out my arms to clasp her to me she vanishes, and I am left with only her memory in my heart. But when she comes the whole world is clothed in a terrible beauty.'

'That's more than she is clothed in, anyway,' Frans said, 'judging from what you have told us about her.'

'She's a spirit. She's the spirit of the veld,' De Swardt murmured, 'she whispers strange and enchanting things. Her coming is like the whisper of the wind. She's not of the earth at all.'

'Oh, well,' Frans said shortly, 'you can keep these Uitlander ghost-women of yours. A Boer girl is good enough for ordinary fellows like me and Schalk Lourens.'

So the days passed.

John de Swardt finished a few more bits of rock and drought-stricken khaki-bos, and I had got so far as to persuade him to label the worst-looking one 'Frans Welman's Farm'.

Then one morning he came to me in great excitement.

'I saw her again, Oom Schalk,' he said, 'I saw her last night. In a surpassing loveliness. Just at midnight. She came softly across the veld towards my tent. The night was warm and lovely, and the stars were mad and singing. And there was low music where her white feet touched the grass. And sometimes her mouth seemed to be laughing, and sometimes it was sad. And her lips were very red, Oom Schalk. And when I reached out with my arms she went away. She disappeared in the maroelas, like the whispering of the wind. And there was a ringing in my ears. And in my heart there was a green fragrance, and I thought of the pale asphodel that grows in the fields of paradise.'

'I don't know about paradise,' I said, 'but if a thing like that grew in my mealie lands I would see to it at once that the kafirs pulled it up. I don't like this spook nonsense.'

I then gave him some good advice. I told him to beware of the moon, which was almost full at the time. Because the moon can do strange things to you in the bushveld, especially if you live in a tent and the full moon is overhead and there are weird shadows amongst the maroelas.

But I knew he wouldn't take any notice of what I told him. Several times after that he came with the same story about the Veld Maiden. I started getting tired of it.

Then, one morning when he came again, I knew everything by the look he had in his eyes. I have already told you about that look.

'Oom Schalk,' he began.

'John de Swardt,' I said to him, 'don't tell me anything. All I ask of you is to pack up your things and leave my farm at once.'

'I'll leave tonight,' he said, 'I promise you that by tomorrow morning I will be gone. Only let me stay here one more day and night.'

His voice trembled when he spoke, and his knees were very unsteady. But it was not for these reasons or for his sake that I relented. I spoke to him civilly for the sake of the look he had in his eyes.

'Very well, then,' I said, 'but you must go straight back to Johannesburg. If you walk down the road through the poort before sun-up you will be able to catch the Government lorry to Zeerust.'

He thanked me and left. I never saw him again.

Next day his tent was still there behind the maroelas, but John de Swardt was gone, and he had taken with him all his pictures. All, that is, except the Veld Maiden one. I suppose he had no more need for it.

And, in any case, the white ants had already started on it. So that's why I can hang the remains of it openly on the wall in my voorhuis, and the Predikant does not raise any objection to it. For the white ants have eaten away practically all of it except the face. As for Frans Welman, it was quite a long time before he gave up searching the Marico for his young wife, Sannie.

The Music-Maker

Of course, I know about history – Oom Schalk Lourens said – it's the stuff children learn in school. Only the other day, at Thys Lemmer's post office, Thys's little son Stoffel started reading out of his history book about a man called Vasco da Gama, who visited the Cape. At once Dirk Snyman started telling young Stoffel about the time when he himself visited the Cape, but young Stoffel didn't take much notice of him. So Dirk Snyman said that that showed you.

Anyway, Dirk Snyman said that what he wanted to tell young Stoffel was that the last time he went down to the Cape a kafir came and sat down right next to him in a tram. What was more, Dirk Snyman said, was that people seemed to think nothing of it.

Yes, it's a queer thing about wanting to get into history.

Take the case of Manie Kruger, for instance.

Manie Kruger was one of the best farmers in the Marico. He knew just how much peach brandy to pour out for the tax-collector to make sure that he would nod dreamily at everything Manie said. And at a time of drought Manie Kruger could run to the Government for help much quicker than any man I ever knew.

Then one day Manie Kruger read an article in the *Kerkbode* about a musician who said that he knew more about music than Napoleon did. After that – having first read another article to find out who Napoleon was – Manie Kruger was a changed man. He could talk of nothing but his place in history and of his musical career.

Of course, everybody knew that no man in the Marico could be counted in the same class with Manie Kruger when it came to playing the concertina.

No Bushveld dance was complete without Manie Kruger's concertina. When he played a vastrap you couldn't keep your feet still. But after he had decided to become the sort of musician that gets into history books, it was strange the way that Manie Kruger altered. For one thing, he said he would never again play at a dance. We all felt sad about that. It was not easy to think of the Bushveld dances of the future. There would be the peach brandy in the kitchen; in the voorkamer the feet of the dancers would go through the steps of the schottische and the polka and the waltz and the mazurka, but on the riempies bench in the corner where the musicians sat, there would be no Manie Kruger. And they would play 'Die Vaal Hare en die Blou Oge' and 'Vat Jou Goed en Trek, Ferreira', but it would be another's fingers that swept over the concertina keys. And when, with the dancing and the peach brandy, the young men called out 'Dagbreek toe' it would not be Manie Kruger's head that bowed down to the applause.

It was sad to think about all this.

For so long, at the Bushveld dances, Manie Kruger had been the chief musician.

And of all those who mourned this change that had come over Manie, we could see that there was no one more grieved than Letta Steyn.

And Manie said such queer things at times. Once he said that what he had to do to get into history was to die of consumption in the arms of a princess, like another musician he had read about. Only it was hard to get consumption in the Marico, because the climate was so healthy.

Although Manie stopped playing his concertina at dances, he played a great deal in another way. He started giving what he called recitals. I went to several of them. They were very impressive.

At the first recital I went to, I found that the front part of Manie's voorkamer was taken up by rows of benches and chairs that he had borrowed from those of his neighbours who didn't mind having to eat their meals on candle-boxes and upturned buckets. At the far end of the voorkamer a wide green curtain was hung on a piece of string. When I came in the place was full. I managed to squeeze in on a bench between Jan Terblanche and a young woman in a blue kappie. Jan Terblanche had been trying to hold this young woman's hand.

Manie Kruger was sitting behind the green curtain. He was already there when I came in. I knew it was Manie by his veldskoens, which were sticking out from underneath the curtain. Letta Steyn sat in front of me. Now and again, when she turned round, I saw that there was a flush on her face and a look of dark excitement in her eyes.

At last everything was ready, and Joel, the farm kafir to whom Manie had given the job, slowly drew the green curtain aside. A few of the younger men called out 'Middag, ou Manie,' and Jan Terblanche asked if it wasn't very close and suffocating, sitting there like that behind that piece of green curtain.

Then he started to play.

And we all knew that it was the most wonderful concertina music we had ever listened to. It was Manie Kruger at his best. He had practised a long time for that recital; his fingers flew over the keys; the notes of the concertina swept into our hearts; the music of Manie Kruger lifted us right out of that voorkamer into a strange and rich and dazzling world.

It was fine.

The applause right through was terrific. At the end of each piece the kafir closed the curtains in front of Manie, and we sat waiting for a few minutes until the curtains were drawn aside again. But after that first time there was no more laughter about this procedure. The recital lasted for about an hour and a half, and the applause at the end was even greater than at the start. And during those ninety minutes Manie left his seat only once. That was when there was some trouble with the curtain and he got up to kick the kafir.

At the end of the recital Manie did not come forward and shake hands with us, as we had expected. Instead, he slipped through behind the green curtain into the kitchen, and sent word that we could come and see him round the back. At first we thought this a bit queer, but Letta Steyn said it was all right. She explained that in other countries the great musicians and stage performers all received their admirers at the back. Jan Terblanche said that if these actors used their kitchens for entertaining their visitors in, he wondered where they did their cooking.

Nevertheless, most of us went round to the kitchen, and we had a good time congratulating Manie Kruger and shaking hands with him; and Manie spoke much of his musical future, and of the triumphs that would come to him in the great cities of the world, when he would stand before the curtain and bow to the applause.

Manie gave a number of recitals after that. They were all equally fine. Only, as he had to practise all day, he couldn't pay much attention to his farming. The result was that his farm went to pieces and he got into debt. The court messengers came and attached half his cattle while he was busy practising for his fourth recital. And he was practising for his seventh recital when they took away his ox-wagon and mule-cart.

Eventually, when Manie Kruger's musical career reached that stage when they took away his plough and the last of his oxen, he sold up what remained of his possessions and left the Bushveld, on his way to those great cities that he had so often talked about. It was very grand, the send-off that the Marico gave him. The Predikant and the Volksraad member both made speeches about how proud the Transvaal was of her great son. Then Manie replied. Instead of thanking his audience, however, he started abusing us left and right, calling us a mob of hooligans and soulless Philistines, and saying how much he despised us.

Naturally, we were very much surprised at this outburst, as we had always been kind to Manie Kruger and had encouraged him all we could. But Letta Steyn explained that Manie didn't really mean the things he said. She said it was just that every great artist was expected to talk in that way about the place he came from.

So we knew it was all right, and the more offensive the things were that Manie said about us, the louder we shouted 'Hoor, hoor vir Manie'. There was a particularly enthusiastic round of applause when he said that we knew as much about art as a boomslang. His language was hotter than anything I had ever heard – except once. And that was when De Wet said what he thought of Cronje's surrender to the English at Paardeberg. We could feel that Manie's speech was the real thing. We cheered ourselves hoarse that day.

And so Manie Kruger went. We received one letter to say that he had reached Pretoria. But after that we heard no more of him.

Yet always, when Letta Steyn spoke of Manie, it was as a child speaks of a dream, half wistfully, and always, with the voice of a wistful child, she would tell me how one day, one day he would return. And often, when it was dusk, I would see her sitting on the stoep, gazing out across the veld into the evening, down the dusty road that led between the thorn-trees and beyond the Dwarsberg, waiting for the lover who would come to her no more.

It was a long time before I again saw Manie Kruger. And then it was in Pretoria. I had gone there to interview the Volksraad member about an election promise. It was quite by accident that I saw Manie. And he was playing the concertina – playing as well as ever, I thought. I went away quickly. But what affected me very strangely was just that one glimpse I had of the green curtain of the bar in front of which Manie Kruger played.

In the Withaak's Shade

Leopards? – Oom Schalk Lourens said – Oh, yes, there are two varieties on this side of the Limpopo. The chief difference between them is that the one kind of leopard has got a few more spots on it than the other kind. But when you meet a leopard in the veld, unexpectedly, you seldom trouble to count his spots to find out what kind he belongs to. That is unnecessary. Because, whatever kind of leopard it is that you come across in this way, you only do one kind of running. And that is the fastest kind.

I remember the occasion that I came across a leopard unexpectedly, and to this day I couldn't tell you how many spots he had, even though I had all the time I needed for studying him. It happened about midday, when I was out on the far end of my farm, behind a koppie, looking for some strayed cattle. I thought the cattle might be there because it is shady under those withaak trees, and there is soft grass that is very pleasant to sit on. After I had looked for the cattle for about an hour in this manner, sitting up against a tree-trunk, it occurred to me that I could look for them just as well, or perhaps even better, if I lay down flat. For even a child knows that cattle aren't so small that you have got to get on to stilts and things to see them properly.

So I lay on my back, with my hat tilted over my face, and my legs crossed, and when I closed my eyes slightly the tip of my boot, sticking up into the air, looked just like the peak of Abjaterskop.

Overhead a lonely aasvoël wheeled, circling slowly round and round without flapping his wings, and I knew that not even a calf could pass in any part of the sky between the tip of my toe and that aasvoël without my observing it immediately. What was more, I could go on lying there under the withaak and looking for the cattle like that all day, if necessary. As you know, I am not the sort of farmer to loaf about the house when there is a man's work to be done.

The more I screwed up my eyes and gazed at the toe of my boot, the more it looked like Abjaterskop. By and by it seemed that it actually was Abjaterskop, and I could see the stones on top of it, and the bush trying to grow up its sides, and in my ears there was a far-off humming sound, like bees in an orchard on a still day. As I have said, it was very pleasant.

Then a strange thing happened. It was as though a huge cloud, shaped like an animal's head and with spots on it, had settled on top of Abjaterskop. It seemed so funny that I wanted to laugh. But I didn't. Instead, I opened my eyes a little more and felt glad to think that I was only dreaming. Because otherwise I would have to believe that the spotted cloud on Abjaterskop was actually a leopard, and that he was gazing at my boot. Again I wanted to laugh. But then, suddenly, I knew.

And I didn't feel so glad. For it was a leopard, all right – a large-sized, hungry-looking leopard, and he was sniffing suspiciously at my feet. I was uncomfortable. I knew that nothing I could do would ever convince that leopard that my toe was Abjaterskop. He was not that sort of leopard: I knew that without even counting the number of his spots. Instead, having finished with my feet, he started sniffing higher up. It was the most terrifying moment of my life. I wanted to get up and run for it. But I couldn't. My legs wouldn't work.

Every big-game hunter I have come across has told me the same story about how, at one time or another, he has owed his escape from lions and other wild animals to his cunning in lying down and pretending to be dead, so that the beast of prey loses interest in him and walks off. Now, as I lay there on the grass, with the leopard trying to make up his mind about me, I understood why, in such a situation, the hunter doesn't move. It's simply that he can't move. That's all. It's not his cunning that keeps him down. It's his legs.

In the meantime the leopard had got up as far as my knees. He was studying my trousers very carefully, and I started getting embarrassed. My trousers were old and rather unfashionable. Also, at the knee, there was a torn place, from where I had climbed through a barbed wire fence, into the thick bush, the time I saw the Government tax-collector coming over the bult before he saw me. The leopard stared at that rent in my trousers for quite a while, and my embarrassment grew. I felt I wanted to explain about the Government tax-collector and the barbed wire. I didn't want the leopard to get the impression that Schalk Lourens was the sort of man who didn't care about his personal appearance.

When the leopard got as far as my shirt, however, I felt better. It was a good blue flannel shirt that I had bought only a few weeks ago from the

Indian store at Ramoutsa, and I didn't care how many strange leopards saw it. Nevertheless, I made up my mind that next time I went to lie on the grass under the withaak, looking for strayed cattle, I would first polish up my veldskoens with sheep's fat, and I would put on my black hat that I only wear to Nagmaal. I could not permit the wild animals of the neighbourhood to sneer at me.

But when the leopard reached my face I got frightened again. I knew he couldn't take exception to my shirt. But I wasn't so sure about my face. Those were terrible moments. I lay very still, afraid to open my eyes and afraid to breathe. Sniff-sniff, the huge creature went, and his breath swept over my face in hot gasps. You hear of many frightening experiences that a man has in a lifetime. I have also been in quite a few perilous situations. But if you want something to make you suddenly old and to turn your hair white in a few moments, there is nothing to beat a leopard – especially when he is standing over you, with his jaws at your throat, trying to find a good place to bite.

The leopard gave a deep growl, stepped right over my body, knocked off my hat, and growled again. I opened my eyes and saw the animal moving away clumsily. But my relief didn't last long. The leopard didn't move far. Instead, he turned over and lay down next to me.

Yes, there on the grass, in the shade of the withaak, the leopard and I lay down together. The leopard lay half-curled up, on his side, with his forelegs crossed, like a dog, and whenever I tried to move away he grunted. I am sure that in the whole history of the Groot Marico there have never been two stranger companions engaged in the thankless task of looking for strayed cattle.

Next day, in Fanie Snyman's voorkamer, which was used as a post office, I told my story to the farmers of the neighbourhood, while they were drinking coffee and waiting for the motor-lorry from Zeerust.

'And how did you get away from that leopard in the end?' Koos van Tonder asked, trying to be funny. 'I suppose you crawled through the grass and frightened the leopard off by pretending to be a python.'

'No, I just got up and walked home,' I said. 'I remembered that the cattle I was looking for might have gone the other way and strayed into your kraal. I thought they would be safer with the leopard.'

'Did the leopard tell you what he thought of General Pienaar's last speech in the Volksraad?' Frans Welman asked, and they all laughed.

I told my story over several times before the lorry came with our letters, and although the dozen odd men present didn't say much while I was talking, I could see that they listened to me in the same way that they listened when Krisjan Lemmer talked. And everybody knew that Krisjan Lemmer was the biggest liar in the Bushveld.

To make matters worse, Krisjan Lemmer was there, too, and when I got to the part of my story where the leopard lay down beside me, Krisjan Lemmer winked at me. You know that kind of wink. It was to let me know that there was now a new understanding between us, and that we could speak in future as one Marico liar to another.

I didn't like that.

'Kêrels,' I said in the end, 'I know just what you are thinking. You don't believe me, and you don't want to say so.'

'But we do believe you,' Krisjan Lemmer interrupted me, 'very wonderful things happen in the Bushveld. I once had a twenty-foot mamba that I named Hans. This snake was so attached to me that I couldn't go anywhere without him. He would even follow me to church on Sunday, and because he didn't care much for some of the sermons, he would wait for me outside under a tree. Not that Hans was irreligious. But he had a sensitive nature, and the strong line that the Predikant took against the serpent in the Garden of Eden always made Hans feel awkward. Yet he didn't go and look for a withaak to lie under, like your leopard. He wasn't stand-offish in that way. An ordinary thorn-tree's shade was good enough for Hans. He knew he was only a mamba, and didn't try to give himself airs.'

I didn't take notice of Krisjan Lemmer's stupid lies, but the upshot of this whole affair was that I also began to have doubts about the existence of that leopard. I recalled queer stories I had heard of human beings that could turn themselves into animals, and although I am not a superstitious man I could not shake off the feeling that it was a spook thing that had happened. But when, a few days later, a huge leopard had been seen from the roadside near the poort, and then again by Mtosas on the way to

Nietverdiend, and again in the turf-lands near the Malopo, matters took a different turn.

At first people jested about this leopard. They said it wasn't a real leopard, but a spotted animal that had walked away out of Schalk Lourens' dream. They also said that the leopard had come to the Dwarsberge to have a look at Krisjan Lemmer's twenty-foot mamba. But afterwards, when they had found his spoor at several water-holes, they had no more doubt about the leopard.

It was dangerous to walk about in the veld, they said. Exciting times followed. There was a great deal of shooting at the leopard and a great deal of running away from him. The amount of Martini and Mauser fire I heard in the krantzes reminded me of nothing so much as the First Boer War. And the amount of running away reminded me of nothing so much as the Second Boer War.

But always the leopard escaped unharmed. Somehow, I felt sorry for him. The way he had first sniffed at me and then lain down beside me that day under the withaak was a strange thing that I couldn't understand. I thought of the Bible, where it is written that the lion shall lie down with the lamb.

But I also wondered if I hadn't dreamt it all. The manner in which those things had befallen me was also unearthly. The leopard began to take up a lot of my thoughts. And there was no man to whom I could talk about it who would be able to help me in any way. Even now, as I am telling you this story, I am expecting you to wink at me, like Krisjan Lemmer did.

Still, I can only tell you the things that happened as I saw them, and what the rest was about only Africa knows.

It was some time before I again walked along the path that leads through the bush to where the withaaks are. But I didn't lie down on the grass again. Because when I reached the place, I found that the leopard had got there before me. He was lying on the same spot, half-curled up in the withaak's shade, and his fore-paws were folded as a dog's are some-times. But he lay very still. And even from the distance where I stood I could see the red splash on his breast where a Mauser bullet had gone.

The Rooinek

Rooineks, said Oom Schalk Lourens, are queer. For instance, there was that day when my nephew Hannes and I had dealings with a couple of Englishmen near Dewetsdorp. It was shortly after Sanna's Post, and Hannes and I were lying behind a rock watching the road. Hannes spent odd moments like that in what he called a useful way. He would file the points of his Mauser cartridges on a piece of flat stone until the lead showed through the steel, in that way making them into dum-dum bullets.

I often spoke to my nephew Hannes about that.

'Hannes,' I used to say. 'That is a sin. The Lord is looking at you.'

'That's all right,' Hannes replied. 'The Lord knows that this is the Boer War, and in war-time He will always forgive a little foolishness like this, especially as the English are so many.'

Anyway, as we lay behind that rock we saw, far down the road, two horsemen come galloping up. We remained perfectly still and let them approach to within four hundred paces. They were English officers. They were mounted on first-rate horses and their uniforms looked very fine and smart. They were the most stylish-looking men I had seen for some time, and I felt quite ashamed of my own ragged trousers and veldskoens. I was glad that I was behind a rock and they couldn't see me. Especially as my jacket was also torn all the way down the back, as a result of my having had, three days before, to get through a barbed wire fence rather quickly. I just got through in time, too. The veldkornet, who was a fat man and couldn't run so fast, was about twenty yards behind me. And he remained on the wire with a bullet through him. All through the Boer War I was pleased that I was thin and never troubled with corns.

Hannes and I fired just about the same time. One of the officers fell off his horse. He struck the road with his shoulders and rolled over twice, kicking up the red dust as he turned. Then the other soldier did a queer thing. He drew up his horse and got off. He gave just one look in our direction. Then he led his horse up to where the other man was twisting and struggling on the ground. It took him a little while to lift him on to his horse, for it is no easy matter to pick up a man like that when he is helpless. And he did all this slowly and calmly, as though he was not concerned about the fact that the men who had just shot his friend were lying only a few hundred yards away. He managed in some way to support the wounded man across the saddle, and walked on beside the horse. After going a few yards he stopped and seemed to remember something. He turned round and waved at the spot where he imagined we were hiding, as though inviting us to shoot. During all that time I had simply lain watching him, astonished at his coolness.

But when he waved his hand I thrust another cartridge into the breach of my Martini and aimed. I aimed very carefully and was just on the point of pulling the trigger when Hannes put his hand on the barrel and pushed up my rifle.

'Don't shoot, Oom Schalk,' he said. 'That's a brave man.' I looked at Hannes in surprise. His face was very white. I said nothing, and allowed my rifle to sink down on to the grass, but I couldn't understand what had come over my nephew. It seemed that not only was that Englishman queer, but that Hannes was also queer. That's all nonsense not killing a man just because he's brave. If he's a brave man and he's fighting on the wrong side, that's all the more reason to shoot him.

I was with my nephew Hannes for another few months after that. Then one day, in a skirmish near the Vaal River, Hannes with a few dozen other burghers was cut off from the commando and had to surrender. That was the last I ever saw of him. I heard later on that, after taking him prisoner, the English searched Hannes and found dum-dum bullets in his possession. They shot him for that. I was very much grieved when I heard of Hannes's death. He had always been full of life and high spirits. Perhaps Hannes was right in saying that the Lord didn't mind about a little foolishness like dum-dum bullets. But the mistake he made was in forgetting that the English did mind.

I was in the veld until they made peace. Then we laid down our rifles and went home. What I knew my farm by, was the hole under the koppie where I quarried slate-stones for the threshing-floor. That was about all that remained as I left it. Everything else was gone. My home was burnt down. My lands were laid waste. My cattle and sheep were slaughtered. Even the stones I had piled for the kraals were pulled down. My wife came out of the concentration camp and we went together to look at our old farm. My wife had gone into the concentration camp with our two children, but she came out alone. And when I saw her again and noticed the way she had changed, I knew that I, who had been through all the fighting, had not seen the Boer War.

Neither Sannie nor I had the heart to go on farming again on that same place. It would be different without the children playing about the house and getting into mischief. We got paid out some money by the new Government for part of our losses. So I bought a wagon and oxen and we left the Free State, which was not even the Free State any longer. It was now called the Orange River Colony.

We trekked right through the Transvaal into the northern part of the Marico Bushveld. Years ago, as a boy, I had trekked through that same country with my parents. Now that I went there again I felt that it was still a good country. It was on the far side of the Dwarsberge, near Derdepoort, that we got a Government farm. Afterwards other farmers trekked in there as well. One or two of them had also come from the Free State, and I knew them. There were also a few Cape rebels whom I had seen on commando. All of us had lost relatives in the war. Some had died in the concentration camps or on the battlefield. Others had been shot for going into rebellion. So, taken all in all, we who trekked into that part of the Marico that lay nearest the Bechuanaland border were bitter against the English.

Then it was that the rooinek came.

It was in the first year of our having settled around Derdepoort. We heard that an Englishman had bought a farm next to Gerhardus Grobbelaar. This was when we were sitting in the voorkamer of Willem Odendaal's house, which was used as a post office. Once a week the post-cart came up with letters from Zeerust, and we came together at Willem Odendaal's house and talked and smoked and drank coffee. Very few of us ever got letters, and then it was mostly demands to pay for the boreholes that had been drilled on our farms or for cement and fencing materials. But every week regularly we went for the post. Sometimes the post cart didn't come, because the Groen River was in flood, and we would most of us have gone home without noticing it, if somebody didn't speak about it.

When Koos Steyn heard that an Englishman was coming to live amongst us he got up from the riempies bank.

'No, kêrels,' he said, 'always when the Englishman comes, it means a little later the Boer has got to shift. I'll pack up my wagon and make coffee, and just trek first thing tomorrow morning.'

Most of us laughed then. Koos Steyn often said funny things like that. But some didn't laugh. Somehow, there seemed to be too much truth in Koos Steyn's words.

We discussed the matter and decided that if we Boers in the Marico could help it the rooinek would not stay amongst us too long. About half an hour later one of William Odendaal's children came in and said that there was a strange wagon coming along the big road. We went to the door and looked out. As the wagon came nearer we saw that it was piled up with all kinds of furniture and also sheets of iron and farming implements. There was so much stuff on the wagon that the tent had to be taken off to get everything on.

The wagon rolled along and came to a stop in front of the house. With the wagon there were one white man and two kafirs. The white man shouted something to the kafirs and threw down the whip. Then he walked up to where we were standing. He was dressed just as we were, in shirt and trousers and veldskoens, and he had dust all over him. But when he stepped over a thorn-bush we saw that he had got socks on. Therefore we knew that he was an Englishman.

Koos Steyn was standing in front of the door.

The Englishman went up to him and held out his hand.

'Good afternoon,' he said in Afrikaans. 'My name is Webber.'

Koos shook hands with him.

'My name is Prince Lord Alfred Milner,' Koos Steyn said

That was when Lord Milner was Governor of the Transvaal, and we all laughed. The rooinek also laughed.

'Well, Lord Prince,' he said, 'I can speak your language a little, and I hope that later on I'll be able to speak it better. I'm coming to live here, and I hope that we'll all be friends.'

He then came round to all of us, but the others turned away and refused to shake hands with him. He came up to me last of all; I felt sorry for him, and although his nation had dealt unjustly with my nation, and I had lost both my children in the concentration camp, still it was not so much the fault of this Englishman. It was the fault of the English Government, who wanted our gold mines. And it was also the fault of Queen Victoria, who didn't like Oom Paul Kruger, because they say that when he went to London Oom Paul spoke to her only once for a few minutes. Oom Paul Kruger said that he was a married man and he was afraid of widows.

When the Englishman Webber went back to his wagon Koos Steyn and I walked with him. He told us that he had bought the farm next to Gerhardus Grobbelaar and that he didn't know much about sheep and cattle and mealies, but he had bought a few books on farming, and he was going to learn all he could out of them. When he said that I looked away towards the poort. I didn't want him to see that I was laughing. But with Koos Steyn it was otherwise.

'Man,' he said, 'let me see those books.'

Webber opened the box at the bottom of the wagon and took out about six big books with green covers.

'These are very good books,' Koos Steyn said. 'Yes, they are very good for the white ants. The white ants will eat them all in two nights.'

As I told you, Koos Steyn was a funny fellow, and no man could help laughing at the things he said.

Those were bad times. There was drought, and we could not sow mealies. The dams dried up, and there was only last year's grass on the veld. We had to pump water out of the boreholes for weeks at a time. Then the rains came and for a while things were better.

Now and again I saw Webber. From what I heard about him it seemed that he was working hard. But of course no rooinek can make a living out of farming, unless they send him money every month from England. And we found out that almost all the money Webber had was what he paid on the farm. He was always reading in those green books what he had to do. It's lucky that those books are written in English, and that the Boers can't read them. Otherwise many more farmers would be ruined every year. When his cattle had the heart-water, or his sheep had the blue-tongue, or there were cutworms or stalk-borers in his mealies, Webber would look it all up in his books. I suppose that when the kafirs stole his sheep he would look that up, too.

Still, Koos Steyn helped Webber quite a lot and taught him a number of things, so that matters did not go as badly with him as they would have if he had only acted according to the lies that were printed in those green books. Webber and Koos Steyn became very friendly. Koos Steyn's wife had had a baby just a few weeks before Webber came. It was the first child they had after being married seven years, and they were very proud of it. It was a girl. Koos Steyn said that he would sooner it had been a boy; but that, even so, it was better than nothing. Right from the first Webber had taken a liking to that child, who was christened Jemima after her mother. Often when I passed Koos Steyn's house I saw the Englishman sitting on the front stoep with the child on his knees.

In the meantime the other farmers around there became annoyed on account of Koos Steyn's friendship with the rooinek. They said that Koos was a handsopper and a traitor to his country. He was intimate with a man who had helped to bring about the downfall of the Afrikaner nation. Yet it was not fair to call Koos a handsopper. Koos had lived in the Graaff-Reinet district when the war broke out, so that he was a Cape Boer and need not have fought. Nevertheless, he joined up with a Free State commando and remained until peace was made, and if at any time the English caught him they would have shot him as a rebel, in the same way they shot Scheepers and many others.

Gerhardus Grobbelaar spoke about this once when we were in Willem Odendaal's post office.

'You are not doing right,' Gerhardus said; 'Boer and Englishman have been enemies since before Slagtersnek. We've lost this war, but some day we'll win. It's the duty we owe to our children to stand against the rooineks. Remember the concentration camps.'

There seemed to me to be truth in what Gerhardus said.

'But the English are here now, and we've got to live with them,' Koos answered. 'When we get to understand one another perhaps we won't need to fight any more. This Englishman Webber is learning Afrikaans very well; and some day he might almost be one of us. The only thing I can't understand about him is that he has a bath every morning. But if he stops that and if he doesn't brush his teeth any more you will hardly be able to tell him from a Boer.'

Although he made a joke about it, I felt that in what Koos Steyn said there was also truth.

Then, the year after the drought, the miltsiek broke out. The miltsiek seemed to be in the grass of the veld, and in the water of the dams, and even in the air the cattle breathed. All over the place I would find cows and oxen lying dead. We all became very discouraged. Nearly all of us in that part of the Marico had started farming again on what the Government had given us. Now that the stock died we had nothing. First the drought had put us back to where we were when we started. Now with the miltsiek we couldn't hope to do anything. We couldn't even sow mealies, because, at the rate at which the cattle were dying, in a short while we would have no oxen left to pull the plough. People talked of selling what they had and going to look for work on the mines. We sent a petition to the Government, but that did no good.

It was then that somebody got hold of the idea of trekking. In a few days we were talking of nothing else. But the question was where we could trek to. They would not allow us into Rhodesia for fear we might spread the miltsiek there as well. And it was useless going to any other part of the Transvaal. Somebody mentioned German West Africa. We had none of us been there before, and I suppose that really was the reason why, in the end, we decided to go there.

'The blight of the English is over South Africa,' Gerhardus Grobbelaar said. 'We'll remain here only to die. We must go away somewhere where there is not the Englishman's flag.'

In a few weeks' time we arranged everything. We were going to trek across the Kalahari into German territory. Everything we had we loaded up. We drove the cattle ahead and followed behind on our wagons. There were five families: the Steyns, the Grobbelaars, the Odendaals, the Ferreiras and Sannie and I. Webber also came with us. I think it was not so much that he was anxious to leave as that he and Koos Steyn had become very much attached to one another, and the Englishman did not wish to remain alone behind.

The youngest person in our trek was Koos Steyn's daughter Jemima, who was then about eighteen months old. Being the baby, she was a favourite with all of us.

Webber sold his wagon and went with Koos Steyn's trek.

When at the end of the first day we outspanned several miles inside the Bechuanaland Protectorate, we were very pleased that we were done with the Transvaal, where we had had so much misfortune. Of course, the Protectorate was also British territory, but all the same we felt happier there than we had done in our country. We saw Webber every day now, and although he was a foreigner with strange ways, and would remain an Uitlander until he died, yet we disliked him less than before for being a rooinek.

It was on the first Sunday that we reached Malopolole. For the first part of our way the country remained bushveld. There were the same kind of thorn-trees that grew in the Marico, except that they became fewer the deeper into the Kalahari that we went. Also, the ground became more and more sandy, until even before we came to Malopolole it was all desert. But scattered thorn bushes remained all the way. That Sunday we held a religious service. Gerhardus Grobbelaar read a chapter out of the Bible and offered up a prayer. We sang a number of psalms, after which Gerhardus prayed again. I shall always remember that Sunday and the way we sat on the ground beside one of the wagons, listening to Gerhardus. That was the last Sunday that we were all together.

The Englishman sat next to Koos Steyn and the baby Jemima lay down in front of him. She played with Webber's fingers and tried to bite them. It was funny to watch her. Several times Webber looked down at her and smiled. I thought then that although Webber was not one of us, yet Jemima certainly did not know it. Maybe in a thing like that the child was wiser than we were. To her it made no difference that the man whose fingers she bit was born in another country and did not speak the same language that she did.

There are many things that I remember about that trek into the Kalahari. But one thing that now seems strange to me is the way in which, right from the first day, we took Gerhardus Grobbelaar for our leader. Whatever he said we just seemed to do without talking very much about it. We all felt that it was right simply because Gerhardus wished it. That was a strange thing about our trek. It was not simply that we knew Gerhardus had got the Lord with him – for we did know that – but it was rather that we believed in Gerhardus as well as the Lord. I think that even if Gerhardus Grobbelaar had been an ungodly man we would still have followed him in exactly the same way. For when you are in the desert and there is no water and the way back is long, then you feel that it is better to have with you a strong man who does not read the Book very much, than a man who is good and religious, and yet does not seem sure how far to trek each day and where to outspan.

But Gerhardus Grobbelaar was a man of God. At the same time there was something about him that made you feel that it was only by acting as he advised that you could succeed. There was only one other man I have ever known who found it so easy to get people to do as he wanted. And that was Paul Kruger. He was very much like Gerhardus Grobbelaar, except that Gerhardus was less quarrelsome. But of the two Paul Kruger was the bigger man.

Only once do I remember Gerhardus losing his temper. And that was with the Nagmaal at Elandsberg. It was a Sunday and we were camped out beside the Crocodile River. Gerhardus went round early in the morning from wagon to wagon and told us that he wanted everybody to come over to where his wagon stood. The Lord had been good to us at that time, so that we had had much rain and our cattle were fat. Gerhardus explained that he wanted to hold a service, to thank the Lord for all His good works, but more especially for what He had done for the farmers on the northern part of the Groot Marico District. This was a good plan, and we all came together with our Bibles and hymn-books. But one man, Karel Pieterse, remained behind at his wagon. Twice Gerhardus went to call him, but

Karel Pieterse lay down on the grass and would not get up to come to the service. He said it was all right thanking the Lord now that there had been rains, but what about all those seasons when there had been drought and the cattle had died of thirst. Gerhardus Grobbelaar shook his head sadly, and said there was nothing he could do then as it was Sunday. But he prayed that the Lord would soften brother Pieterse's heart, and he finished off his prayer by saying that in any case, in the morning, he would help to soften the brother's heart himself.

The following morning Gerhardus walked over with a sjambok and an ox-riem to where Karel Pieterse sat before his fire, watching the kafir making coffee. They were both of them men who were big in the body. But Gerhardus got the better of the struggle. In the end he won. He fastened Karel to the wheel of his own wagon with the ox-riem. Then he thrashed him with the sjambok while Karel's wife and children were looking on.

That had happened years before. But nobody had forgotten. And now, in the Kalahari, when Gerhardus summoned us to a service, it was noticed that no man stayed away.

Just outside Malopolole is a muddy stream that is dry part of the year and part of the year has a foot or so of brackish water. We were lucky in being there just at the time when it had water. Early the following morning we filled up the water barrels that we had put on our wagons before leaving Marico. We were going right into the desert, and we did not know where we would get water again. Even the Bakwena kafirs could not tell us for sure.

'The Great Dorstland Trek,' Koos Steyn shouted as we got ready to move off. 'Anyway, we won't fare as badly as the Dorstland Trekkers. We'll lose less cattle than they did because we've got less to lose. And seeing that we are only five families, not more than about a dozen of us will die of thirst.'

I thought it was bad luck for Koos Steyn to make jokes like that about the Dorstland Trek, and I think that others felt the same about it. We trekked through the day, and it was all desert. By sunset we had not come across a sign of water anywhere. Abraham Ferreira said towards evening that perhaps it would be better if we went back to Malopolole and tried to find out for sure which was the best way of getting through the Kalahari.

But the rest said that there was no need to do that, since we would be sure to come across water the next day. And, anyway, we were Doppers and, having once set out, we were not going to turn back. But after we had given the cattle water our barrels did not have too much left in them.

By the middle of the following day all our water had given out except a little that we kept for the children. But still we pushed on. Now that we had gone so far we were afraid to go back because of the long way that we would have to go without water to get back to Malopolole. In the evening we were very anxious. We all knelt down in the sand and prayed. Gerhardus Grobbelaar's voice sounded very deep and earnest when he besought God to have mercy on us, especially for the sake of the little ones. He mentioned the baby Jemima by name.

It was moonlight. All around us was the desert. Our wagons seemed very small and lonely; there was something about them that looked very mournful. The women and the children put their arms round one another and wept a long while. Our kafirs stood some distance away and watched us. My wife Sannie put her hand in mine, and I thought of the concentration camp. Poor woman, she had suffered much. And I knew that her thoughts were the same as my own: that after all it was perhaps better that our children should have died then than now.

We had got so far into the desert that we began telling one another that we must be near the end. Although we knew that German West was far away, and that in the way we had been travelling we had got little more than into the beginning of the Kalahari, yet we tried to tell one another lies about how near water was likely to be. But of course we told those lies only to one another. Each man in his own heart knew what the real truth was. And later on we even stopped telling one another lies about what a good chance we had of getting out alive. You can understand how badly things had gone with us when you know that we no longer troubled about hiding our position from the women and children. They wept, some of them. But that made no difference then. Nobody tried to comfort the women and children who cried. We knew that tears were useless, and yet somehow at that hour we felt that the weeping of the women was not less useless than the courage of the men. After a while there was no more weeping in our camp. Some of the women who lived through the dreadful things of the days that came after, and got safely back to the Transvaal, never again wept. What they had seen appeared to have hardened them. In this respect they had become as men. I think that is the saddest thing that ever happens in this world when women pass through great suffering that makes them become as men.

That night we hardly slept. Early the next morning the men went out to look for water. An hour after sun-up Ferreira came back and told us that he had found a muddy pool a few miles away. We all went there, but there wasn't much water. Still we got a little, and that made us feel better. It was only when it came to driving our cattle towards the mudhole that we found our kafirs had deserted us during the night. After we had gone to sleep they had stolen away. Some of the weaker cattle couldn't get up to go to the pool. So we left them. Some were trampled to death or got choked in the mud, and we had to pull them out to let the rest get to the hole. It was pitiful.

Just before we left, one of Ferreira's daughters died. We scooped a hole in the sand and buried her.

So we decided to trek back.

After his daughter was dead Abraham Ferreira went up to Gerhardus and told him that if we had taken his advice earlier on and gone back, his daughter would not have died.

'Your daughter is dead now, Abraham,' Gerhardus said. 'It is no use talking about her any longer. We all have to die some day. I refused to go back earlier. I have decided to go back now.'

Abraham Ferreira looked Gerhardus in the eyes and laughed. I shall always remember how that laughter sounded on the desert. In Abraham's voice there was the hoarseness of the sand and thirst. His voice was cracked with what the desert had done to him; his face was lined and his lips were blackened. But there was nothing about him that spoke of grief for his daughter's death.

'Your daughter is still alive, Oom Gerhardus,' Abraham Ferreira said, pointing to the wagon wherein lay Gerhardus's wife, who was weak, and the child to whom she had given birth two years before. 'Yes, she is still alive . . . so far.'

Ferreira turned away laughing, and we heard him a little later explaining to his wife in cracked tones about the joke he had made.

Gerhardus Grobbelaar watched the other men walk away without saying anything. So far we had followed Gerhardus through all things, and our faith in him had been great. But now that he had decided to trek back we lost our belief in him. We lost it suddenly, too. We knew that it was best to turn back, and that to continue would mean that we would all die on the Kalahari. And yet, if Gerhardus had said we must still go on we would have done so. We would have gone through with him right to the end. But now that he as much as said he was beaten by the desert we had no more faith in Gerhardus. That is why I have said that Paul Kruger was a greater man than Gerhardus. Because Paul Kruger was that kind of man whom we still worshipped even when he decided to retreat. If it had been Paul Kruger who told us that we had to go back we would have returned with strong hearts. We would have retained exactly the same love for our leader, even if we knew that he was beaten. But from the moment that Gerhardus said we must go back we all knew that he was no longer our leader. Gerhardus knew that also.

We knew what lay between us and Malopolole and there was grave doubt in our hearts when we turned our wagons round. Our cattle were very weak, and we had to inspan all that could walk. We hadn't enough yokes, and therefore we cut poles from the scattered bushes and tied them to the trek chains. As we were also without skeis we had to fasten the necks of the oxen straight on to the yokes with strops, and several of the oxen got strangled.

Then we saw that Koos Steyn had become mad. For he refused to return. He inspanned his oxen and got ready to trek on. His wife sat silent in the wagon with the baby; wherever her husband went she would go, too. That was only right, of course. Some women kissed her good-bye and cried. But Koos Steyn's wife did not cry. We reasoned with Koos about it, but he said that he had made up his mind to cross the Kalahari, and he was not going to turn back for just nonsense.

'But, man,' Gerhardus Grobbelaar said to him, 'you've got no water to drink.'

'I'll drink coffee then,' Koos Steyn answered, laughing as always, and took up the whip and walked away beside the wagon. And Webber went off with him, just because Koos Steyn had been good to him, I suppose. That's why I have said that Englishmen are queer. Webber must have known that if Koos Steyn had not actually gone wrong in the head, still what he was doing now was madness, and yet he stayed with him.

We separated. Our wagons went slowly back to Malopolole. Koos Steyn's wagon went deeper into the desert. My wagon went last. I looked back at the Steyns. At that moment Webber also looked round. He saw me and waved his hand. It reminded me of that day in the Boer War when that other Englishman, whose companion we had shot, also turned round and waved.

Eventually we got back to Malopolole with two wagons and a handful of cattle. We abandoned the other wagons. Awful things happened on that desert. A number of children died. Gerhardus Grobbelaar's wagon was in front of me. Once I saw a bundle being dropped through the side of the wagon-tent. I knew what it was. Gerhardus would not trouble to bury his dead child, and his wife lay in the tent too weak to move. So I got off the wagon and scraped a small heap of sand over the body. All I remember of the rest of the journey to Malopolole is the sun and the sand. And the thirst. Although at one time we thought we had lost our way, yet that did not matter much to us. We were past feeling. We could neither pray nor curse, our parched tongues cleaving to the roofs of our mouths.

Until today I am not sure how many days we were on our way back, unless I sit down and work it all out, and then I suppose I get it wrong. We got back to Malopolole and water. We said we would never go away from there again. I don't think that even those parents who had lost children grieved about them then. They were stunned with what they had gone through. But I knew that later on it would all come back again. Then they would remember things about shallow graves in the sand, and Gerhardus Grobbelaar and his wife would think of a little bundle lying out in the Kalahari. And I knew how they would feel.

Afterwards we fitted out a wagon with fresh oxen; we took an abundant supply of water and went back into the desert to look for the Steyn family. With the help of the Bechuana kafirs, who could see tracks that we could not see, we found the wagon. The oxen had been outspanned; a few lay dead beside the wagon. The kafirs pointed out to us footprints on the sand, which showed which way those two men and that woman had gone.

In the end we found them.

Koos Steyn and his wife lay side by side in the sand; the woman's head rested on the man's shoulder; her long hair had become loosened, and blew softly in the wind. A great deal of fine sand had drifted over their bodies. We never found the baby Jemima. She must have died somewhere along the way and Koos Steyn must have buried her. But we agreed that the Englishman Webber must have passed through terrible things; he could not even have had any understanding left as to what the Steyns had done with their baby. He probably thought, up to the moment when he died, that he was carrying the child. For, when we lifted his body, we found, still clasped in his dead and rigid arms, a few old rags and a child's clothes.

It seemed to us that the wind that always stirs in the Kalahari blew very quietly and softly that morning.

Yes, the wind blew very gently.

A Bekkersdal Marathon

At Naudé who had a wireless set, came into Jurie Steyn's voorkamer, where we were sitting waiting for the Government lorry from Bekkersdal, and gave us the latest news. He said that the newest thing in Europe was that young people there were going in for non-stop dancing. It was called marathon dancing, At Naudé told us, and those young people were trying to break the record for who could remain on their feet longest, dancing.

We listened for a while to what At Naudé had to say, and then we suddenly remembered a marathon event that had taken place in the little dorp of Bekkersdal – almost in our midst, you could say. What was more, there were quite a number of us sitting in Jurie Steyn's post office who had actually taken part in that non-stop affair, and without knowing that we were breaking records, and without expecting any sort of a prize for it, either.

We discussed that affair at considerable length and from all angles, and we were still talking about it when the lorry came. And we agreed that it had been in several respects an unusual occurrence. We also agreed that it was questionable whether we could have carried off things so successfully that day if it had not been for Billy Robertse.

You see, our organist at Bekkersdal was Billy Robertse. He had once been a sailor and had come to the bushveld some years before, travelling on foot. His belongings, fastened in a red handkerchief, were slung over his shoulder on a stick. Billy Robertse was journeying in that fashion for the sake of his health. He suffered from an unfortunate complaint for which he had at regular intervals to drink something out of a black bottle that he always carried handy in his jacket-pocket.

Billy Robertse would even keep that bottle beside him in the organist's gallery in case of a sudden attack. And if the hymn the predikant gave out had many verses, you could be sure that about half-way through Billy Robertse would bring the bottle up to his mouth, leaning sideways towards what was in it. And he would put several extra twirls into the second part of the hymn.

When he first applied for the position of organist in the Bekkersdal church, Billy Robertse told the meeting of deacons that he had learnt to play the organ in a cathedral in Northern Europe. Several deacons felt, then, that they could not favour his application. They said that the cathedral sounded too Papist, the way Billy Robertse described it, with a dome 300 ft. high and with marble apostles. But it was lucky for Billy Robertse that he was able to mention, at the following combined meeting of elders and deacons, that he had also played the piano in a South American dance hall, of which the manager had been a Presbyterian. He asked the meeting to overlook his unfortunate past, saying that he had had a hard life, and anybody could make mistakes. In any case, he had never cared much for the Romish atmosphere of the cathedral, he said, and had been happier in the dance hall.

In the end, Billy Robertse got the appointment. But in his sermons for several Sundays after that the predikant, Dominee Welthagen, had spoken very strongly against the evils of dance halls. He described those places of awful sin in such burning words that at least one young man went to see Billy Robertse, privately, with a view to taking lessons in playing the piano.

But Billy Robertse was a good musician. And he took a deep interest in his work. And he said that when he sat down on the organist's stool behind the pulpit, and his fingers were flying over the keyboards, and he was pulling out the stops, and his feet were pressing down the notes that sent the deep bass tones through the pipes – then he felt that he could play all day, he said.

I don't suppose he guessed that he would one day be put to the test, however.

It all happened through Dominee Welthagen one Sunday morning going into a trance in the pulpit. And we did not realise that he was in a trance. It was an illness that overtook him in a strange and sudden fashion.

At each service the predikant, after reading a passage from the Bible, would lean forward with his hand on the pulpit rail and give out the number of the hymn we had to sing. For years his manner of conducting the service had been exactly the same. He would say, for instance: 'We will now sing Psalm 82, verses 1 to 4.' Then he would allow his head to sink forward on to his chest and he would remain rigid, as though in prayer, until the last notes of the hymn died away in the church.

Now, on that particular morning, just after he had announced the number of the psalm, without mentioning what verses, Dominee Welthagen again took a firm grip on the pulpit rail and allowed his head to sink forward on to his breast. We did not realise that he had fallen into a trance of a peculiar character that kept his body standing upright while his mind was a blank.

We learnt that only later.

In the meantime, while the organ was playing over the opening bars, we began to realise that Dominee Welthagen had not indicated how many verses we had to sing. But he would discover his mistake, we thought, after we had been singing for a few minutes.

All the same, one or two of the younger members of the congregation did titter, slightly, when they took up their hymn-books. For Dominee Welthagen had given out Psalm 119. And everybody knows that Psalm 119 has 176 verses.

This was a church service that will never be forgotten in Bekkersdal.

We sang the first verse and then the second and then the third. When we got to about the sixth verse and the minister still gave no sign that it would be the last, we assumed that he wished us to sing the first eight verses. For, if you open your hymn-book you'll see that Psalm 119 is divided into sets of eight verses, each ending with the word '*Pouse*'.

We ended the last notes of verse eight with more than an ordinary number of turns and twirls, confident that at any moment Dominee Welthagen would raise his head and let us know that we could sing '*Amen*'.

It was when the organ started up very slowly and solemnly with the music for verse nine that a real feeling of disquiet overcame the congregation. But, of course, we gave no sign of what went on in our minds. We held Dominee Welthagen in too much veneration.

Nevertheless, I would rather not say too much about our feelings, when verse followed verse and Pouse succeeded Pouse, and still Dominee

Welthagen made no sign that we had sung long enough, or that there was anything unusual in what he was demanding of us.

After they had recovered from their first surprise, the members of the church council conducted themselves in a most exemplary manner. Elders and deacons tiptoed up and down the aisles, whispering words of reassurance to such members of the congregation, men as well as women, who gave signs of wanting to panic.

At one stage it looked as though we were going to have trouble from the organist. That was when Billy Robertse, at the end of the 34th verse, held up his black bottle and signalled quietly to the elders to indicate that his medicine was finished. At the end of the 35th verse he made signals of a less quiet character, and again at the end of the 36th verse. That was when Elder Landsman tiptoed out of the church and went round to the Konsistorie, where the Nagmaal wine was kept. When Elder Landsman came back into the church he had a long black bottle half hidden under his *manel*. He took the bottle up to the organist's gallery, still walking on tiptoe.

At verse 61 there was almost a breakdown. That was when a message came from the back of the organ, where Koster Claassen and the assistant verger, whose task it was to turn the handle that kept the organ supplied with wind, were in a state near to exhaustion. So it was Deacon Cronje's turn to go tiptoeing out of the church. Deacon Cronje was head warder at the local goal. When he came back it was with three burly Native convicts in striped jerseys, who also went through the church on tiptoe. They arrived just in time to take over the handle from Koster Claassen and the assistant verger.

At verse 98 the organist again started making signals about his medicine. Once more Elder Landsman went round to the Konsistorie. This time he was accompanied by another elder and a deacon, and they stayed away somewhat longer than the time when Elder Landsman had gone on his own. On their return the deacon bumped into a small hymn-book table at the back of the church. Perhaps it was because the deacon was a fat, red-faced man, and not used to tiptoeing.

At verse 124 the organist signalled again, and the same three members of the church council filed out to the Konsistorie, the deacon walking in front this time.

It was about then that the pastor of the Full Gospel Apostolic Faith Church, about whom Dominee Welthagen had in the past used almost as strong language as about the Pope, came up to the front gate of the church to see what was afoot. He lived near our church and, having heard the same hymn-tune being played over and over for about eight hours, he was a very amazed man. Then he saw the door of the Konsistorie open, and two elders and a deacon coming out, walking on tiptoe – they having apparently forgotten that they were not in church, then. When the pastor saw one of the elders hiding a black bottle under his *manel*, a look of understanding came over his features. The pastor walked off, shaking his head.

At verse 152 the organist signalled again. This time Elder Landsman and the other elder went out alone. The deacon stayed behind in the deacon's bench, apparently in deep thought. The organist signalled again, for the last time, at verse 169. So you can imagine how many visits the two elders made to the Konsistorie altogether.

The last verse came, and the last line of the last verse. This time it had to be 'Amen'. Nothing could stop it. I would rather not describe the state that the congregation was in. And by then the three Native convicts, red stripes and all, were, in the Bakhatla tongue, threatening mutiny. 'Aa-m-e-e-n' came from what sounded like less than a score of voices, hoarse with singing.

The organ music ceased.

Maybe it was the sudden silence that at last brought Dominee Welthagen out of his long trance. He raised his head and looked slowly about him. His gaze travelled over his congregation, and then, looking at the windows, he saw that it was night. We understood right away what was going on in Dominee Welthagen's mind. He thought he had just come into the pulpit, and that this was the beginning of the evening service. We realised that, during all the time we had been singing, the predikant had been in a state of unconsciousness.

Once again Dominee Welthagen took a firm grip on the pulpit rail. His head again started drooping forward on to his breast. But before he went into a trance for the second time, he gave the hymn for the evening service.

'We will,' Dominee Welthagen announced, 'sing Psalm 119.'

Glossary

Aasvoël	General term for a vulture (of any species)
Baas	Master: term of address generally by black worker to his employer
Bakkop	A cobra snake
Biltong	Strips of dried meat
Blesbok	Small African antelope
Blinkblaar	Any of several species of tree or shrub with shiny leaves
Boomslang	Highly venomous, tree-living snake
Bult	A low ridge or sandy hill
Bywoner	A landless, white, tenant farmer or farm overseer, paid with board and lodging and allowed to occupy and work a small plot of farmland for his own account. The word normally refers to someone quite poor
Dagbreek toe	Until dawn
Dagga	The intoxicating plant, Indian hemp – equivalent to marijuana
Dominee	Minister or pastor of the Dutch Reformed Church
Dopper	Member of the strictly Calvinist wing of Gereformeerde Kerk (Dutch Reformed Church)
Flag Bill	Act of parliament passed in 1925 to prescribe the form of the new flag of the Union of South Africa
Floute	Fainting spell or blackout
Gallamsiekte	A serious bacterial disease in cattle
Goël	Magician; ghostly spirit
Haarwurm	Intestinal worm which affects livestock
Handsopper	A derogatory term applied to those Boers who surrendered to the British in the Anglo Boer War
Harde beskuit	Hard biscuits or rusks
Hoogte	Heights; hill or raised ground
Huisbesoek	House call or visit made by a clergyman or minister to a member of his church or by a politician to a constituent
Induna	Headman or senior adviser in a black community
Jong	Fellow or chap; familiar form of address between young men
Kameeldorings	Camel thorn. A type of thorny acacia tree
Kêrels	Chap, fellow, bloke; a young man
Kerkbode	The title of the official publication of the Nederduitse Gereformeerde Kerk (Dutch Reformed Church)
Kerk-plein	Church square
Klinkpenne	Wooden dowels

Kloof	Ravine, gorge
Koppie	Small hill or rocky outcrop
Krantz	Rock outcrop or cliff, often at the summit of a hill
Kremetartboom	Alternative name for the baobab tree, the roots of which are edible
Kweekgras	A type of grass
Laager / Lager	Defensive circle of wagons formed around a camp
Landdrost	Local magistrate
Lyddite	High explosive used by the British forces in the Anglo Boer War
Mampoer	A raw brandy distilled from fruits such as peaches and marula fruit
Manel	A black, frock coat often worn by senior members of the church
Maroela / Marula	Medium sized trees of open woodland with a plum like fruit
Martini	Type of single shot rifle
Mauser	German-made rifle. Imported in large numbers, it became the standard weapon of the Boer forces during the Anglo Boer War
Meneer	Respectful form of address to a man; sir or mister
Mielies	Maize
Miltsiek	Anthrax: a deadly bacterial disease that can affect all livestock
Moepels	A type of evergreen tree
Mosleyites	Followers of the British Fascist leader of the 1930's, Oswald Mosely
Nagmaal	Holy Communion: celebrated by the Dutch Reformed churches every three months
Obiit Mafeking	Latin phrase meaning, 'died at Mafeking'
Ouderling	An elder of the Dutch Reformed churches; a member of the governing body of the church
Outspan	To un-yoke or un-harness oxen from wagons
Ox-riem	Rawhide straps or thongs, often used to lock the wheels of an ox wagon
Picannin	A black child: it would nowadays be regarded as an offensive term
Platteland	Rural areas far from the cities and urban life
Polgras	Tufted grass
Poort	Narrow pass through hills or mountains
Pouse	Pause; interval
Predikant	Minister of the Dutch Reformed Church
P. W. D.	Public Works Department
Rant	Ridge or hill
Ribbok / Rietbok	Reedbuck. A small grey medium sized antelope
Riempies	Leather thongs interlaced to make the seats of chairs and benches
Riempies-stoel	A stool made with riempie leather
Rinderpest	Highly infectious disease which affects cattle and other livestock

Ringhals	Ring-necked spitting cobra
Rooinek	Redneck: term of abuse for Englishmen – soldiers and settlers
Rusbank	Couch or settee
Ruspe	Caterpillar
Seksie	Section of soldiers; platoon
Sjambok	A long, rawhide whip
Steenbok	Small reddish brown antelope
Stoep	Open verandah at the front of a house
Swarthaak	Black thorn-tree
Tamboekie	A type of grass which grows very tall
Uitlander	Foreigner. Particularly used of those who came to the Witwatersrand during the gold rush
Vas staan	Stand fast: hold your ground
Vastrap	Traditional Afrikaans folk dance
Veldkornet	A non commissioned officer in the Boer forces
Veldskoen	Simple shoes made of rawhide
Vierkleur	The green, red, white and blue flag of the old Transvaal Republic, adopted in 1857
Vlakte	Plains
Vlei	Area of standing water or swamp
Volksraad	Parliament or legislative body of the old South African Republics
Voorhuis / voorkamer	Front room or sitting room
Wag-'n-bietjie	Literally, wait a while. A type of shrub with hooked thorns
Withaak	A white thorn-tree, a member of the acacia family